1
Khyber Pakhtunkhwa Province, Pakistan

Wars start in so many ways. This one was to be a holy war. Throughout history, some of the cruelest wars have been launched in the name of religion: just and holy to the true believer; bigoted and merciless to the non-believer. This war was launched on a chilly April evening, in a crumbling, red-tile-roofed villa, three kilometers off the N35 Highway, midway between Islamabad and Abbottabad.

Inside, a group of bearded and turbaned men sat on cushions on the floor of a dank room dimly lit by kerosene lanterns. They had arrived separately by devious routes. Their drivers and vehicles waited nearby in a secluded vacant lot, while a platoon of heavily armed men surrounded the house. They heard a car pull up and then the creak of a door opening. A tall man walked in. He had a long beard flecked with gray that matched the gray of his robe. The men got up and greeted him with great ceremony. The newcomer used a cane to walk around, stooping to embrace each man. He was a Sheikh—a Saudi of great dignity, a holy man, and their leader. He sat down and was served a cup of tea by one of the younger men. The Sheikh took a sip of tea, stroked his beard, and inquired politely of the gathered men's health and families. After niceties had been exchanged, he took another sip and began, "I am honored you could attend tonight. You've traveled far and taken great risks." Heads leaned forward to catch his voice. "Tonight we shall decide on our most important project to hasten the creation of the new Caliphate. We've done grave harm to the American devils with our 9/11 airplane attacks and it's time to launch our next project. This time we will create chaos and inflict serious economic damage on the infidels in their homeland. Ayman, the Hakim, and I have a proposal to present to you tonight. I will let him tell you of it."

The Hakim, an Egyptian physician with a frizzy beard, wore a brown vest over his white robe, and a white turban framing a brown birthmark on his forehead. He was a stocky man with a stern look, who lacked the Sheikh's polished charm. He stood up and squinted as he used a flashlight to read from notes.

The listeners nodded in approval as he read them in entirety, then sat down again. The Sheikh took it in, smiled, and said, "That is the plan. We have recruited highly qualified personnel, all devout believers in our just cause. We've enlisted a brilliant university professor who has developed the technical details." He took a sip of tea and continued. "This will be a complex, multistage operation and all components must be compartmentalized. Secrecy is everything in this war; only you are to know the entire battle plan. So what do you think of the proposal my brothers?"

After a short discussion, they agreed that the planned action was justified and righteous based on recent fatwas. They next turned to the budget; 14 million US dollars was a large sum and not easy to move across international borders covertly. Some nodded their approval and others frowned when the Sheikh informed them that the Iranians would provide half the funds. He addressed those who seem displeased by saying, "I know some of you are concerned by our partnering with the unholy Shia, but much can be accomplished by working together against our common enemy."

An older man with a full white beard, a noted Sunni cleric, cleared his throat and asked, "But how can we trust those treacherous Shia dogs?"

"Ayman and I have met with their Quds Force leaders and hammered out an agreement for joint attacks against the Americans. We believe it will work and not compromise our plan."

"So what price did we have to pay for the apostates' unexpected generosity?" the old man asked.

"My elder brother, the only price we've paid is agreeing to attack those sites chosen by the Iranians. We will decide the timing of the attacks. They don't know our battle plans and we don't know theirs. We thought it was a reasonable deal."

The old man raised his bushy eyebrows and muttered, "Inshallah."

The Hakim elaborated on the project's feasibility. Then they decided who would oversee various components of the operation. At the end, all agreed it was a brilliant plan and the likely effects of the attacks justified the costs and risks.

"My brothers, we've made an historic decision," the Sheikh declared. "Our attacks will bring the Great Satan to his knees and turn his attention away from our holy lands. Since we're dispersed now, there is no single country for him to attack in rage. Allah willing, we will succeed and establish our new and glorious Caliphate." The others nodded and murmured, "Inshallah." The Sheikh got up and walked around the room to embrace each man. He stopped at the Hakim, put a hand on his shoulder, and nodded as he said, "Well, Ayman, you shall have your dream of a bioterror attack and I shall have my holy war." He turned and smiled as he left.

2
Santa Fe, New Mexico, USA.

The snoring in the room was punctuated by the phone ringing. The source of the snoring shook his head and groped for the phone, his eyes still shut. He mumbled, "Hello?"

There was a man's voice on the other end. "Is this Dr. Winston Sage?"

"Yeah."

"My name is John Grant. I'm the New Mexico State Epidemiologist. I was given your name by the people at the University of New Mexico Medical School as someone who might be interested in serving on a new State Advisory Committee on Bioterrorism."

"Huh?" Sage said as he shook his head and opened his eyes.

"We need a well-qualified physician-epidemiologist for the Committee."

Sage was blinking, both from the brilliant Santa Fe sun outside and from the two glasses of wine he'd had with lunch. "My field isn't infectious diseases. I was a cancer epidemiologist," he replied.

"I understand you're a leading expert on investigating disease clusters and that your Doctor of Public Health dissertation at Harvard was on evaluating possible person-to-person transmission of cancer. Sounds like an infectious disease to me."

"My research was on cancer clusters. It involves different approaches," Sage mumbled.

"I also learned you worked in Ethiopia and saw a lot of tropical infectious diseases."

Sage assumed he had learned of the lecture he'd given to first-year UNM medical students on his experiences while teaching at the Gondar Public Health College in Ethiopia. He had shown some horrendous slides of infectious diseases, including pictures of one of the last cases of smallpox in Africa. "I guess I know something about tropical diseases," he remarked. "I had training in tropical diseases during my M.P.H. training and then I taught courses in tropical medicine in Ethiopia, but that's a long time ago."

Grant seemed undeterred. "You've probably seen more of the diseases our Committee will be concerned with than anybody in our State. We just received a federal grant to start a model bioterrorism education and surveillance program and we need someone like you."

Sage was fully awake now and suspected that this committee was probably nothing more than a federally funded boondoggle. "Why did the feds pick New Mexico for a bioterrorism program? We don't have large population centers or large, crowded facilities for an attack."

"The Government was interested in using our successful Hanta virus surveillance program as a model. Our Senators made this point effectively and we got a large grant."

Sage realized that this really was a Federal pork-barrel project. Nevertheless, he was becoming intrigued by the chance to learn about bioterrorism while combatting the boredom of retirement. In the end he agreed to join the Committee, with the caveat that he wasn't sure he'd be adding much.

"I'm sure you can contribute a lot more than you think," Grant said. I'll be sending you a formal invitation to serve on the committee and we'll call you regarding the first meeting—it'll be in Santa Fe. Thanks, Dr. Sage. I look forward to meeting you."

After hanging up, Sage sat there wondering what he had just gotten himself into. In his grogginess he'd failed to ask what the committee appointment entailed in terms of time commitment and responsibility. Well, at least he could stay current in infectious diseases. Besides when it came to combatting senility, he was a believer in the "use it or lose it" theory. He raised the back of his overstuffed recliner and sat up, yawning as he reached down to pick up the medical journal he'd been reading and looked at his empty wine glass on the side table. He got up and went looking for his wife Julia who was also a physician and an epidemiologist; they'd met 31 years ago as classmates in the Master of Public Health program at Harvard.

He found Julia sitting on the living room couch, reading. "Hey Julia, guess what; I'm going to serve on a New Mexico committee on bioterrorism."

Julia looked at him as if he he'd just stepped out of a UFO. "Are you for real, Win? You know beans about bioterrorism. And why would New Mexico need a bioterrorism program?"

"Well, New Mexico has a model surveillance program for Hanta virus they can build on. I remember watching something about it on TV."

"That's nuts," she said.

"Look, I'm retired, bored, and in need of some occupational therapy for my aging brain; I have nothing to lose but excess time."

"Hanta virus is spread by rodents, not terrorists. This reminds me of the joke about the drunk who loses his keys outside a bar and goes down the street to look for them under a streetlight because the light's so much better there. At least you didn't dream up this lame-brained project."

"No, I'm not that crazy," Win said as he went over and kissed Julia on the forehead.

"You know Julia, we're epidemiologists; we're supposed to be medical detectives. This could be my big chance to be a real-world sleuth. Can't you just see the newspaper headline: 'Santa Fe doctor uncovers terrorist plot in New Mexico.' I'll be a hero," Win said with a bow.

"Don't get carried away, Buster. This is New Mexico and there ain't going to be any bioterrorism here."

3
Agha Khan University Hospital, Karachi, Pakistan

It was late afternoon in the Emergency Clinic at the Agha Khan University Hospital in Karachi—hot, humid, and smelly. Adwalla Rahman sat holding her seven-year-old son on her lap, fanning him with a piece of cardboard. The walls were stained and bare, save for a plaque with a ceramic picture of the Agha Khan and a crescent below it. They had been waiting for two hours and the waiting-room crowd finally seemed to be dwindling. Adwalla waved a fly off her son's face, which was red and sweaty. She was worried because she had left her other three children with a neighbor and it was getting close to the time for their evening meal. No one at the front desk seemed to know how much longer she would have to wait.

Finally, a man in a tan uniform asked her to bring her boy inside to be seen by the hakim. The boy was sleeping and she hated to disturb him, but he needed to be seen.

A soiled green curtain separated the waiting room from the examining rooms. The inside area reeked of disinfectant and was even hotter than outside because of all the lights. An aide ushered her into a curtained-off cubicle and instructed her to undress her son so he could be examined. A nursing sister came in after a few minutes and asked if Adwalla was the boy's mother. While chatting with Adwalla, she took the boy's pulse and temperature and shook her head after looking at the thermometer.

"About a week ago he developed a fever," Adwalla said. "For a few days it got higher and higher and it has never come down. He told me his head and belly hurt and he's weak. Today he complained that he couldn't move his bowels and he vomited twice. He also developed a funny rash on his chest. For two days now he's been coughing too. I saw something like this in my nephew and he died from it."

"When was that?"

"A few years ago."

"How old is your boy?"

"He's seven and my oldest child."

"Is anyone at home sick with the same thing?"

"No, I don't think so."

"Has he had diarrhea?"

"No."

"Okay, we'll have to wait for the doctor, but first I need to draw some blood from his arm for tests. It will only hurt a little." Just as she said, when the nurse drew the blood, the sick boy didn't cry or move. She left and they were alone again.

After another long wait, a doctor in green scrubs and a long white coat entered their cubicle with the sister they had seen before. "Salaam; how are you this evening?"

"Honored hakim, my son is sick with the fever and he's very weak."

"That's what the sister told me. She said he has a high fever, 41.2 degrees, and a slow heart rate. The laboratory called to let us know his white blood cell count is low, but…."

"Is he going to die?" she interrupted him, too panicked to be polite.

"No, my sister; it means he's likely to have typhoid fever and we now have drugs that can cure it. Do you see these rose-colored spots on his chest and belly? They are classic for typhoid. We'll have to admit him to the hospital and keep him here for about a week. Don't worry about the charges; we are a charity hospital supported by our namesake's generosity."

8

"Can I leave him alone for a while? I must make arrangements for my other children."

The nurse answered, "We'll take good care of him in your absence. Don't worry."

Adwalla, who could neither read nor write, had to place Xs and thumbprints where they instructed her to sign the admission forms. She hugged her boy and told him she was going home to take care of the family and would be back later. He began sobbing, so she left quickly.

Once she was gone, the doctor followed her out of the examining room and found a phone on a corner desk. He dialed and asked for Tahir. After a few seconds he said, "My esteemed brother, we have a source for one of the agents for which we've been waiting. I'm admitting the carrier to the pediatric ward. He's a seven-year-old with almost certain typhoid fever. He hasn't been having diarrhea and is constipated so we may have to give him a laxative or use suppositories to get our samples. I'll keep him off antibiotics for as long as I can without losing him. Go to the ward and tell the staff I ordered the collection of stool samples by any means. Tell them it's essential for making an accurate diagnosis. I'll place him in an isolation room. Praised be Allah!" and he hung up.

The doctor went back into the examining cubicle and gave his instructions to the nursing sister who dutifully wrote them down on an order sheet that the doctor then signed. As he left, he said, "You've done a good job, sister."

The doctor was elated by this opportunity. His family had fled Kashmir when the Indians took over and he felt honored that the organisms he collected would be used against the despised Indians in New Delhi.

4
Red Crescent Hospital, Dhaka, Bangladesh

It was dreadful, sitting and waiting endlessly in the Emergency Clinic at the Red Crescent Hospital on a steamy afternoon in Dhaka. There was no air conditioning, only a slowly rotating ceiling fan that churned the fetid air. Mohammed Arwad, a low-ranking civil servant, sat on a rickety bench cradling his elderly mother. She'd been having severe diarrhea for two days and now with the vomiting, she could keep little down. They'd been waiting for three hours and Mohammed worried she might die before the doctor saw her. At least she had no fever or rashes he could see, given her devoutly modest dress. He kept brushing flies from her face with his handkerchief.

Finally, one of the nursing sisters came over and said they could come inside to see the doctor. "Sorry about the wait," she said. "We've been tied up by a multi-vehicle traffic accident." The sister helped his feeble mother onto a wooden examining table. She drew a plastic curtain around the table, took the patient's temperature and blood pressure, and proceeded to take a medical history.

"How old are you, Auntie?" the sister asked.

"I think I'm 64 years old; I don't know for sure," she answered faintly.

"Tell me, what's the problem you're here for?"

"I have diarrhea and vomiting too."

"When did it begin, Auntie?"

"About two days ago."

"How bad is it?"

"It's very bad. I have diarrhea almost every hour and vomit after everything I try to drink or eat." She was short of breath after answering.

"Did you pass any blood with your diarrhea?"

"No. I don't think so."

Mohammed stroked his mustache, looked down and winced as he listened to his mother providing such intimate information.

"Have you had fever or chills?"

"No."

The nurse continued with her singsong litany of questions that seemed to follow the rhythm of the slowly turning ceiling fan. "Have you had any pain in your belly or cramps?"

"No; that's what's so strange."

Mohammed felt so embarrassed, he left the room to wait outside. He could still hear his mother, but it helped not to have to look at her while she discussed her bodily functions.

"Tell me Auntie, what does this diarrhea look like?"

"It's strange; it looks like gray water."

"Does it look like the water from washing rice?"

"How did you know?"

"I think I know what may be wrong with you." The nurse frowned and went on. "Why didn't you come in sooner?"

"I had no way of getting here. My son came to see me and he brought me here."

"Well, you're lucky to be alive."

"What do I have, Sister? Am I going to die?"

"We'll wait for the doctor to make the diagnosis. He should be here soon. You're very sick and I need to give you some fluids straight away." The nurse went out for a minute and returned with a beat-up metal pole on wheels, with an arm-like structure from which hung a bottle of liquid with a red rubber tube attached.

Mohammed, who was pacing up and back outside witnessed this with alarm and followed the nurse back into the cubicle. He looked away as the nurse helped his mother into a Johnny gown and started an intravenous drip. The nurse then drew several tubes of blood for the laboratory. "Auntie, with this drip, we will probably save your life. So lie back and rest."

Mohammed asked in a tremulous voice, "What's wrong with her?"

"I'm sure it's cholera," she whispered, "but we'll wait for the doctor to make the final diagnosis. I think she's going to be fine in short order."

Mohammed suspected the Sister knew what she was talking about, but wasn't that what they said about all patients, even when they were dying? He shrugged and sat down on a chair to wait. "Inshallah," he muttered.

It was a half-hour before a middle-aged man in a long white coat came into the room, followed by several younger men in white coats and two nursing sisters in starched white uniforms. The leader studied her medical chart and said, "Mrs. Arwad, I'm Doctor Haddad. How are you feeling?"

"Very weak."

"Sister Amina told me your story. Have you had cramps or fever with your diarrhea?"

"I don't own a thermometer, but I never felt hot and I never had even a small cramp."

As they were talking, he lifted the skin over her abdomen to estimate her degree of dehydration. He looked at her eyes and everted her lower eyelids to see if she was anemic. He felt her forehead, which was cool and clammy. "Sister Amina told me your diarrhea was like rice water; is that true?"

"Yes. She knew about it before I even told her."

"Auntie, I think you have cholera and you came to the hospital just in time. The treatment is replacing the water and salts your body lost from the diarrhea and vomiting. That loss is what makes you so sick, and can lead to death. We're going to keep you in the hospital for a few days. First, we'll do some tests to make sure it is cholera and then we'll nurse you back to health. Allah willing, I think you'll be well in a day or two." He patted her hand and turned to go. But before he left, one of his assistants asked, "Should we start her on antibiotics when she gets to the ward?"

"No. She'll do fine on replacement therapy. We'll collect her stools for the next few hours to run some tests."

Haddad left the entourage and went to the nurse's desk where he dialed a phone number, waited briefly and asked, "Achmed, is that you? We have a special case for you to process in the lab. Her name is Arwad and I'm admitting her to Ward 3-2. She has one of the diseases for which we've been waiting. I'll write orders to keep her off antibiotics and to collect all stool specimens for special lab studies. Go to the ward immediately and instruct the staff in how to handle the specimen collection. Tell them it's a special research project of mine and they are to follow the protocol properly or else! Peace be with you my brother."

Haddad was the son of Palestinian refugees who had taken up residence in Bangladesh. They'd become prosperous merchants who could afford to send their eldest son to medical school in Syria. His parents had never recovered from the loss of their ancestral land to the Zionist devils; their hatred of the Zionists was like a cancer gnawing at their innards. So Haddad was extremely proud to have been enlisted to collect cholera organisms to be used to spread the disease in Tel Aviv.

He rejoined the group and announced, "It looks like we saw our first cholera case of the year. Let's hope Allah will spare us another epidemic. All right, we have two more cases to see here and then we'll make ward rounds."

5
Karachi, Pakistan

The warehouse was a dilapidated affair near the docks of Karachi Harbor. Rashid Hussein and Jalal Mohammed made their way to it by a roundabout route to lessen chances of being followed. The sign on the door read, "Red Crescent Pharmaceuticals, Godown Offices." From the doorstep they could see the vast harbor below, filled with huge tankers and container ships. A faint smell of petrol wafted up from the ships. Rashid looked around to ensure they were alone before he knocked on the rusted door. They waited until the door opened a crack and a man's voice asked who they were. Rashid replied, "Messengers of Allah," and they were invited inside.

Rashid and Jalal could easily pass for two salesmen selling pharmaceutical products or equipment. But in fact, Rashid was a professor of microbiology currently on leave from the Dow Medical College in Karachi to tend to his elderly parents, while Jalal was a recent engineering graduate of the University of Technology and Science in Islamabad. They had come to inspect shipments of equipment and supervise their repackaging for transshipment to a manufacturing facility.

Inside they were greeted by an older man with a full, white beard. He was wearing the shalwar qameez, a long, loose tunic over baggy trousers, an open vest, and an elaborately embroidered taqiyah, the short round cap worn by devout Muslims; it had been a gift from the Sheikh. His name was Ahmed Tarkani, and he ran a large shipping company in Rawalpindi. Tarkani was a trusted friend of the Sheikh; he had delivered high security shipments for the Brothers for many years, a resourceful expert in shipping sensitive items to difficult places, who had never lost a shipment. There were also two younger men in the godown, dressed in navy coveralls.

Rashid, who looked concerned, pulled Tarkani aside to ask if the two young men could be trusted. "I would trust them with my life; they are my sons," Tarkani retorted. Rashid, new to this cloak-and-dagger business, blushed.

"Come let me show you what we've received," Tarkani said as he took Rashid by the arm. "These wooden crates arrived first; they were in a container from China. We took them out of the container but didn't uncrate them until we received instructions from you." Rashid scanned the dank warehouse and saw it was nearly full with the shipments.

Rashid took out several sheets of paper from his briefcase. He checked them and found that this must be the shipment of stainless steel fermentation vats they'd ordered. The cargo manifest tacked to the crate confirmed this. "Let's uncrate these. We'll need to repackage them in bubble wrap and cardboard boxes for shipment inland; it'll be much lighter." Tarkani signaled to his sons, who picked up crowbars and began the process.

Tarkani pointed out to Rashid the crates received from the US, France, Germany, and Switzerland. Rashid checked each shipment off his list. They stopped in front of two large generators that stood on wooden pallets and were packed in shrink-wrapped plastic. "These pieces are heavy and will be almost impossible to ship to your destination," Tarkani said. He pulled Rashid away from the others and whispered, "Why on earth do you want to ship all this heavy equipment to such a remote place? Why can't you set up here in Karachi? It would be so much easier and less expensive."

"We considered it, but our facility must be in an isolated setting, away from prying eyes and where our workers will be far from their families and friends, to prevent innocent betrayal of secrecy. The Brothers were adamant about this."

Tarkani scowled and said, "It borders on lunacy to try to transport this heavy equipment to your destination. There are no roads near your site. We'll have to rely on camels to get it over the rough terrain."

"I've heard you're a miracle worker when it comes to getting supplies to impossible places," Rashid said with a smile.

Tarkani chortled and said, "I think my reputation is about to be damaged. Well, Inshallah, we will get it to your location although these pieces of equipment may not work well after a rough camel ride."

Rashid and Tarkani continued the inspection of the cargo while Jalal supervised the sons unpacking. Everything they'd ordered had arrived and the cartons and crates looked undamaged. They couldn't afford the time it would take to assemble and test the equipment and then disassemble it for shipment. There was also the matter of not wanting others to know what the equipment was.

It was dark when they finished. Repackaging would take several days and then the transportation process would begin. As Rashid and Jalal were leaving, they thanked Ahmed and his sons and marveled at how everything had worked out. "This man is supposed to be a genius at shipping things. He'll get it to our site and in good shape, I'm sure. Now I'm looking forward to getting started on our great mission, "Rashid said as they walked down the street.

"I'm young, I guess. I'm just looking forward to being paid for my work and being able to buy a house for my family," Jalal said.

6
Santa Fe

It was Win's big day: his first Bioterrorism Committee meeting. He wanted to fit in, so he wore a denim sports coat, a blue shirt, khaki pants and, instead of a conventional tie, the Hopi, silver bola tie that Julia had given him. Feeling suitably stylish, Win drove to the meeting at the State Health Department downtown and found the place with ease.

He entered the 1970-era office building and made his way to the Committee's meeting room. A guy with a ponytail sat at the head of the Formica-topped conference table; Win assumed he was the State Epidemiologist. He wore a rumpled navy blazer, plaid shirt, and a huge turquoise and silver bola, which made Win glad about his own sartorial selection. Some of the people were chatting, but Win didn't know a soul there until another two men straggled in. Win instantly recognized one of them, Tom Shaw, an FBI agent from Albuquerque, whom he had met soon after he'd moved to Santa Fe, when he'd become involved in a messy investigation of a neighbor's missing wife. Win thought Shaw was competent, but too uptight. Shaw was the only guy in the room with a real tie on.

The pony-tailed guy started the meeting, introducing himself as John Grant, the State Epidemiologist. Then he asked everyone to introduce themselves by going around the table, identifying their areas of expertise and whom they would represent. The committee was a modern-day Noah's ark. There were two government computer scientists, representatives of the New Mexico Medical Society and the State Hospital Association, an Air Force major who was a microbiologist, a local emergency medicine physician, a State Police captain, the FBI dude, Win, and a Department of Agriculture veterinarian. The only member that really belonged on the Committee was Bill Applegate, a young medical school professor. He wore a university uniform of wire-rimmed glasses, a wrinkled plaid shirt, torn blue jeans, and hiking boots. He was an infectious disease specialist with an interest in Hanta virus infection, and was involved with the State's Hanta virus program. It looked like John was a skilled bureaucrat and had included all the relevant political constituencies, a formula sure to guarantee limited results.

Grant told them he was a physician-epidemiologist with training in infectious diseases. He had worked in the Indian Health Service for 20 years and took this job when he retired. He introduced his Department's staff, singling out a woman named Judy Smith, who was a Registered Nurse and would be the Executive Secretary for the Committee.

John began, "I'd first like to give you an overview of the history of this project." He described the discovery in New Mexico in 1993 of a new respiratory ailment with a high fatality rate. "This outbreak led to the discovery of a new class of Hanta viruses. Good field epidemiology helped find that the reservoir for this infection was a rodent, the deer mouse. This led to a program that trapped deer mice to monitor population size and infection rates in the animals. A human surveillance program was added to alert health authorities to new human outbreaks. Combined with educational programs for high-risk populations, these systems have been a success."

He went on, "After the 9/11 terrorist attacks, officials at local and national levels started identifying potential targets for terrorist attacks. Several experts expressed concern about attacks on New Mexico facilities. Although we don't have a large population, we house some important national defense sites. We have two nuclear development facilities—the Los Alamos and Sandia National Labs—Kirtland, Holloman and Cannon Air Force Bases, Fort Bliss Military Reservation and the White Sands Missile Range with the NASA Test Facility, for starters. As part of a State anti-terrorism program, the Governor and our US Senators held a series of meetings about our vulnerable targets. When the subject of bioterrorism came up, the Governor suggested we build a disease surveillance and educational program modeled on our Hanta virus program. With passage of the Homeland Security Act, our senators secured federal funding for such a project and arranged for use of the computing facilities of LANL and Sandia. We also secured funding from the Federal Government's Recovery and Reinvestment Act. So that's how we got here today. We have a great opportunity to build a model program in New Mexico."

Win tuned out as Grant went on. "I thought I'd provide a brief overview of the likely types of bioterrorism. Let me start with the candidate agents for bioterrorism. Using the CDC's classification, the most likely agents are in Category A. This group is characterized by being easily introduced or transmitted from person to person. It includes: Anthrax; botulism; plague—remember the Black Death; smallpox; tularemia or rabbit fever; and the scary group of viral hemorrhagic fevers and arenaviruses that include Ebola and Marburg viruses and Lassa fever. These last diseases occur mostly in Africa, are highly contagious, and have a high fatality rate."

John droned on covering Category B and C agents. Halfway through the Category C spiel, Win's eyes closed and his head slumped. He was awakened by the sound of Tom Shaw clearing his throat. Shaw, who had the demeanor of a mortician, said, "That's correct; our current thinking at the F.B.I is that our biggest threat is from Category A agents, particularly anthrax. You're all aware, I'm sure, of the anthrax mailings to the Congress and a newspaper office. It's an agent well suited for terrorism, particularly in the form that was used."

Shaw finished and John picked up on his canned talk, "The way the Governor and our Department envision the system is that it would collect health data from emergency departments, hospital admission records, several sentinel clinics and practices, the Indian Health Service, the University Hospital, and clinical labs around the State."

Win grimaced at the thought of this huge data collection and processing operation. Analysis of a massive amount of medical data was a real challenge, and then interpreting it quickly enough to take any action would add to a messy situation. He didn't think the State people had the foggiest notion of what they were getting into. Grant didn't even specify what data they'd collect.

John slogged on, "We'll also beef up our program for reporting infectious diseases in the State. We've obtained funding from Washington to provide dedicated PCs in key locations for entry of surveillance data. These computers will feed directly into our central data bank and should be usable by most clinical staff. We'll also mount an educational program in the State to alert our doctors and nurses to the signs and symptoms of diseases like anthrax, plague and smallpox."

Win was reminded of his public health days, particularly in the classrooms at Harvard, with cloistered academics proposing grandiose programs that had no hope of succeeding out where the rubber met the road. Unfortunately, practicing physicians were too busy coping with managed care, short staffing, government forms and regulations, and bulging clinic populations to be able to give any time to a project such as John was proposing. Anything reported, would be done by the least skilled and lowest paid workers.

John would never win any awards for teaching. Win guessed at least half of the people listening had no idea what he was saying, but John was oblivious. "I envision the Committee will subdivide into working groups such as an animal diseases group, food-borne and water-borne infection groups, a diagnostic algorithm development group, a response group, or others we think might be needed. The Committee should meet as a whole, at least once a month and the working groups will meet in between those meetings."

Win noted that John hadn't thought of a data group. But then, Win was an epidemiologist and this was the thing that concerned him most. This lack of concern about the nitty-gritty of collecting the data, processing it, and analyzing it didn't bode well for the program's success. As an outsider, Win decided not to bring this up at the first meeting.

John suggested they adjourn and chat over coffee and doughnuts. Win, who couldn't wait to get out of the meeting, was relieved that this wasn't a diehard "nuts and berries" group. They moved next door to a staff lunchroom with the usual vending machines, refrigerator, microwave and Formica-topped tables.

Win stood there, stretching his arms and shaking his head, when Tom Shaw came up to him and whispered, "Well, well; if it isn't Win Sage, the Dr. Strangelove of Santa Fe. When I first saw you here I cringed. I know we're headed for trouble with you on this Committee."

"Now Tom, your analogy is wrong. I'm more like General Jack D. Ripper in the Strangelove movie, the guy obsessed with maintaining the purity of our bodily fluids. We aren't heading for any trouble, since you know as well as I there's a snowball's chance in hell of any terrorism occurring in this State. Besides, their surveillance system isn't going to work."

"I don't know, Sage, particularly after the trouble you got yourself into as a bumbling detective looking for your neighbor's wife. Trouble seems to have a way of finding you, but let's hope it was a one-off event. At least, you put your sophomoric sense of humor aside for this meeting."

Win quipped, "Well, you seem to have lightened up a bit since we last worked together. You know, you look much better in a gray suit than a black one. You're less likely to be mistaken for a Mormon missionary now."

"And you haven't changed a bit."

"Anyway Tom, I don't know a lot about bioterrorism, but I once participated in a conference on food safety and it scared the hell out of me."

"By the way, the Bureau's concerned that the next act of terrorism on our soil could be biologic. That's why I take things like this Committee a lot more seriously than you do."

Win raised his right hand and said, "Tom, I'll be on my best behavior, Scout's Honor. I'm going to mix with the crowd."

"I'll join you."

The twosome chatted with the other members, most of whom seemed personable and knowledgeable. Win was relieved that the two Government computer wallahs shared his skepticism about the feasibility of the data operations. The emergency doc had his head screwed on straight and would lend some practicality to the group, and the veterinarian seemed to be a data trap for animal infectious diseases. The others seemed sharp and, more importantly, practical. Win thought that all in all this was a good group, but their charge was impossible, not to mention irrelevant. Anyway, he could learn some interesting new stuff.

7
South Waziristan Agency, Federally Administered Tribal Areas, Pakistan

The news arrived a month after the fateful meeting with the Sheikh. In remote South Waziristan, the Hakim was sitting in his garden behind vine-covered, stone walls. He was deep in discussion with an aide when an assistant came into the garden and hesitantly handed him a note. The Hakim grabbed the folded paper, opened it, and read the note twice. He turned ashen and appeared to be in a trance as tears rolled down his cheeks

"What is it?" the aide asked.

"It's the Sheikh! The Americans killed him in his home in front of his family."

"Can this be true? How could they have known where he was? We've been so careful. Will this change our plans?"

The Hakim sighed. "It is true, my son. The infidels' cursed leader appeared on television to announce it. It was on Al Jazeera and CNN. One of our men in Abbottabad confirmed the report."

The only sound was the tinkling of the fountain in the center of the garden as the Hakim stared at the flowering fruit trees and thought for a while before going on. "No, my son, we will proceed as planned. The American dogs will pay a greater price now. Our Leader's death will not have been in vain. This will be his last war and we'll make it one that will be remembered for generations." He pounded his fist on the arm of his chair and said, "My brother's death will be avenged!"

8
Islamabad, Pakistan

Achmed Nirwal was in his laboratory at the Ministry of Health's Central Public Health Laboratories on the outskirts of Islamabad. He was proud of his government job that gave him prestige and a stable, if modest, income. He had worked diligently for his Bachelor's and Master's degrees in microbiology and this was his reward, and a just one, he believed. Allah had blessed him with intelligence and the drive to succeed.

These were the nation's central reference laboratories and he found the work there fascinating. His most recent assignment was working in the bacteriology lab that did the identification and typing of difficult or unusual specimens from across the country. They were often called on to review the identification of organisms from large or dangerous disease outbreaks. The initial identifications were usually done by less experienced personnel out in the field or in poorly equipped hospital laboratories.

He was currently investigating specimens from an outbreak of severe, bloody diarrhea in Karachi. The initial investigators suspected it was likely food-borne, and the food the patients had eaten in common was ground beef from a local grocery. The hospital, where one of the patients had died, thought they had isolated both Salmonella and pathogenic E. coli from the patient's stool and blood. They shipped their specimens to Achmed's lab for confirmation. He knew that the bloody diarrhea was more likely related to E. coli than to Salmonella infection, particularly if it was one of the enterohemorrhagic types.

Ali, his lab tech, was working under a glass hood and suddenly exclaimed, "Achmed, come look at this! The child probably died of pathogenic E. coli infection. The typing of the specimens from Karachi shows it's the 0157:H7 strain."

"That's nasty stuff and can kill," Achmed said. "So it looks like we have another outbreak of meat-borne, enterohemorrhagic E. coli infection. In the West, most of these outbreaks seem to occur after eating hamburgers at those abominable fast food restaurants. It's too bad it doesn't occur commonly in pork. Are you sure about the typing?"

"Yes, I ran it three times as you taught me."

"We'll have to notify the Ministry of Health since the public could get alarmed by this news. Make sure you clean up well and store the plates safely in the incubator. We don't want to destroy them until we're certain the outbreak is contained."

"Yes, Hajji Achmed. Is it all right if I take a tea break after I clean things up?"

"You've worked hard this afternoon and should take a break. I'll ring up the Deputy Minister's secretary to give him the bad news."

Ali stored his culture plates in the secure incubator. They routinely stored dangerous specimens in an incubator that could be locked at night. Some ignorant oaf could get into the specimens and spread dangerous bugs around. Worse yet, some lunatic could steal dangerous specimens to poison people. Ali then carefully disposed of his plastic instruments and the workplace paper liners, washed his hands thoroughly with disinfectant soap, and took off for a much-needed break.

After Ali left, Achmed, who was seated at his desk, took out his worn leather wallet and retrieved a small piece of paper with a telephone number on it. He dialed the number and waited.

A male voice answered, "Good day; how may I help you?"

Achmed answered with the required response, "It's a good day indeed."

"Ah; so it is you. Do you have something for us?"

"Yes, my brother. I have some 0157:H7 E. coli."

"When can you deliver it?"

"Tonight, if you wish."

"That would be perfect. You must be careful in coming here."

"I should arrive at about 9:00 PM Peace be with you my brother." Achmed hung up and sat back in his chair. He was proud to be involved in helping his brothers in their jihad. Achmed firmly believed that it was his religious duty to aid in the destruction of the Great Satan. He was delighted these organisms would be used in Afghanistan against the Americans and their running dog allies. "Praise be to Allah," he said.

He beamed as he dialed the number for the Ministry of Health.

9

North Waziristan Agency, Federally Administered Tribal Areas, Pakistan

Rashid Hussein, the microbiology professor, was up at the crack of dawn to prepare for an important visit by his new leader. The sound of a rooster crowing in the village nearby and the smell of smoky, morning cook-fires reminded him of childhood in his parents' village. The Brothers had made the difficult decision to locate near a village, giving up some of the secrecy surrounding the project, but it wasn't logistically feasible to run the operation solely on power from generators. They needed to be able to tap into power lines for electricity. He nodded as he surveyed the barren compound with its tents and Quonset huts and the surrounding mountains. The compound and the nearby village were on the only pieces of level ground amid the steep hills.

He had worked around the clock for the past month to get the equipment installed and working in time for this visit and he was exhausted. After skipping dinner last night he was starved, so he washed, dressed and headed down to one of the buildings that smelled of porridge and tea. He was the first for breakfast and was greeted by the cook, a rotund man in traditional Pakistani garb.

"Welcome, my brother. Would you like your usual breakfast?"

"Yes. Today's a special day, so I'll need a hearty meal. The Hakim is coming to review our progress; it's a great honor."

"He's a great man leading a great cause, my Imam has said."

Rashid wolfed down a fortifying breakfast of porridge, fried eggs, naan and several glasses of tea. Setting up a full-fledged biologics manufacturing facility in the middle of nowhere was an incredible challenge and he could hardly believe they'd done it. He had meant to impress the Hakim with his ability to get an impossible job done well and on time. It was sad that the Sheikh wasn't alive to see the fruition of their shared dream. Rashid finished his meal and left to make the rounds of the different buildings with their newly installed equipment.

He entered the first and largest building, which was brightly lit with fluorescent lighting that made the stainless steel tanks inside gleam. He toured the tanks and all seemed to be in operational order. The next building contained an area with Plexiglas cubicles covered by stainless steel exhaust hoods on one side and laboratory benches covered with glassware on the other. His office was at the back of this building, partitioned off from the laboratory area by a floral-printed curtain. He entered one of the cubicles and turned on the laminar flow fan to make sure it was working. He went off to a more distant hut that contained several freezers and low-temperature centrifuges and had side rooms enclosed by double sets of glass doors. Everything was completed at last and he closed his eyes as in prayer. He smiled when he went outside and saw that the men were up and about. He called to one of them, "Jalal, I need to talk to you."

Jalal ran over and greeted Rashid, "Salaam. It's a great day today. How can I be of help?"

"We need to do several last minute checks before the Hakim and his people arrive. I need you to take some men to check the perimeter fencing and the razor wire we installed the other day. Also, check the fuel tanks to make sure they're still full. Were you able to fix that cranky refrigerated centrifuge last night?"

"Yes. We have it running like a top now. Let's hope, Allah willing, that it all works today during the Hakim's visit."

The call of a muezzin in the nearby village reminded Rashid it was time for his morning prayers. He went back to his small house on a hill overlooking the dusty compound where he carefully washed, unfurled a fine Afghan prayer rug—a gift from the Sheikh—and faced its mihrab towards Mecca. He knelt and said his prayers. He was a truly devout man, an hafiz, one who had completely memorized the Qur'an.

It was 8:40 AM when they saw the first sign of the Hakim's retinue. Rashid noticed at least a dozen armed men on horseback off in the distance. As they got closer to the compound they fanned out searching the inhospitable terrain. They dismounted at the high points overlooking the camp where they assumed firing positions. Rashid turned to look at the rear of the compound and noticed additional armed guards behind the camp. The Hakim was a survivor because he left nothing to chance. About ten minutes later, Rashid saw a smaller party approaching, led by two men on horseback at its head. One of the two men was short and heavyset, the other tall and lean. Both wore black tribal outfits, carried automatic weapons, and had full beards. They looked like armed mullahs to Rashid. The group rode directly into camp and dismounted at the headquarters building where Rashid and Jalal were waiting.

"Salaam aleikem, my honored brothers," Rashid said.

"Aleikem salaam. It's a beautiful day today and an important one. This is my aide Tariq," the Hakim said as he pointed to the younger man.

"It's an honor to have you visit"

The Hakim said, "So Rashid, do you think you're ready to begin receiving the materials for production?"

"Yes, my esteemed leader. All of the equipment has been received, assembled, and is in working order."

"Why don't you take us on a tour? I was once a physician, so I may still know of the things you'll be doing here. We cannot stay long."

Rashid took them through each of the buildings explaining the function of each piece of equipment, with Jalal trailing behind them. The Hakim asked some pointed questions and seemed sharp as a tack but he had the annoying traits of finding minor cleanliness problems everywhere and scowling the whole time.

Rashid inquired politely, "May we serve you some tea?"

The Hakim looked at his watch and then the sky and said, "Yes. That would be nice," although he didn't look enthusiastic about spending more time there.

They went into the mess hall where hot tea was waiting. The Hakim took several sips of tea and said, "As you know, we're concerned about security in this area with all the bandits and warlords about. We'll leave a contingent of men behind to protect the place and will unload arms and camouflage equipment. To keep this place as quiet as possible, none of your men is to leave the compound until the project is completed. The people in the village below are loyal followers and believers, but I fear outsiders. Also, your men are to lead devout lives and there is to be no alcohol here. You also must be aware of possible spies from above—satellites and those cursed drones—so the compound has to look like abandoned military barracks rather than a laboratory." He fixed Rashid with a stare and asked, "Do you truly believe you're ready to begin production?"

"Yes, my leader. We're ready and eager for the day when we ship our products for use."

"Good! We'll have the culture supplies delivered in two days and the feeder stock should arrive shortly after. We have obtained all the types of feeder stock you requested from our medical brothers. You'll need some volunteers to test the products and we'll provide them when you're ready. We must be absolutely certain the products work." He sighed and went on, "It's been my dream for years to mount a biologic attack on the American dogs. You give me hope, Rashid, that my desire will be fulfilled. You have done a remarkable job and it shall be rewarded. Give my praise to your men too for serving our cause so well." They went outside where some of the Hakim's men were unloading wooden crates from camels. One of the men came over to join them.

"This is Yusuf Khan," the Hakim said. "He will be the leader of the security force we'll leave behind. I believe you have sufficient housing here to accommodate him and his men."

"Yes, my leader."

"Good, then; we'll be leaving. May Allah speed you and protect you."

The Hakim and his aide got on their horses with help from Yusuf, and headed out of the compound. The Hakim leaned over and said to his aide, "This Rashid is a competent man and a true believer. It's rare to find an accomplished university professor who can also build a laboratory and manufacturing facility and finish it on time in such an isolated place. We must take good care of him for future operations. We'll reward the others too. These are good men."

Rashid frowned as he watched the caravan leave. He had preferred to work with the Sheikh. The Hakim was a brilliant man, but rough and uncharming. Rashid wondered whether it was piety or hatred that drove the Hakim and decided it was probably both. He sighed and turned to study Yusuf and the long scar on his face that distorted his left eye and twisted his lip in a half-snarl. He looked menacing and it worried Rashid.

10
Astoria, Queens, New York City

Nasir al Fakrah had to slow his pace down to avoid attracting attention as he walked from the subway to his meeting. But he didn't want to keep the Imam waiting. The unseasonably warm weather was making him sweat. Although he'd lived in the New York City area for two years, he still found it difficult to travel about the city using public transportation. He finally arrived at the five-story, red-brick building where the Imam lived. His apartment was over a bustling, noisy Greek restaurant and bar, the Mykonos, but the old man liked where he lived. Nasir hurried up the three flights of stairs two steps at a time. He knocked on the apartment door and was let in by the Imam himself.

"Peace be with you my son Nasir. It's good to see you."

"Peace be with you my respected Imam. You're looking well."

"Come in my son." The Imam led Nasir into a living room furnished with an old blue couch, two overstuffed blue upholstered chairs, and some large cushions on the plush carpeted floor. He steered Rashid to one of the cushions and turned on a radio at high volume before he took a seat on another. The room also had a noisy fan turned up to high speed. On top of this, the faint sound of Greek music drifted up to the apartment.

He asked in Arabic, "How is your family, Nasir?"

Nasir had to move closer to the Imam to hear him, as the din almost completely obscured what he was saying. "They are well, Sir. My oldest son is about to begin at the madrasah next month. It's been hard on my wife, being alone, but my family is watching her well. I look forward to going home when all is done with our charity work here."

"I expect it will not be too long. So how is your youth project going?"

"Quite well. We've enrolled 11 well-qualified young men. They're upstanding, devout Muslims who'll profit greatly from our religious training program."

"Tell me, how did you choose your students?"

"We found them through several mosques. We had a profile for the ideal candidates. We wanted our scholars to have been born in the US to parents from the Middle East. Most parents are from Iraq and Pakistan. Since this is also a rehabilitation program, we searched for troubled youth. The boy's fathers were unemployed and could never fit in well to their adopted country. Almost all of our boys had trouble in school or finding a job, so they feel like outsiders and are angry at the US. Fortunately, they are all religious and have been transformed by their new roles as soldiers of Allah."

"Are the boys intelligent enough for our educational program?"

"Yes, I think so. All have learned their lessons well and have memorized them."

"That is a delight to my ears. Do you have adequate funds for your program?"

"Yes, the Brothers have been most generous in their support."

"Do your boys all have the proper credentials now?"

"Yes, that part has worked out well."

"Have the sites for their field work been selected?"

"Yes, the sites are small cities spread across the US. Unfortunately, the Iranians insisted on these sites; we preferred large cities. I'm now getting the boys set up with housing and educational programs."

"That's good. Have you arranged their return travel after their field work is completed?"

"Yes, it's important to get them back to their homes safely and quickly after the fieldwork. Their parents will be anxious to see them."

"Have you arranged for their medical care? We want them to be fit and have all their immunizations up to date. There are many infections they can get in their schools."

"Yes, they've been seen by trustworthy physicians and are physically fit and fully immunized."

"If any of your boys are harmed, can they be traced back to you?"

"I've been most careful in my dealings with them. They don't know who I really am or who's supporting them. As in all our charity work, we want to keep ourselves compartmentalized and anonymous. I think our arrangements are secure."

The Imam nodded. "You've been well trained, my son. We can never be too careful. I understand this time we will be kinder to the non-believers, aiming more at their wallets than their lives."

Nasir moved closer to the Imam and whispered in his ear, "That is the intent, Imam. We will have an important economic impact with our program. We aim to wage economic jihad to show the non-believers our resolve. This project, combined with the high price of oil, will really hurt their economy. The Iranians are doing a good job of sustaining fear of disruption of oil supplies to keep prices high."

"Yes, we may someday spread righteousness in this land of non-believers. You must keep me informed of progress with this important work. Come Nasir, let's have some tea." The Imam led Nasir to the kitchen where they made small talk over glasses of tea. He silently passed a large black, nylon briefcase to Nasir and then ushered him out and said, "Salaam aleikem, my son."

Nasir walked at a normal pace this time as he found his way back to the subway with no trouble. He felt relieved and proud that the Imam was pleased with his progress.

11
North Waziristan

After the Hakim and his small army departed, Yusuf Khan got to work immediately. He moved the wooden boxes of arms to a storage shed and posted one of his men there as a guard. He had his other men, ten in number, move their gear to a dormitory Quonset hut where they would bunk during this operation. Next, he dispatched his men to start on the needed fortifications of the compound. They were a rough looking lot and the word charm was clearly not in their vocabulary. They were all tall, bearded and dressed in local black tribal clothing that could have used a good wash. They looked like they'd been recruited from one of the fierce tribal groups that populated the inhospitable mountains of the Afghanistan-Pakistan border. The men began digging foxholes at the four corners of the compound and filling sandbags to be piled around the foxholes. The facility was on a steep hill, with sweeping views of all approaches. Two of the men began placing plastic camouflage nets over the buildings in the compound and anchoring them securely to the ground with metal pegs. Yusuf eyed all of this silently as he stood at the top of the hill near the rear of the compound. The men were well trained and had the seasoned caution of troops who had fought many guerilla battles. Yusuf knew well that this operation needed tight security even though they were in friendly territory. They could not risk a security lapse at this secure end of the operation; there would be far greater risks as the operation shifted closer to its targets.

Rashid saw the Hakim's lieutenant and walked over to join him. "Well Yusuf, I see you and your men have lost no time."

"As the Hakim said, we'll need to start your operations here in a few days and we need to beef up security to be prudent. My men are good, but we need to fortify this place. We survive because we are careful and trust no one. Speaking of protection, we'll need to immunize your workers to protect them from any accidental infection. One of my men, Mahmoud, is a trained nurse and is ready to give your men their shots. Why don't you round them up in half an hour so he can do his work? We can give the shots in the dining tent."

Rashid agreed and said, "It should be done. These immunizations require a few days to reach peak effectiveness and we'll be starting production in a few days. Did you bring the vaccines with you?"

"Yes, one of the boxes we unloaded contains the shot materials in freezer packs. We need to use it soon."

"Then I will make it a priority for my men."

"Thank you, Rashid. Oh, one more item remains. We've brought camouflage uniforms for your men to wear. After the men get their shots we'll distribute them. We want them to wear these clothes whenever they're outside to minimize being spotted from overhead."

Rashid was surprised, but agreed it was prudent. He was feeling proud of himself as he made the rounds of his facility and personally ordered all the staff to show up for their shots in half an hour.

In the meantime, Yusuf found Mahmoud, the nurse, and ordered him to get set up in the dining tent to give the personnel their shots. He saluted Yusuf and said, "Immediately, Sir."

Mahmoud found the dining hut and enlisted the help of the cook and dishwasher to get things set up. He carefully laid out his instructions and the two lists of personnel, one with a red mark at the top of the page and the other with a blue mark. He assumed this was because the workers would have different exposures to the infectious agents. He carefully unpacked the vials of vaccines from their freezer packs and placed those with red marks by the "red" list and the vials with blue marks by the "blue list." He next unpacked the disposable syringes and needles he would use to administer the vaccines and packets of antiseptic wipes. He asked the cook for a large garbage bag, surveyed his handiwork and was set to begin.

The workers began to trickle into the dining tent. Yusuf's men also came. Rashid and Yusuf entered and greeted their men as they made their way to the table where Mahmoud had set things up. Yusuf looked to Rashid, who stood up on a bench and began, "My esteemed brothers, we are working on an important mission here that involves the handling of some bacteria and viruses that could make us sick if we were exposed to them accidentally. To protect ourselves we need to be immunized. The Hakim has generously provided us with the vaccines we will use today. The shots will hurt a bit and the places where you get the shots may become sore. Our colleague, Mahmoud, who will give you the shots, is a trained nurse who can help you if you feel sick afterwards. I will go first to show you that the shots aren't really bad."

Rashid got down from his perch and rolled up his sleeves. He walked over to Mahmoud's table and said, "I'm your first victim, I guess," evoking laughs from the rank and file. Mahmoud searched the lists for Rashid's name and the shots he was to receive. Rashid was on the blue list and received 5 separate shots from the blue vials. He rolled down his sleeves and quipped, "That wasn't too bad and you can see I'm still standing."

Jalal, Rashid's deputy, went next and also received 5 shots from the blue vials. Their men followed them into line, looking a bit worried. They all received 5 shots from the red vials and flinched and joked as they underwent their ordeal. Yusuf and his men went next and they were all on the blue list. They looked stern and showed no discomfort as they got their shots.

Yusuf announced, "My brothers, we will soon begin production, Allah willing. It will become important for us to work with speed when our supplies and feeder stocks arrive. We'll change over to shift work to run the operation efficiently and you'll have to stay in camp full-time from now on. We need you to be available at any time and also we do not wish to accidentally spread the agents to our friends in the village nearby. We will also be distributing camouflage uniforms to you. The Great Satan has satellites in the heavens and flies drones over our Province looking for targets. You must wear these clothes when you're outside so you are less visible from above. May Allah protect us and speed us in our noble cause."

Rashid scowled as he left the building deep in thought. He was no longer in charge.

12
Santa Fe

Win was looking forward to the second meeting of the Bioterrorism Surveillance Advisory Committee, "the B-sack" as he now called it. Win was compulsive and easily became obsessed with problems, particularly thorny ones. After extensive on-line reading, he was concerned about the vulnerability of the US to bioterrorism attack, though he was still convinced the likelihood of New Mexico being involved was low. America is generally lax in security of vulnerable sites like water supply facilities, HVAC facilities in big office complexes and shopping malls, or food supplies. It would be prohibitively expensive to beef up security for all possible weak points nationally, and besides, who'd want to pay for it? It was like health insurance, which pays far more for surgical procedures than preventive services, allowing most of the damage to have been done. But politicians don't get reelected for garnering money for projects that have no visible benefits to brag about. When prevention is done well, there should be little to show for it other than some statistics that nobody cares to see. Meanwhile, the world is becoming full of fanatics and nut-cases hell-bent on destroying the US and it's going to cost the country more and more to prevent attacks.

It was another magnificent day in Santa Fe—with bright sun and turquoise skies—putting Win in good spirits on the drive into town. He turned on the car radio and tuned in the local country and western music station. Win always contended that this music was America's opera, with better and more sophisticated, heart-rending librettos than Italian opera. Unfortunately, he couldn't get anybody to agree with him. He pulled into the parking area between the state buildings and found a visitor's parking spot.

Win was the first to arrive for the meeting, aside from Tom Shaw, the FBI dude, so he sat down next to him.

"Hi, Tom. What are you and the Bureau up to these days in preventing bioterrorism?"

"Well, well, if it isn't Dr. Sage. How've you been?"

"I've been fine, but getting concerned about our vulnerability to bioterrorism attacks in the US. You didn't answer my question."

"The Bureau is up to a lot and most of it's classified."

"You haven't changed a bit, even though you've lightened up in your dress."

"And you haven't changed in your sophomoric wit."

"Yup, it looks like we've established a nice, mutual understanding."

"To be serious, what do you think the Committee ought to do as a priority, Win?"

"I would go with the simplest and most 'doable' things first. I would beef up communicable disease reporting and mount an educational program to teach docs and nurses how to recognize diseases that might be involved in a bioterrorist attack. An elaborate, computer-based system to pick up an epidemic of suspect diseases is fanciful nonsense. You'd get the most 'bang for your buck' by putting up posters with pictures of patients with diseases like anthrax, smallpox or plague in doctors' offices or emergency rooms."

"Now that sounds reasonable for a change."

At that point John Grant, his staff and a gaggle of committee members arrived. There were greetings all around followed by John's calling the meeting to order. He welcomed everybody and began in his nerdy style, reporting that he'd received calls from Committee members regarding the feasibility of his proposed program. "So let's discuss what you think we should be doing. Does anybody have ideas?"

Tom kicked Win under the table, startling him, and then suggested that he begin the discussion. Win had no choice but to give his two bits worth of advice, so he repeated what he'd said to Tom. "As part of the new program, we could print up posters with pictures of some of the diseases we'd expect in a terrorist attack," he suggested. "Not many practicing docs or nurses know the differences in the appearance of smallpox and chickenpox. The same goes for the eschar in anthrax patients or the buboes in bubonic plague. For the non-docs or nurses here, that means the characteristic black scab in anthrax or the enlarged lymph nodes in plague. Getting these posters up in health care facilities should at least get people to think of these diseases when they see patients. As part of this, you could post a hot-line telephone number to call if any of these diseases are seen. The odds are it'll never get used, but it's still a good idea just in case. Of course, you'd need to have trained people to answer and field any hot-line calls that did come in. This might be done by training a group of nurses and having one of them on call, 24-7. That's a quick and easy way to get real-time reporting. You could also run continuing medical education courses around the state on infectious diseases. Everybody is looking for easy and free CME credits for their medical license renewal nowadays. This would give us more time to set up the sophisticated data systems you talked about last time."

The computer lady from Los Alamos looked like she wanted to kiss Win. "I think these are great ideas," she said. "The development of an elaborate computer system is going to take at least a year, and probably two, but we could get the rest of this going right away."

The Executive Director of the State Medical Society also jumped on the bandwagon. "I bounced the discussion from our first meeting off some of our doctors. They all expressed concern about the feasibility and real costs of having a full-blown computerized reporting system. I think Win's ideas are a good first step. The State Medical Society could help with the CME courses, which I think our docs would welcome. We just need to keep the courses short, close to home, and after practice hours. Maybe even serve them a nice supper. Our docs can't be away from their practices for too long in the current economic environment."

Bill Applegate, the infectious disease guy from UNM added, "I agree this would be a good beginning. I could get some of our ID faculty and fellows to do some of the teaching. My only concern is that not all of the potential bioterrorism diseases lend themselves to pictures. For example, how would you illustrate diarrhea from shigellosis so it can be differentiated from that due to a benign summer enterovirus infection? The same goes for pathogenic E. coli infections. I don't think doctors are going to hang pictures of stool samples on their office walls. So maybe we could have a poster that just has readable text and provides some differential diagnosis information on diarrheal diseases or unexplained fevers. The problem is the more you put on the posters, the less likely a busy person is to read it. So my thoughts are to keep any posters simple and supplement them by mailings of informational materials or running short courses."

Several others echoed strong support for Win's ideas. Grant looked upset. He raised his hand to stop the discussion and declared, "I disagree with the priorities you've proposed. Our Governor and Senators worked hard to get us access to the computing facilities at Los Alamos and Sandia Labs and if we don't use them, we'll lose access to them. Getting data systems set up should be our top priority. That will also protect our funding."

Win waved his hand as he interrupted Grant. "John, you can make it a priority, but that's not going to speed things up. The data collection system you're proposing couldn't get implemented for at least a year, and likely more, no matter what resources you put behind it. You'd have nothing to show for your efforts after a year; wouldn't that jeopardize your funding even more? Why not move ahead with your data system and also do some of the projects we've just suggested? At least you'll have something to show early on. It'll also give the program quick visibility and raise bioterrorism awareness."

John looked resigned and said, "Well, so long as development of our data collection system remains the top priority, I guess we can pursue some of your suggestions in tandem." He called for a vote of the committee members on whether to go ahead with this approach. The vote was unanimously in favor, with most members looking down as they raised their hands. John went on, "Now we'll need to have some subcommittees: one on developing the posters or mailing materials; another on setting up ID courses and arranging for CME accreditation; and a third on the recruiting and training of nurses and how to handle the incoming reports." He asked for volunteers and Win chose the third group.

John asked, "Does anyone else have other thoughts we should discuss?"

The government veterinarian raised his hand. "We also should be thinking about animal bioterrorism. I'd like to explore the possibility of a parallel educational program for our State's vets. They need to be alerted to the possible terrorist introduction of things like foot-and-mouth disease or swine fever into the state's livestock."

John responded, "That's an important area for us to pursue. Why don't you go ahead and organize a sub-committee on bioterrorist-spread animal infections. We'll need a volunteer or two from the Committee and you might also want to get an outside expert on animal ID involved. Any other thoughts?"

Bill Applegate raised his hand and said, "You know there's another important area we haven't discussed, and that's the identification of the source of any outbreak of one of these diseases, should the unthinkable happen. When there's an outbreak of something like salmonella infection or staph food poisoning, we usually do an intensive search to identify a point source for the epidemic. The CDC has a whole series of training materials available on the investigation of community disease outbreaks. A lot of it's focused on outbreaks of food-borne diseases. You know, the proverbial scenario of chopped chicken liver or potato salad sitting around at a Bar Mitzvah. I suggest we have a subcommittee on how to investigate the source of any unusual disease outbreak."

John said, "That's a great idea. Bill, why don't you round up some people for a working group on outbreak investigation. Let's adjourn and chat over coffee next door."

"What about a data processing and analysis group?" Win interjected.

"I'm thinking about it and we'll discuss it at our next meeting," John answered as he exchanged glances with Judy. "Let's head next door."

As the group moved next door, Win felt relieved that some practicality had prevailed.

13
Hanford, Washington

It was a warm, March day in Hanford, a small city in south-eastern Washington State. Samir Fakri read the sign on the outside of Robertson's Supermarket one more time before he went in. He headed to the service desk and politely inquired if this was the place where he could apply for the job posted outside. The sign said, "Help Wanted." He chatted up the middle-aged lady at the desk about how his family had just moved to Hanford since his father had taken a job with the Department of Energy to oversee the cleanup of the old nuclear facility there. He told her he was a senior in high school and hoped to earn some money for a car, since they were living outside of town.

She gave him a once-over and asked, "Are you over 16?"

Samir smiled warmly and said, "I'm actually 17, Ma'am."

"Do you have a driver's license or some other ID?"

"I have a learner's permit from Pennsylvania where we used to live. It's got my picture on it."

"That'll be fine. Why don't you fill out this form; it'll take a few minutes." She passed him a pen and a form attached to a clipboard. The form asked for name, address, social security number, previous employment and so on. Samir filled it out quickly, while leaning on the counter. He printed clearly and neatly, and took it back to the lady. He smiled pleasantly at her and said, "I think everything you need is here. I tried to write so you could read it easily."

"Oh, you do have neat handwriting. Most young people today are terrible at writing. I think it's because everybody types on computers now." She looked at his application and asked, "I see you have a foreign-sounding name. Are you a US citizen?"

"Yes; I was born in State College, Pennsylvania. I've got a passport at home if you need to see it. My dad has a top security clearance at Hanford, if that helps."

"Sorry to ask, but nowadays we need to check all applications because we could get checked by immigration officials. We have a lot of illegal immigrants working in our orchards in this State, you know."

"Of course, Ma'am. You're doing your job and we really need to be careful about people nowadays."

"Do you have your Social Security card with you?"

"Yes Ma'am. I thought you might need it."

"Well, it looks like everything we need is here. You know, we usually give the application to our manager who then reviews it and if he thinks you're good, he'll call you back. You seem like such a nice young man, I'm sure he'd like you. This is a slow time of day for us, so let me see if he can interview you now. Why don't you sit over there, you could use the seat of the blood pressure machine."

"That's nice of you, Ma'am. I'd be glad to wait. My dad would be proud of me if I came home with a job so soon. He was happy when I got a job on my own at McDonalds in State College." Samir smiled as the nice lady placed a call to the manager's office and got back to her work. Ten minutes later, a young guy wearing a short-sleeved shirt and tie came over to the service desk and began talking to the lady behind the counter. She showed him Samir's application and pointed in his direction.

The manager came over and asked if the young man was Samir. Samir nodded and the manager introduced himself. "I'm Jim Olson, the Store Manager. June, behind the desk, tells me you're looking for a job as a bagboy. Have you had any previous experience working in a supermarket?"

"Yes, a couple of weeks of part-time work in our local supermarket back in State College, Pennsylvania, Sir. I worked as a bagboy and also helped with cleaning the store. I worked part-time at McDonalds during my junior year."

"What sort of cleaning did you do?"

"When things got slow, the manager asked for volunteers to help sweep and mop the floors. I don't like standing around doing nothing, so I always offered to help."

"I see. When did you move to Hanford?"

"A couple of weeks ago. My Dad took a job at the Hanford labs. He used to teach at Penn State; he's an engineer. He's involved with the cleanup of the old facility; that's his specialty."

"You know, you're the best-mannered young man we've had apply for a job in a long time. You sure charmed June, and she's a real sourpuss. We need someone from 3:30 to 7:30 PM Would that fit in with your school hours?"

"That would work perfectly! When can I start?"

"We need to do some background checks and submit the paperwork to our regional office. We should have all of that done by next week. Could you start next Thursday?"

"Yes, that would be perfect since we're still unpacking at home from the move. I need to help my mom because it's a lot of work for her. My dad is already busy in his new job."

"Okay, you're on then. Do you go by the name Samir or do you have a nickname?

"I've been called Sam since I was a little kid."

"Okay Sam, welcome to the Robertson's family."

Sam thanked the manager profusely and shook his hand. He went over to the service desk and thanked June as well. He said, "I'm so happy to get a job here and I really appreciate your interest in me. I'll do a good job and won't disappoint you."

After Samir left, Jim, the manager, went over to talk with June. "That young man has got to be one of the most serious and well-mannered applicants I've met in a long time. He's also clean and well dressed. I wish more teenagers could be like that."

"That's why I wanted you to meet him right away. I hope he turns out to be as good as he seems."

Sam left the store with a smile on his face. He had thoroughly rehearsed for this day in front of Uncle Abdullah, who would be pleased to learn that he'd put on such a winning performance. It was beginning to look like he'd get his chance to prove his manhood in the great jihad against the detested American devils. There'd be no more bullying in school; he was on the path to Paradise. He dreamed of Shahada, dying in combat for Allah someday, and the 72 dark-eyed virgins Allah would bestow upon him for his martyrdom.

14
North Waziristan

There was an air of expectancy at the camp in remote Waziristan. Rashid, Yusuf and their men were anxiously awaiting the supplies to get the factory up and running. To Rashid this represented the culmination of a long and difficult process that had seemed doomed at times. The plant had to be built far from prying eyes and surveillance aircraft routes, which placed it in this God-forsaken place with no passable roads, reliable electricity, or even telephones. He hoped he never saw a camel again after this operation. It was mid-morning and the caravan was supposed to have arrived last night.

To Yusuf, this moment meant something different. This was the beginning of the endgame of an operation that would be as important as that of his immortal brothers who flew their airplanes into the Twin Towers in New York, and he was determined that he and his men should protect this plant with their lives.

One of Yusuf's men came up to Rashid to alert him to a line of camels on the horizon. Rashid thanked the tall, bearded man and ran off to tell his men to prepare for unpacking the long-awaited supplies. At last they'd see whether the plant would truly work.

Rashid's men gathered in the central courtyard, with carts for moving the materials. Yusuf's men, ever cautious, took up combat positions in their fortified foxholes. Yusuf was scanning the horizon with a pair of binoculars. He came over to Rashid and told him, "The caravan is ours; my brother is at the head of the column. I estimate they'll be here in about 20 minutes, so get your men ready.

After we unload, we'll need to hurry, as the shipment of feeder stock is due here in another 3 days."

Rashid was puzzled by how Yusuf managed to stay so well informed of operations without a radio or even a cell phone, which wouldn't work here anyway. He shrugged off his curiosity and got his men ready.

It wasn't long before a tall, bearded man on horseback rode into the compound. He saw Yusuf and headed towards him shouting, "Salaam aleikem, my brother."

Yusuf answered, "Aleikem salaam. I'm glad you arrived safely, but why were you late?"

"Unfortunately, a bridge was washed out as well as a section of the track we followed. Our camel drivers are good and we managed to make up some of the lost time."

"Why don't you wash the dust off and then join me for some tea. I need to hear about this road problem. Let me show you to my quarters where you can clean up."

Yusuf took his brother to his hut and then rejoined the group. Rashid asked politely, "Is he really your brother? He doesn't look much like you."

"He's my half-brother. My father, rest his soul, had three wives."

"It's good to have a relative in charge. It must have been a hard trip; he looks totally worn out."

"He knows the importance of this trip, and must have driven himself and his men hard."

The camel train arrived and entered the compound with an assortment of bellows, moans and groans from the camels, who suddenly realized they were facing a respite from their heavy loads. The camel drivers helped with the unloading, though their chief job seemed to be to control the camels that were kicking wildly at Rashid's men. The containers hidden under wraps were clearly marked in an Urdu code. Rashid, who had a list of the coded packages and what they contained, directed the containers to specific Quonset huts. He was pleased when it was done and he could see that all the needed supplies had arrived. His first priority was to check the viability of the cell culture materials he would use for virus production. These cells were fastidious, and Rashid was hoping their temperature control arrangements had worked to keep the cells alive.

Suddenly the camp was bustling with men in high spirits. This was what they'd been waiting for after their hard work. They had scant time to get all the solutions and media mixed and the cell lines established and ready to go when the feeder stock would arrive in three days. Many of the other aspects of the operation were already underway in different places, and getting each component to converge at the same time was becoming critical now. For security purposes, most of the men had only faint ideas of what they were doing. Only two, Rashid and Yusuf, knew what the end products would be used for.

"So far, so good, "Rashid said to his aide. "It's now in Allah's hands."

15

Livermore, California

On an early spring morning in the small city of Livermore, California, a neatly dressed Emanuel Farwal stood in front of the Earth Source Food Market, searching the windows for help-wanted signs. He couldn't find any, but went in anyway, approaching a harried looking middle-aged woman behind the service counter.

"Excuse me, Ma'am." He smiled pleasantly. "I'm new to the community and was looking to see if there were any jobs available at your Market. I'd like to find a job as a bagboy or anything like that. I'm going to enter college this fall and wanted to make some money to buy a car. Our new house is outside the city, so I really need a car. My dad is a physicist at Lawrence Livermore Lab; he just started there."

The lady looked up from her computer screen and said, "Sorry, young man, but I don't think we need any help right now."

"That's too bad, because I have experience working in a natural foods store just like this back in Detroit where we just moved from. Could I at least talk to the manager? I'm a good worker and serious about my jobs Ma'am."

She sized up Emanuel and said, "Well, you look like a nice young man. I'll see if he's free to talk to you." She dialed a number and all Emanuel could hear of her conversation was, "a nice and well-mannered boy." She told Emanuel that the manager would be there to talk with him shortly, and gave him an application form to fill out while he waited.

Before long, a man dressed in a plaid shirt and jeans came over introducing himself as Jim Macalester, the store manager. "Are you the young fellow that's looking for a job?"

"Yes, Sir. My name is Emanuel Farwal, my friends call me Manny."

"What kind of work are you looking for?"

"Back in Detroit I worked in the Whole Earth Super Market as a bagboy, and when the manager needed extra help I also worked on the cleanup crew. I really like to work in a natural foods store. You get nice people coming to shop in these stores, and besides, I'm a vegetarian, so I get great tips from the customers on diet and recipes. Oh, I forgot to mention that my family just moved here from Detroit. My dad's a physicist at the Livermore Lab."

Macalester studied Manny's application form and asked, "Were you born here in the US?"

"Yes, I was born in Detroit."

"Well your name sounds foreign—like Middle Eastern."

"My parents moved to the US before I was born. They're from Iraq and came here to escape from Sadam Hussein's regime. They're US citizens and my Dad works for the Government now."

Macalester scowled as he said, "Well, we don't need any help right now. We'll keep your application and call you if something comes up. Thanks for your interest in Earth Source."

Manny thanked him and looked down as he left. He knew this was a brush-off and sensed it was due to anti-Muslim prejudice; he'd faced a lot of it back home. Yes, he'd get back at these evil heathens and their Zionist masters.

Macalester stopped to chat with the lady at the service desk giving her Manny's application to throw out.

"He seemed so earnest and pleasant," she protested

"He's a damn Arab and from Iraq to boot. I hate those savages. My brother was killed in Iraq by some bastard suicide bomber. I bet if we hired this kid, he'd start showing up for work with a damned towel on his head and he'd steal from us. There'll be no Arabs working in my store!"

As Macalester left, the lady shrugged and muttered, "Wow, I didn't know that about Jim. How sad."

16
Rawalpindi, Pakistan

Ahmed Tarkani was beside himself with anger on the phone shouting at the garage owner whose shop he always used. "Azlan, you knave, you promised me you'd get that truck ready to roll tonight. I don't care if you can't get a part. Steal one or cannibalize another truck. It had better be ready!" He slammed the phone into its cradle. He needed the old Mercedes truck for the rough run into Waziristan. It had special fittings installed for this shipment.

He turned around to his oldest son. "Can you imagine such bad luck? First, the truck breaks down and then Azlan claims he can't get a part to fix it. We have to leave tonight. All the packages are scheduled to arrive this afternoon and they're time sensitive."

"Father, don't worry. Azlan is a genius at fixing things and getting spare parts by any means possible. He'll come through. You made your point clearly."

This was a special job, directly ordered by the Hakim, who'd told Ahmed he would be carrying a perishable cargo worth more than gold. It required refrigeration and speedy delivery despite the incredibly rough terrain. Tarkani would use only his family members for delivery of such valuable and important cargo; you couldn't trust anyone else these days. They would be carrying Kalashnikovs, escorted by a Land Rover filled with more armed relatives. They would carry written orders from the Hakim's group as additional protection in the lawless country they would pass through. The Hakim and the Brotherhood were revered in those parts, so a note from him would carry great weight, presuming that any bandits they might encounter could read.

Tarkani asked, "Did Jamil leave yet for Islamabad airport to pick up the shipments?"

"Yes, father. He left about an hour ago with the small, refrigerated truck. We already received one shipment by truck from Islamabad that's safe in our refrigerator in back."

"The air shipment from Dhaka should be arriving in an hour, and the one from Calcutta an hour after that. I'm lucky to have sons to do these tasks for me, praise Allah."

"Mother and Auntie are preparing our meals for the trip. They should be delivering the food at about dusk. We plan to start out at dark. Jamil has estimated it will take us two days to reach the farthest point to which we can drive. We've arranged for camels to rendezvous with us at that point. It will take the camels another day from there. The camel drivers are relatives and can be trusted. They also know this trip is for the Hakim personally. We'll pack the cargo with dry ice for the trip and use the special containers that'll keep the contents cold without freezing them. If we can start tonight, we should get the delivery to Waziristan on time. I'll call Azlan again in about an hour to check on the status of our truck."

It was a typical, busy day at the shipping company, but the upcoming VIP shipment had everybody jumpy. It wasn't long before Jamil called in from the airport. His father took the call.

"Father, I have the shipment from Dhaka in the refrigerated truck. The package looks in perfect shape and there was no problem clearing customs; Cousin Ibrahim is on duty at the customs desk this afternoon. The flight from Calcutta is showing to be on time and Ibrahim will clear that shipment for us too."

"Very good, my son. Just drive under the speed limit without making any stops."

"Yes Father."

Tarkani told his eldest son, "Well, at least the air shipments are going well. Now we need our dear friend Azlan to work his magic."

As if on cue, the phone rang and it was Azlan. Ahmed took the call. "Well my rogue friend, have you been able to fix my precious truck?" There was a long pause while Tarkani listened. "May Allah heap blessings on you and your family. You don't have to worry; I will never inquire as to how you got the part. When can we pick it up? Oh, good. I am greatly in your debt, my friend. Salaam."

Ahmed sat down and let out a loud sigh. "My son, Allah has been good to us today; the truck will be ready later this afternoon. From the sound of it, Azlan stole the part we needed from a government truck. He's a bandit, but a loyal friend. So we're on schedule for tonight's shipment, praise Allah."

17
White Rock, New Mexico

Salim Chowdry sat on the carpeted floor of his tiny apartment in White Rock, a small town northwest of Santa Fe that was a bedroom community for Los Alamos National Laboratory. He was dreading the call he had to make to his mentor, Uncle Abdullah. He had failed miserably trying to land a job at either of the nearby Brown's supermarkets, even though he had dressed neatly, poured on all his charm, and spouted the prepared stories about needing to raise money for college and how his father had just taken a new position at the Los Alamos Lab. These were small towns and there were just no jobs – unless he had somehow turned people off at both stores.

Salim had Abdullah's telephone number memorized. He dialed and awaited his disgrace.

A voice at the other end answered, "Hello, Ibrahim's Halal Grocery."

Salim answered, "This is Omar reporting from Site 6."

He was instructed to hang up and wait for a call.

After ten minutes, Uncle Abdullah rang. "Yes my son; how are you doing?"

"I'm fine, but without a job."

"Did you apply in both towns and use the recommended script?"

"Yes. They claimed they had no jobs. I asked about all types of jobs, full and part-time. They had nothing or just didn't want to hire me."

Abdullah was silent for a long time before he responded. "I believe they truly had no jobs. You're a fine, upstanding young man and you've been well trained. You would have gotten something if there were positions available. For now, just stay in your apartment for a few days. You can go out to sightsee or shop, but keep a low profile. We have an alternative plan for you in nearby Santa Fe, but we'll have to find an apartment for you and that'll take a few days. This may prove a blessing in disguise. Santa Fe is the State capital and draws people from a wide area for shopping. Trust in Allah; it will be for the best. So be patient my son. Salaam."

Abdullah had anticipated that even his best and most attractive boy might have a problem getting hired in these two small towns. He needed to make a few phone calls now.

18
Santa Fe

Early on a sunny and chilly morning in high desert Santa Fe, Win was outside walking his two dogs, who enjoyed walking down the hill with him every morning to get the newspaper at the base of the driveway. He'd had no luck in training either dog to fetch the paper on their own, unlike their predecessor, his first Dandie Dinmont terrier, who'd been so good at it that one morning, when he came back with no paper, Win scolded him and sent him back out—so he went and stole the neighbors' paper.

This was going to be an interesting morning. Win was going to attend two subcommittee meetings for the Bioterrorism Surveillance Program, the first on how to train and prepare nurses to staff infectious disease hotlines, and the second to investigate sources of potential outbreaks of disease from bioterrorist attacks. As if to prove that the work they were doing might be needed, an article on page one of the day's paper described another major suicide bombing in Iraq. Win muttered to the dogs, "This terrorism stuff is serious all right!" The dogs weren't big fans of Win's musings on current events and ignored him on the way up the hill.

Win fed the dogs, got some coffee to Julia, dressed and headed off to his meeting downtown. He parked at the State Office Building and went to the meeting room where he helped himself to coffee and a chocolate and nut covered doughnut. He knew he'd pay the price on his waistline, not to mention the snide remarks from Julia, should he admit to his indulgence. But he needed sustenance for what was likely to be another boring meeting,

The group to prepare nurses consisted of Win, John and a mix of nurses and doctors. Win thought it was a good idea to have nurses on the panel.

John began, "This subcommittee is supposed to deal with the handling of incoming reports of possible disease caused by bioterrorism. We want to recruit and train nurses to be the first responders. Right now, we can make available one full-time nurse from our staff to field the hotline during regular working hours. We'll have to recruit at least two more for night, weekend, vacation, and holiday coverage. We can provide everyone with pagers and cell phones." As John dragged on, discussing how they would recruit and train the nurses, Win noted that he had an unfortunate way of making everything sound boring and bureaucratic, which drove him to a second doughnut.

They finally decided to run an intensive training course for one full-time and three part-time nurses. They would rotate coverage, 24-7, and all would carry pagers, cell phones, and a handbook on communicable diseases. There would be physician back-up in the form of John, Bill and Win, who would also carry pagers and cell phones. Win, who hadn't carried a pager since his last days as an attending physician, and who dreaded the thought of being on call again, tried to wriggle out of this responsibility. His biggest concern was that he was rusty in the practice of medicine, so he'd have to attend all these courses on infectious diseases. But no good deed goes unpunished; it was his idea, and he got roped into implementing it. As the meeting adjourned, John announced the next meeting would focus on what to do when there was a report of one of the "diseases of interest," as he called them.

Despite having been enlisted against his will, Win was pleased that at least the program would be good for the State of New Mexico's economy, and he reassured himself that he probably would never get a call even though wearing a pager still bugged him.

Win's second subcommittee meeting was down the dingy hall. The subject was outbreak investigation, in the event one of the "diseases of interest" was identified and Bill Applegate was the meeting

Chair. Unfortunately, he turned out to be just as boring as John. Maybe it went with the territory of being an infectious disease doc? Win could kick himself for not having gotten another doughnut. Bill laboriously covered the traditional methods of investigating communicable disease outbreaks and searching for infectious sources. The only things Win found of interest were the notions of a pile-on, second strike, much like the suicide bombers who detonate themselves at the site of an earlier bombing after the rescue workers arrive on the scene, and the multiple means for terrorists to spread infectious Agents—via water, air, and foods, as well as sending agents in the mail.

Win piped up, "We're probably better off investing our resources and personnel in confirming diagnoses before we trace sources. If we're dealing with a treatable infectious disease, we'll need adequate supplies of antibiotics to cure the cases that come up, and stop further disease spread. Maybe as part of this overall program, the State should stockpile some drugs like ciprofloxacin for anthrax."

Bill asked if there were any other questions and the emergency medicine physician spoke up. "As one of the people likely to see the first cases of any terrorist-caused diseases, I keep thinking of how I would react if, say, a 50-year-old office worker comes in with anthrax, but presents with a high fever, malaise and some painful swollen lymph nodes with no classic eschar or lung findings. If she looks really sick, I might hospitalize her, but I would probably have no idea of her diagnosis or report her to your hotline. Now if I saw 5 or 10 similar cases, I might call the hotline if I suspected they shared one of your infections of interest—and that's a big 'if.' The bottom line is, it's not going to be easy for me or my ED colleagues to provide the hotline with good information."

Bill said, "Well it looks like we'll need a whole new set of methods for investigating and managing cases of bioterrorist-introduced diseases."

Win muttered to his neighbor, "Yup; this ain't going to be like staph food poisoning from the chopped chicken liver at a Bar Mitzvah."

19
Rawalpindi

Ahmed Tarkani was flittering around his warehouse as nervous as a bridegroom on his wedding day. His truck had come back from Azlan's shop in perfect working order, Jamil had arrived back from Islamabad Airport with both shipments, and the crew for the trip and armed escort were ready to go. Ahmed supervised the loading of the shipment and supplies for the trip. The perishable materials and dry ice were carefully stowed in a large refrigerated compartment lashed to rings on the floor and walls, and covered with insulating blankets.

There were also a dozen or so boxes that were marked fragile and did not require refrigeration. These were light, carefully secured in the non-refrigerated portion of the truck and covered with burlap sacking. The emergency gasoline-powered generator was lashed down securely in another section of the truck. At the back of the truck was an auxiliary gasoline tank.

Ahmed had no idea what any of the contents of the shipment might be and no desire to know. His task was to get them moved quickly and safely to a remote area of Waziristan. He was a holy man and he'd been told this was a holy mission. The Hakim's deputy and he had gone over the shipment requirements and contingency planning in minute detail. Ahmed suspected he'd been chosen for this task because he and his family came from Waziristan and he had successfully performed other missions for the Brothers. He greatly admired the Brothers and would do anything to assist them in their righteous cause. He would also be rewarded handsomely for his work if he got the goods to the destination safely and on time. So far, all was going well, thanks to his friend Azlan, another Waziri.

Ahmed walked to the back of his warehouse where he had some workers move several large wooden crates stacked against the rear wall. There was an ancient, steel wall safe behind the boxes. Ahmed used a memorized combination to open the large lock, pulled open the heavy door and brought out some canvas sacks. He waved to his oldest son to come over and said, "These are the Kalashnikovs the Hakim's people left with us for the mission. There's extra ammunition in the sacks. Distribute them only to our family members. You and Nabil will need to carry two in the truck's cab. Come into my office before you leave. I have some final instructions for you."

It was another twenty minutes or so before Ahmed's eldest son came in to see him. "Father, we're ready to go. The truck's petrol tanks are full and the auxiliary tank as well. We have extra tires and a portable compressor. I'm looking forward to going back to our homeland. I miss the mountains and our people."

"Son, you must drive fast, but remain cautious. There may be some checkpoints where the Army will stop you to inspect the truck. You must be polite and inform them you are delivering some supplies for the Hakim and the Brotherhood. They will be expecting you and will allow you to pass. I am more worried about bandits, but they too have great respect for the Brothers and you have a document to prove you're working for them. Once you are out of Pindi, distribute the weapons to our family group. With some hardheads, Kalashnikovs can be more persuasive than a letter. Our cousins will meet you at the end of the passable road. You and Nabil must carefully supervise the loading of the camels. Everything must be lashed securely to the saddles. Also, take note of any road problems on the way; you'll have to go back again. May Allah protect you."

"Don't worry, Father; we'll be careful and vigilant."

Ahmed watched as the truck and the Land Rover escort pulled out of the warehouse to begin their journey. He said softly, "Inshallah."

The two sons drove slowly until they were outside the city limits where they pulled over and quickly wrapped their heads in the

traditional Waziri loose turban of yellowish-tan homespun cloth.
Nabil said, "We're going home, my brother."

"Yes, Nabil. Now we must drive like demons."

20
White Rock and Santa Fe

It had been a tough week for Salim Chowdry. He had failed miserably trying to land a job in Los Alamos or White Rock and had to sit around his tiny apartment with no TV and nothing to do except study the Qur'an while waiting to hear from Uncle Abdullah. On the seventh day, the call finally came. Salim was to move to Santa Fe the next day. He was instructed to pick up a reserved and pre-paid U-Haul and to move his furniture and belongings to a new apartment on the south side of Santa Fe. Having few belongings, he could load the trailer himself. Abdullah was optimistic about Salim's prospects for finding a job in Santa Fe. Salim wrote down the address of his new apartment and directions to get there and thanked his uncle for his kindness. Abdullah promised to call again tomorrow evening.

The move went without a hitch. Salim spent the morning taking apart his Ikea furniture and the afternoon reassembling everything. Just as he was finishing his dinner of canned ravioli, Uncle Abdullah called his cell phone, inquiring about how Salim's move had gone and whether he liked his new apartment.

"It's a really nice place and the move was easy," Salim said.

"Did anyone see you or talk to you when you loaded and unloaded your stuff?"

"I didn't notice anybody when I was loading in White Rock," Salim replied. "A couple of women with children saw me unloading in Santa Fe, but they just smiled at me and said nothing. The woman in the apartment office was nice and welcomed me. She showed me to the apartment and gave me the keys and some instructions on how to use the air conditioner and the laundry in the basement."

"Very good, Salim. Tomorrow you're to begin looking for a job. Get a pen and paper and write these names and addresses down." He dictated the names and addresses of six supermarkets, instructing Salim to start with the first name and continue down the list in order. "Just remember your training. Dress neatly and be polite."

"Yes Uncle. I won't disappoint you this time." Uncle Abdullah had been the first person in Salim's life to treat him with respect and to show him a path to greatness. He clenched his fists and resolved to make his uncle proud of him.

21
Santa Fe

It was Tuesday, and Win was at his desk admiring his new T-shirt as he waited for his buddy, Herky. Now that he was retired, Win loved his routine Tuesday trips into town for lunch with his neighbor, Charles Herkimer, a.k.a. Herky. Herky, a retired banker, was a classic Santa Fe eccentric and an amusing companion. His Achilles heel was an obsession with physical fitness in his quest to find the fountain of youth to keep up with his ever-younger series of wives. With more time on his hands, Win dreamed of finally getting around to doing all the things he'd always wanted to do but had put off for decades, so he'd created a Mañana List to work through systematically. Win was adamant that this wasn't a bucket list; he wasn't ready to kick the bucket for a long time. High on his list was the creation of a series of literary T-shirts. His first T-shirt, which read, "Chaucer is a Pysser," came from an idea he'd hatched many decades ago in a freshman college English class. He had a new one today that he was raring to get made.

Although he was anticipating his arrival, he was nonetheless startled when Herky silently materialized at his study door. Herky was wearing a green, camouflage T-shirt, desert-camo cargo shorts and a floppy tan-camo hat with a chinstrap.

Win chuckled and asked, "What are you all dressed up for Herk? Are you working as an extra in an Indiana Jones movie?"

"Ha. Ha. Aren't you funny?'

"What's with the camouflage? It's not hunting season."

"I was out hiking this morning. These are stylish and utilitarian clothes."

"Herk, are you part of some fringy paramilitary group?"

"Win, I think your bioterrorism committee stuff is getting to you. Is that a new T-shirt in the works?"

"Yeah, I got the creative juices flowing again. You'll like this one; it's right up your alley."

"You know Win; you should grow up and give up your juvenile projects. You're an old man now."

"That's precisely why I'm doing these projects. I may grow old, but I don't have to grow up! I aim to stay young mentally, by thinking and acting young, maybe even immature. These projects are important to me."

"I still think you should tackle more serious things that are appropriate for your age. You've hung around universities too long. Get a life Win, an adult life!"

"Herky, you're making me feel like I should get ready for the grave. I'm going to pursue my juvenile tasks with a passion. Now, where are we going for lunch today?"

"Today, I chose Tina's Restaurant near the Rail Yard. It's very popular."

"So I heard and they don't take reservations. I don't fancy long waits for any restaurant."

"This one's worth a wait, but it's Tuesday and early, so we won't have much of a wait." "Well, I was planning to visit the new galleries at the Rail Yard and Site Santa Fe."

"Okay. Then let's go to your T-shirt maker first."

Win was glad Julia didn't notice him leaving with another T-shirt creation under his arm. She really got on him about his "asinine" T-shirts. Win was surprised to see Herky driving his wife's Lexus. "Hey Herky, what happened to your old truck? Did it finally give up the ghost?"

"No, it's in the shop having a new transmission put in."

"I'm sure the new transmission costs more than your truck's worth. Why don't you just junk it and get a new one?"

Herky looked aghast. "Win, do you see that vase on the back seat? It holds the ashes of my wife's last dog. I have the same relationship with my truck."

Win looked at Herky sideways and said, "That is weird, Herky and your logic escapes me. A truck is an inanimate object. Also, why on earth are your wife's dog's ashes on the back seat?"

"Aren't you the smart-ass academic?" Herky quipped. "My wife's late dog's favorite place to be was in this car with her, so she decided to honor her dog by keeping his ashes here."

Win shook his head and said, "Only in Santa Fe."

Win had touched a nerve with Herky and he drove silently to their first stop, Sam's Tees. Win entered the shop, domain of Morris, the Grand Wallah of T-shirts. The shop was dimly lit and a mess, with piles of T-shirts everywhere. Morris, all tattooed and pierced, was behind the counter working. He lit up when he saw Win, and shouted, "Hi Doc; how've you been? I've been looking forward to your next Mañana List project. Whatcha got for me today?"

"Morris, I think I've got a good one that might get you reading important literature again."

"Awesome; let's take a look."

Win proudly showed Morris his sketches and Morris looked puzzled.

"What language is that in, Doc?"

"It's in French, actually Middle French."

"Gee Doc, I didn't know there were different sections of French. But since I can't speak any section of French, I guess it doesn't matter. Tell me more about this line and where it comes from so I can do some research on it."

Win gave him a short lecture on the line's origin and its meaning which got Morris all fired up. "Doc, I think I'm going to like totally dig this. I'll have it ready for you this afternoon."

"That'd be great. I've wanted to do this for a long time and can't wait to see it."

"One last thing, Doc. Did Middle French use different script from regular French?"

"You know Morris, I don't know."

"Don't worry, I'll check it out on the web and see what I can come up with. You have a good day on the town."

So Win headed out into the blinding sunlight and joined Herky, who remained silent as they drove to Tina's, obviously still miffed. But when he pulled into the parking lot he said, "Okay, you're forgiven. I shouldn't hold your academic impairment against you."

22
Santa Fe

Herky was right; they didn't have to wait at the restaurant. They got a corner booth and ordered a round of iced tea. "Whatcha going to order, Win? You know, I think those terrorist committee meetings with all the doughnuts are putting weight on you."

Win wished he hadn't told Herky about the doughnuts. "I think I'll have the chicken enchiladas with green chili and go light on the queso."

Herky smiled his approval. "I'm going to have their tamale plate."

"Hey Herk, tamales are made with lard. That's a lot of calories, not to mention the fat load."

Herky waved his finger and pronounced, "When you have an exercise program as vigorous as mine, you can eat anything and not put on weight. And the doc tells me my coronary arteries are clean as a whistle. He says I can live to 100 and I'm working hard to reach that goal."

"Hey, Herk, if you live that long, you might end up with another wife or two."

"Not by divorce, I hope. I can't afford another divorce. Hmm, I hadn't thought about that issue. Now let's talk about your longevity strategy." Win braced himself for a lecture and capitulated. "I know, I know; I need to step up my diet and exercise program."

Herky had to nod his agreement because his mouth was stuffed with tortilla chips and salsa, and then he tore into his tamales when they arrived. Win thought he must have had a pretty vigorous hike that morning.

While Herky was chomping on his meal, Win announced that he was giving up his usual Tuesday visits to Canyon Road, the main art center of Santa Fe. "I'm going to tour the new galleries at the Rail Yard District this afternoon, and then I'll visit Site Santa Fe. They have an interesting avant-garde show on. I can walk over there from here."

Herky emerged from his plate and said, "Too bad the Farmers Market isn't open today. You could buy some wholesome, organic fruits and vegetables there."

Herky finished his lunch and used two paper napkins to clean his face.

It was a beautiful, cool day so Win walked briskly. After a few minutes he reached his first destination, a gallery specializing in Japanese bamboo baskets, some of which had been made by "Living National Treasures" of Japan and commanded breathtaking prices. It reminded Win of his days in Japan as a US Air Force doctor, when he and Julia would spend their spare time visiting the art galleries in Tokyo. He was on his way to his second destination, a sleek gallery specializing in American paintings when he passed the site of the Farmer's Market, which was closed today. He found an empty bench and sat down to ponder the Market as a potential site for bioterrorism. Most of what was sold there were fresh vegetables, salad greens, and fruit—raw foods that could easily spread infectious agents. Among these, pre-washed salad greens and fruit would probably top the list, assuming an attack used foods rather than an aerosol delivery of agents.

Win scratched his head, chiding himself for becoming obsessive. He got up and visited two more galleries and SITE Santa Fe—the local contemporary art museum—before heading over to meet Herky, who beckoned Win to get in the car. "So how was your adventure in a new part of town," he asked.

"It's nice to visit new galleries. There are some incredibly up-scale galleries at the Rail Yard." Win didn't mention his obsessive interlude at the market.

"Okay, Win, let's get over to your T-shirt place. I'm dying to see what silly project you came up with this time."

23
Santa Fe

Win was anxious to see Morris' handiwork too and when he entered, he found him waiting with a big grin on his face.

"Hey Doc, this was an epic project and I think you'll like what I've made for you. I had a great time reading about this dude Villon and his Ballade on the Internet. I assume he's another one of your dead, white, European guys—I think you called them DWEMs."

"I'm glad you enjoyed learning about Villon. Yeah, he's another DWEM. So let's see what you created."

With a loud "Ta, Da," Morris unfurled the new T-shirt. "I made up six shirts with your text and six with mine. The usual agreement holds; if you don't like mine, you get them free."

There it was, red print on a navy T-shirt reading:

**Reprendre les
neiges d'antan
From Sage Advice to the Elderly
(With apologies to Francois Villon)**

"Morris, it looks just beautiful. I'm going to wear it proudly."

"Okay Doc, now let me show you my version, but first let me apologize for not being able to come up with some medieval French fonts for it." With another flourish and "Ta Da," he unrolled his version that added, "16th Century poet, thief and vagabond," after Villon's name and an English translation, **"Recapture the snows of yesteryear,"** on the back.

"So what do you think, Doc? I used the English on the back so you won't get asked all the time what the front means."

"What can I say? You never cease to amaze me. You know, reprendre can be interpreted several different ways, but you chose the interpretation that captures exactly what I had in mind. Also, where did you get the biographical info on Villon?"

"It's easy Doc; I just Googled 'Villon, and snows of yesteryear.' This dude Villon is awesome, someone I want to know more about. He was a crook and a great poet, but he spent most of his time in jail, in taverns, and on the road to avoid going to jail. You know, most of what's known about him comes from his criminal rap sheets. I also learned the word yesteryear was coined by Dante Gabriel Rossetti, when he translated the Ballade in the 19th Century, only he spelled it yester-year."

"You know Morris, you're a born scholar and you soak up knowledge like a sponge. You should've been a college professor."

"Aw no, Doc. I was a terrible student and everybody always told me I was dumb. I did go to college, but I was at the bottom of my class and barely graduated."

"Did you think you were dumb, Morris?"

"Well not really, but when enough people call you dumb you start to believe it."

"Morris, you aren't dumb! You're a blanking genius."

"Thank you, Doc. By the way, how come you never use curse words?"

"You really don't need to if you have a good vocabulary and use it well. Don't get me wrong, if somebody ran a red light and crashed into my car, the curse words would certainly flow."

"You know, I like the 'Sage Advice to the Elderly' you came up with. Are you writing a book for the elderly?"

"No, Morris. I'm thinking of it as a collection of aphorisms for gray panthers, to be used on T-shirts."

"That's great, whatever aphorisms are. I wish I'd had some teachers like you in college; I might have learned something."

"I hate to say it, but I never taught like this, Morris. That line—'where are the snows of yesteryear—always makes me feel sad. It makes me think about all the coulda, woulda, shouldas in my life." Win took out a handkerchief and dabbed his eyes.

"Are you okay, Doc?"

"I'm fine. I'm just getting old, I guess," Win said as he collected his treasures, paid Morris, and gave him a bear hug and a thumbs-up sign as he left.

When Herky asked to see Morris's latest creation, Win unfolded one of the shirts and held it up. Herky studied it and said, "This is classy for a change. I like this one."

"It's all yours. Now let's head home."

24
Newark, New Jersey

Ibrahim Nasrullah, one of Nasir al Fakrah's deputies, ambled cautiously down the street towards the Cedars of Lebanon Freight Forwarding sign. The roar of the planes taking off and landing at nearby Newark Airport was deafening. From outside, the office looked like a dump.

Ibrahim opened the steel front door and stepped inside, triggering a soft alarm. Leaving the bright sunshine, it took a few seconds for his eyes to adjust to the dim interior. As they did, he made out a mess of strewn boxes and packing materials. A tall, bearded man wearing a white skullcap appeared through a back entry covered by a curtain of strung beads.

"How may I help you?" he inquired.

"I'm Abdel and I've come to see Mr. Jumblatt."

"He's expecting you. Wait here a minute."

As he waited, Ibrahim surveyed the place further. He noticed a calendar in Arabic on the wall and a big American flag next to a large Lebanese flag on another wall. This was probably a Lebanese-owned place, with an owner or manager with the name of a prominent Druze family. He raised his eyebrows. Life was full of puzzles.

After a few minutes, the bearded man returned, gesturing for Ibrahim to follow him back though the curtain, where he found a neater and more brightly lit office furnished with upholstered chairs and a low table on an Oriental rug. Sitting in one of the chairs was a dignified-looking, corpulent, elderly man, who invited Ibrahim to take a seat next to him. He wore a fine, gray tweed, three-piece suit, a tie, and an elegant gold chain across his vest.

"Salaam Aleikem, Abdel. I've been expecting you. I am Jumblatt. Will you take some tea?"

"Aleikem Salaam, Mr. Jumblatt. Yes, thank you; that would be nice."

"How are your sons?"

"Nasrullah, Nasir and George are doing well, thank you."

Jumblatt nodded, acknowledging the passwords. "Your colleague has informed me that an important shipment will be arriving from Europe and I am to clear it through customs and deliver it for you. He said you'll provide me with the particulars of its destination here in the US so we can arrange trans-shipment. He also wanted us to handle all aspects of the shipment and not use intermediaries, which I am prepared to do though it could be costly."

Ibrahim raised his eyebrows at the openness of Jumblatt's conversation and Jumblatt picked up on it immediately. "No need to worry, my brother. This place is clean. I don't like talking with noise in the background, so we screen this place thoroughly. Our conversation is safe here."

"Thank you. One can never be too careful. We plan to take receipt of the shipment from you initially. The materials will then be repackaged and returned to you for trans-shipment to several different locations. Since the shipment contains some liquids and medical needles and syringes, it would be much easier for you to handle the trans-shipment than my colleagues. Here is a list of the cities and addresses to which we will need the packages delivered."

Ibrahim handed a sealed envelope from his coat pocket to Jumblatt, who opened the envelope and studied the list of delivery sites. He refolded the paper and put it into an inner jacket pocket. Tea was served in glasses by the bearded man who listened in on the conversation.

Jumblatt took a long sip of tea and then resumed the conversation. "Yes. We can get the shipments to these destinations in 24 to 48 hours as your colleague requested."

Ibrahim reached into his coat again and pulled out a second, thicker envelope that he handed to Jumblatt. "My colleague wanted you to have this in advance. We will complete the payment when the business is done, if that is alright with you."

Jumblatt opened the second envelope and thumbed through the green hundred-dollar bills. He smiled and handed the envelope to his bearded assistant. "This will be fine. We are men of trust and honor in our brotherhood."

Ibrahim and Jumblatt resumed drinking tea and making small talk. The assistant stood nearby to fill their glasses and, a little too obviously, to protect Jumblatt. Eventually, Ibrahim inquired politely as to whether Jumblatt was from Lebanon, hoping he wouldn't appear too forward.

Jumblatt responded that he had indeed grown up in Beirut, and that his family had been Druze who converted to Sunni Islam when he was a boy. He was a shrewd observer, correctly addressing Ibrahim's concern. Jumblatt went on, "Leaving the Druze faith is very serious. My parents were shunned by their families and friends and driven out of their ancestral village; it only made them more devout Sunnis. Such is life!" He shrugged and changed the subject. "I understand the shipment will arrive at Newark Airport in several weeks. We're prepared to handle it, but please let us know the precise delivery information as soon as possible."

After an appropriate amount of time, Ibrahim politely said that he needed to get going. Jumblatt slowly got up from his chair, extended his hand to Ibrahim and said, "Peace be with you my brother." The assistant led Ibrahim out and said nothing.

25
North Waziristan

The production compound in Waziristan was bustling with activity, leaving Rashid in overdrive and fussing over the activities in each building. The cell cultures had survived and were being propagated. To his disbelief, Rashid had pulled off the impossible in one of the most remote corners of the world. Now he was ready for the feeder stock to arrive today. Yusuf and his men scoured the nearby countryside with binoculars, while Rashid looked out over the huge cliffs and steep valleys, marveling that any of the equipment could have reached this forsaken place.

It was afternoon before they first sighted the camel train. Yusuf's men took up their defensive positions, all eyes focused on the approaching caravan. It was dusk when it arrived with its unruly, stinking camels. A handsome, tall Pashtun, led the column into the compound, addressing them, "Which of you is Brother Rashid?"

"I am Rashid."

"I am Hussein and this is your delivery from Pindi. I believe it's in good condition, as the dry ice packages are still cold, but you should inspect the boxes labeled 'Fragile' and 'Glass' after our rough trip. I am to give you these documents." He reached under his tunic and pulled out a long camel-leather pouch that he handed to Rashid.

Rashid examined the documents carefully before inviting the Pashtun and his men to join them for a meal. Out of the corner of his eye, he noticed that Yusuf's men, in the pillboxes, had their guns trained on the camel drivers.

The Pashtun said, "First we must unload our precious cargo and feed and water our camels. Then it will be our pleasure to join you in a meal."

The unloading took longer than Rashid had expected. All the agents he'd requested and the glassware and shipping containers had arrived. He anxiously directed each package to a specific location and instructed his men on how to unpack them. It was after dark when the Pashtun leader and his famished crew of camel drivers joined Rashid, Jalal and Yusuf for a meal of mutton, rice, naan and fresh fruits.

Yusuf asked Hussein, "Was the trip difficult?"

"No. The trails are good at this time of year and no one stopped us on the way. The few government patrols in this area must have been warned away. It was just slow going. There was a bridge washout that was just repaired." Hussein's eyes were fixed on Yusuf's scar as he replied.

Yusuf inquired as to how long they needed to stay at the camp before departing.

Hussein sighed and said, "My camels and men could use rest, but we must leave before dawn. We do not wish to be sighted near your camp. We were told that secrecy of this location is of the utmost importance."

"Yes, that's probably a wise thing and you can rest a distance from here," Yusuf replied.

"I was told I need to come back to pick up a shipment to go to Pindi."

Rashid responded this time, "I expect it will be at least four weeks from now."

Hussein said, "That is what I was told. We are available whenever you summon us. This is the Prophet's work and we will be here when you need us, Allah willing."

Hussein and his men napped briefly, wrapped in their blankets beside their camels. Rashid wouldn't sleep that night so he could oversee the process of getting the cultures going. Yusuf and his men wouldn't sleep either; they would watch over the Pashtun strangers with guns at the ready.

26
Santa Fe

Salim got up early and said his morning prayers before putting on his best clothes, making sure his hair was brushed, and studying the list of potential job sites. His plan was to arrive at the first store at 9:30 AM He had the jitters, not wanting to fail again.

By 11:00 o'clock, Salim hadn't found a position at the first three stores. He hammered his fists on the steering wheel of his car as he screwed up the courage to enter the fourth store on his list, Nature's Harvest Foods. He checked his hair in the rear view mirror, got out, and straightened his clothes before entering. He was glad there was no line at the service desk behind which sat a pretty, buxom woman. She wore no bra and Salim tried to avoid staring at her nipples.

"Excuse me Ma'am," he began. "Is this the place to apply for a job?"

"What kind of job are you looking for?" she asked as she chewed gum.

"I'm looking for a job as a bagboy or stocker, something like that. I just moved here from Berkeley, California. I had a job there as a bagboy in a natural foods store like this. I also helped with stocking the shelves and the fresh foods section. My dad just started a new job at Los Alamos National Lab. He was a professor at UC Berkeley. I need to make some money for college this fall."

"Thanks for the life-story." She smirked. "I think Jerry, our manager, was looking for some help. Why don't you fill out an application?" She chewed her gum loudly as she handed Salim an application on a clipboard and a pen.

He perched on a stack of cartons as he filled out the form with neat handwriting and then returned it to her while checking out her breasts. She paged Jerry, who came over in a few minutes to speak with Salim. Jerry introduced himself and asked if Salim was looking for a job. Salim repeated his rehearsed spiel while Jerry picked at his teeth and then asked Salim if he'd filled out an application.

"Yes, I did Sir. I gave it to the lady at the service desk."

Jerry went over to the service desk to fetch Salim's application. He too checked out the woman's breasts. "You've got a foreign-sounding name. Are you a US citizen?"

"Oh, yes. I was born in Los Angeles when my dad was a graduate student at Cal Tech. I have a passport and birth certificate at home, but I brought along my social security card and my driver's license."

"Okay, those'll be enough." He reviewed Salim's application and asked, "Did you do stocking as well as checkout service in your previous job?"

"Yes and I mopped the floors. I really know how natural food stores work, Sir."

"Well we're a small store and we ask our employees to multi-task with whatever jobs need doing around here."

"That would be fine. I think I'd really like working here."

"Okay. We'll need to do a background check before we can offer you a job. Give your driver's license and social security card to Betsy so she can copy them. We can only offer you the minimum wage to start, but that's high in Santa Fe. Do you go by Salim?"

"Everyone calls me Sal."

"Okay Sal, if everything checks out, you've got a job. We'll call you in about a week to let you know."

Salim shook Jerry's hand and thanked him. He went back to the counter and watched as Betsy copied his IDs. After he was finished, he had to force himself to walk slowly out to his parked car. When he got inside he dropped his head, sighed, and let out a loud cry of "Allahu akbar." He was on his way to manhood and respect; his days as a loser were over. Uncle Abdullah would be proud of him.

27
Astoria

Things had been progressing well and it was time for Nasir to brief the Imam again. He didn't mind the subway trip to Queens as much as the walk to the Imam's apartment above a devilish bar. Nasir sneered as he walked by the noisy Greek restaurant and hurried up the stairs to get away as quickly as possible from the smell of garlic, oregano and beer.

He knocked softly and was quietly ushered inside and invited to sit while the Imam turned his radio to near-din level. "Greetings, Nasir. Have you been well?"

"Yes, Imam. I've been well and our program's pieces are falling into place. I have a small gift here for you; it's imported from Turkey. It's your favorite brand."

He handed a package to the Imam, who opened the box and offered it to Nasir. "Please have a piece," he said, before selecting one for himself. "You remembered my weakness for Turkish delight. Unfortunately, since my diagnosis of diabetes, I've had to go light on sweets, but thank you, my son." He chuckled and added, "I hope you aren't planning to use lokum as a vehicle for our program; it might selectively target our people."

Nasir laughed and began his briefing. "Our boys are all well placed now and accepted in their schools. The religious texts are being restored and should be ready for shipment in several weeks. I've received notification of the final distribution date; it's one of great significance. Our Persian backers are satisfied with that date for their work too. The texts will be shipped through Germany to our Druze friend in New Jersey. I will process the texts before the Druze ships them out to our distribution points. The international shipping will be in the hands of our trusted friends in Pakistan and Germany. They are Waziris and soldiers in the cause. The US shipping part will be handled entirely by our Druze friend. Like many converts to Islam, he's more devout than those born to the religion. That's where we stand."

"My son, I see concern on your brow, or is it doubt?"

Nasir sighed and looked down as he said, "We've worked so hard on developing our plan, but it all hinges on receiving texts that will be authentic. I know you've already decided to do a test of the documents at the preparation facility. We can be somewhat assured if the tests come out positive. If they do not, we can develop a new batch of documents, although this will require that our boys stay longer at their schools than we originally planned. Producing the new texts should be faster than before because of our experience with the process."

"That is the plan, my son."

Nasir went on softly, "Because I'm so focused on the American end of the program, I worry about the international shipping of the documents, then their reconstitution here, the shipment to the boys, and our ability to have the boys deliver them properly to the heathens. The documents may be in good condition back home, but so much can go wrong once they leave the facility. If they are damaged, we can do nothing here to restore them. This leads me to suggest a small alteration in our plans. I think we should do a trial run of a few documents here before we provide all the documents to the scholars. We can try those documents with a short lead-time so we can see quickly how effective they are. It shouldn't result in any harm to our boys if the introduction is on a small scale. We can't risk delivering counterfeit documents or finding the delivery system to the heathens doesn't work, and then disbanding our scholars without any impact. All our elaborate efforts would be for nothing."

"So what you are saying is that even if the documents prove authentic back home, they might not be reliable when they arrive or are used here?"

"Yes. I'm most concerned that the means of getting the documents accepted by the heathens may not work. I consider that our weakest link."

The Imam looked grave and said, "Yes, I see your points. It won't be the same to test the documents at home and here. So, should we only conduct a test when they get here?"

"I don't know. It's probably prudent to do both tests, but only use two documents for the American test, ones that would be simple to introduce to the heathens. The test at home can be used for the documents that take longer and are trickier to authenticate."

"Tell me more of your plan for a test here?" the Imam asked.

Nasir had a well-prepared answer, but pretended to think about it for a moment before replying. "I recommend using those short-onset documents whose effects are most likely to get into the media, since we are dependent on public reports of our documents' influence. If we learn nothing via such sources about this trial, we will be in the dark about the documents' impact. So the next question would be whether to proceed with a full release of the documents or not."

The Imam said, "That would be a problem. Still, I think your proposal seems a reasonable and wise step. How much would it slow down the program?"

"I estimate that once we have the documents here, it should give us answers in about four weeks or less."

"So if we get the requested documents here shortly, it may not slow us down since production of all the documents will take a few more weeks."

"Yes, Imam. Unfortunately, an American trial introduces further complexity, the need to have the texts sent as two separate shipments from the homeland. Now, the amount needed for a small trial wouldn't require a large package and would be much easier to clear customs."

The Imam asked, "How large a box would be needed for this shipment?"

"I estimate it would be about three to four times the size of the lokum box there."

"So it could fit in a suitcase or backpack."

"Yes, but unfortunately I believe it should be sent in a way identical to the main shipment as a test of the safety of the shipment method."

The Imam shook his head and said, "Oh, yet another step for potential discovery. Still, I agree it should be done that way." He closed his eyes and stroked his beard. He took a long time before speaking. "I fear the program may be getting too complex. There are many opportunities to fail. But it must be done in this series of small steps, and we have a great deal invested in it. Inshallah!" Eyes still closed, he went on. "Do you have the trial sites and documents identified?"

Nasir leaned forward and whispered his response in the Imam's ear. He went on, "I recommend we do the trials at sites with few health care facilities and away from big cities. When I was a public health student at Johns Hopkins, I learned that the definition of an epidemic is the occurrence of a disease in excess of normal expectation, so a clear excess must be observed. If a doctor sees one case of cholera, he might just dismiss it as a medical oddity. If that same doctor sees two or three cases, it becomes an epidemic that gets reported to authorities and lands on the Internet. It would be best if all cases were seen at one facility. So I've selected small towns with a single hospital."

"As usual, Nasir, you have thought things out thoroughly. I like your plan, but I must consult with the Shura. In the meantime, go ahead and plan for a trial run."

The Imam got up and led Nasir to the kitchen where they had tea. He passed Nasir a large canvas envelope and put his finger over his mouth to signal silence. They made small talk and the Imam asked, "How is your boy coming along?"

Nasir, the proud father, did some bragging before they exchanged goodbyes.

28
Santa Fe

Salim was excited to start his new job. Abdullah, too, had been excited about Salim's landing a job at Nature's Bounty, as people came from great distances to shop there. Hopefully, some of those customers would be from Los Alamos or White Rock.

As instructed, Salim wore a short-sleeved, white shirt, khaki trousers and rubber-soled shoes to work. He was all smiles as he reported to the service desk to fill out some additional forms. Unfortunately, the bra-less woman wasn't there today. She excited him as much as she repulsed him. The young man at the desk was friendly and called the manager when Salim was done with the forms. The manager turned out to be Jerry Cartwright, the man who'd first interviewed him.

A smiling Jerry greeted Salim cheerfully, "Welcome aboard, Sal. I should take you around and get you oriented. Let's start with the checkout area up front." He led Salim to the front of the store and introduced him to the checkout personnel. He then showed him the paper and plastic bags and instructed him to help customers to their cars when the store wasn't busy, and to insist on it with any elderly patrons." He concluded, "When we do get busy, we may ask you to pitch in and help our supply clerks."

"Got it, boss," Salim said, increasingly annoyed by his breezy, false cheer.

At the back of the store, Jerry pointed out the staff lounge where Salim could hang his clothes and store his stuff while working. It was a communal set-up with open wooden cubes rather than lockers, and a coat rack. Jerry walked across the hall to a cold-room with a glass and stainless steel door. "This is one of our refrigerated rooms. It's used for bulk and packaged salads. We only take them out in small quantities to keep them fresh." He then led Salim through the butcher shop and the rest of the refrigerated rooms.

Salim took it all in and commented "Wow! This is state-of-the-art compared to the store I worked in back in Berkeley." He was particularly pleased by the proximity of the staff lounge to the refrigerated rooms.

Jerry led Salim to the front of the store and turned him over to one of the checkout clerks who would orient him to the checkout area.

Salim had a pleasant first day. It was slow, so nobody asked him to help with stocking or cleaning. The unpredictability of his job duties could pose a problem when the time came, but he'd deal with that. All in all, he was thrilled by the opportunity the store provided to carry out his mission. The layout was perfect. Allah had directed him here. Now he looked forward to the day when he would wipe the stupid smile off Jerry's face.

29
North Waziristan

Rashid was at a microscope, engrossed in examining the tissue cultures they were using for propagating viruses, when he was summoned by one of the guards to join Yusuf outside. Yusuf was talking with two rough-looking strangers on horseback, his armed guards surrounding the riders. Rashid joined the cozy group and asked what was going on.

"These men have a message for you," Yusuf answered. He handed an envelope to Rashid. It was from the Hakim and addressed to him. He turned his back to the men and opened the envelope. The letter read:

"My esteemed Rashid,

There has been a change in our plans. We have decided to conduct a small test of two agents at their delivery sites. This will be done before we do a larger test at the camp. The two agents are cholera and enterohemorrhagic E. coli. I believe you have propagated these already. The agents are to be packaged the same way the larger shipment will be. We need three ampoules of each agent. We need this done immediately. The men delivering this note will wait until the materials are ready.

I look forward to the successful completion of your work and to the day we witness the creation of the new and glorious Caliphate.

Inshallah,

A."

Rashid exhaled loudly, handed the note to Yusuf and said, "It looks like my men have some urgent work to do. We haven't tested the machinery for freeze-drying and packaging the agents yet."

Yusuf finished reading the letter, grimaced crookedly, and asked, "How long do you think it will take to complete this task?"

"My guess is that we can do it in two days. We have enough of these agents produced. It's the processing and packaging that could slow us down."

"Very well then; I'll have these men return in two days."

Yusuf directed the men to camp away from the installation and to return in two days. "You must stay out of open areas and never mention this camp to anyone," he ordered them. Then he turned to Rashid and said, "I don't know what this is all about, but the Hakim wants this urgently. I will put my men on high alert; the messengers could have been followed here."

"Well, I don't think my men and I will be getting much sleep the next two days. But, I believe we can get it done by then, Inshallah."

30
Astoria

Nasir al Fakrah had been summoned to an urgent meeting with the Imam, where he was sure he'd find out the Shura's decision on his proposed trial. He smiled as he envisioned their approval; his plan was too sensible for them to turn down. And sure enough, after he went through his usual routine of turning on the radio and a noisy fan, the Imam announced that he had good news. "The Council and our Leader agree that your plan for an American test should be carried out. They will also conduct the larger-scale test back home. The test documents you requested will be shipped here soon. So you must alert the Druze and give him the necessary shipping documents. Will you deliver the test documents to the boys yourself?"

"Yes."

"You must be careful, my son. Local recruits must do the main delivery of all the documents. After you reconstitute the main shipment, you will leave the country immediately. You know too much."

"I understand."

"I have more good news. The document validation is progressing well." He leaned towards Nasir and whispered. "Even the virus production is going well."

"That is encouraging, but I still worry about our end of the program, but that's my task—to worry about the smallest details."

"I have the shipping information, more cash, and airline tickets for you; I will give them to you when you leave. Come, let us take some tea."

31
North Waziristan

Rashid was spent from the pace at which they were producing the infectious agents. He wasn't young any more. On top of this, he had to deal with power failures and equipment breakdowns. He was lucky to have Jalal as his assistant. Jalal had proved to be a skilled production engineer who could repair anything and his skills had been tested to the extreme. Rashid would have to inform the Hakim about Jalal's great skills for use in future projects. Rashid was pleased that he had arranged for Jalal to be well compensated for his work on this project, as he had a young, pregnant wife and they could use the money.

Rashid went outside and searched for Yusuf, who was at one of the foxholes. The wind was howling and he had to speak loudly. "Salaam, Yusuf. I have some good news. I think we have enough hepatitis virus produced for testing on volunteers and we definitely have enough of the bacterial agents."

"That is good news! Just let me know when you wish to start the testing."

"Yusuf, where are the volunteers coming from and when can they arrive?"

"The volunteers are here. They're your men, and are available when production goals have been reached. You will go on with the freeze-drying and packaging with a skeleton crew while the tests are ongoing."

Rashid turned pale. "But I need my men to complete production. They're good and valuable men. Also, haven't they been immunized against the agents we're producing?"

"Not all received vaccines; some received saline injections. It's best this way. We cannot risk bringing in outsiders. If death claims them, they will find their way to Paradise sooner. This is Jihad and your men are great warriors in the struggle. Allah rewards the righteous Jihadi in Paradise."

Rashid stood silent, stunned by the cynical disregard for his men. It had taken a long time to assemble his team and many were friends. He knew the brothers were hard men who would sacrifice anyone or anything to accomplish their mission, but this turn of events severely tested his devotion to the cause.

He finally asked, "How will the agents be administered, Yusuf, and will the men be treated after they show symptoms?   Most of these diseases can be cured easily."

"The Hakim insists we administer the agents in foods, as will occur in the field. Our nurse, Mahmoud, will work with you and the cook to sprinkle the reconstituted bugs on the foods of selected workers. The cook will be kept in the dark and told this is a special hygienic program. All agents must first be lyophilized and packaged as in actual practice. Your men will, of course, be treated; we do not wish them to suffer. We are devout and true believers, not heartless infidels."

"Will we quarantine the men after they're exposed? They could spread the diseases to the other men."

"The Hakim recommends that they can work for one more day after they are exposed, since the incubation periods are all longer than a day. After this time period, they will be confined to the hospital we will set up. The men exposed to hepatitis can work for at least a week or two after exposure. We can then monitor them for abnormalities in their liver function tests, before they show any clinical signs of hepatitis. Mahmoud has equipment to set up a lab to monitor the liver function of the infected men. We'll have your men go to the dining room for their meals on an assigned schedule. Only two will eat at a time and the cook and Mahmoud will prepare their meals. I'll give you a program of which men are to receive each of the agents and in what sequence. We'll start with hepatitis since it has the longest incubation period. Can we start the feeding program tomorrow?"

"Yusuf, there's a problem with your plan. Soon after hepatitis infection, even before symptoms develop, the patients start shedding virus. The infected workers can infect others."

"Don't worry about that; leave it to us. Can we begin tomorrow? " Yusuf asked

Rashid was about to say something, thought the better of it, and answered, "That will depend on being able to lyophilize the virus and package it tonight. I assume there will be no hitches."

"Very well. We'll announce the new dining room schedule tomorrow morning and administer the virus beginning with tomorrow's evening meal. Work hard, my brother. We are on a tight schedule and this project is of great importance to our righteous cause."

Rashid walked back to his office staring at the ground. He felt torn between his loyalty and love for his men, and the great mission of jihad and bringing down the infidel who defiles the holy sites and spreads heresy throughout the world. But these were devout Muslims who would be under attack. He realized that if he refused to go along, he would be replaced, or worse. Besides, how could he abandon the project that he and the Sheikh had conceived without seeing it through to its end? The larger mission must prevail, he decided with renewed conviction. But he also realized that his first impression of Yusuf was correct; Yusuf was an evil man.

32
North Waziristan

Rashid was engrossed in processing hepatitis A virus for freeze-drying and vacuum packing in glass ampoules. Their Chinese-made lyophilizing equipment had been purchased through several intermediaries; its stainless steel vacuum chambers gleamed as a testament to Rashid's fastidiousness. Despite its recent use, Rashid had been worried it wouldn't work, but so far, the freezing part functioned, and he now needed to test the vacuum system. As he fiddled with the controls, he heard the hissing sound of air being expelled and exclaimed, "Praise be to Allah!"

"All right men, let's load the machine and see if it works. Everyone put on your masks, gowns and gloves and let's fill the vials." They fitted the glass vials onto the nozzles at the bottom of the tanks and slowly filled them. The machine then used a spot weld to melt the glass at the top of the vial to seal it.

Several hours later, they had the needed ampoules neatly resting in their prepared Styrofoam holders. They'd find out if the process worked about a week after the "volunteers" ingested the virus.

"Let's clean the equipment and process the cholera material next," he instructed the team that was trained to clean the machine after each use. It was a slow process as they worked in shifts around the clock processing one agent after another. This was the culmination of Rashid's dream and the adrenaline-flow of a full-scale packaging of the biologic materials kept him going.

It was first light when Yusuf came to visit. He donned a surgical cap, mask, gown and gloves at the door before asking, "Well Rashid, how are things going? I see the Styrofoam containers are being filled, but I think you need some rest. Tired people make mistakes. Why don't you put Jalal in charge and come join me for breakfast and then take a nap."

"We're making excellent progress, but it's going slowly. Everything's working well and we've had no spills or breakage yet. I prefer to watch over my dream come true, and I don't feel the least bit tired."

"You must rest, Rashid. You've told me how competent your assistant Jalal is. So why not put him in charge for a short while?"

"I prefer to stay."

Yusuf fixed Rashid with a glare and said, "You will leave promptly or I'll have my men escort you out."

"All right, I'll get Jalal here and then join you in the dining hut. I could use some hot tea and bread."

Rashid waited until he was alone to let himself scowl. Yusuf was a hard, driven man and Rashid now disliked him intensely. He guessed Yusuf must have suffered severe injuries in some battle, probably in Afghanistan, not that it excused his behavior. Rashid was comforted by the realization that he would soon be home with his family and out of this ruthless, upside-down world.

33
North Waziristan

Rashid and Yusuf stood in the center of the dusty compound facing an assembly of workers. It was early morning, cold and windy, and Rashid began by giving a pep talk. "You have worked hard and performed well," he told the brothers. "We must now work even harder as the completion date for our project nears. We will continue our shift work around the clock and will take our meals in small shift groups. The new work and meal schedules will be posted outside the living quarters. Allah shall reward you for your faithful work on behalf of our great jihad."

The men headed off to study the newly posted schedules as the two leaders watched. Yusuf began, "Well Rashid, we are at the endgame. The processing and packaging appears to be going well and we now have samples to allow testing of the agents. We must test the samples exactly as they will be used in the field. See that I receive two ampoules of each agent immediately because the testing must begin today. Mahmoud and I will handle the testing; there's no need to take you away from your important work. We cannot ship the materials until we know they are biologically active. Let us pray they work."

Rashid went back to his hut to say his morning prayers. He still recoiled at Yusuf's poisoning of his men. As soon as he finished, he went to the laboratories to get the required samples. He went to each workstation and gingerly loaded two samples of each agent into the specialized foam-cushioned carrier they had developed. He was constantly aware of the fragility of their packaging and walked as if on eggs. He finished gathering the samples and went off looking for Yusuf whom he guessed would be in the dining tent.

He found Yusuf there, having breakfast alone. "Yusuf, I have the needed materials for testing. Where do you want them placed?"

"Actually, I'd like them placed on a bench outside in the sun."

Rashid shook his head. "We can't run the risk of damage due to sun exposure or to heating up the specimens."

Yusuf replied, "When the samples are out in the field or at their delivery sites, they may be exposed to sunlight and heat. Part of our testing is to rough up the samples to mimic field conditions."

"But Yusuf, these are fragile agents!"

"Rashid, my careful scientist, our soldiers will not be in a laboratory, but out in real world conditions. If we don't approximate what might happen outside, we run the risk of the specimens arriving at their delivery sites having no biologic activity. We will start testing with the evening meal and the first selected workers."

Their conversation was interrupted by a noisy disturbance outside. They went out and saw two men in tribal regalia on horseback, surrounded by Yusuf's men with rifles at the ready. One of Yusuf's men held a small box, which he passed to Rashid, and reported, "This came for you. The men on horseback say it's important. There's also a letter."

Rashid looked at the letter first. The note was in the Hakim's handwriting; it read:

"Honored Professor,

The bearer of this note has a package that contains a new strain of E. coli that caused an epidemic in Germany. We want you to propagate this strain and add it to your mixes. It will add confusion to the Great Satan's search for causes.

Continue with your fine work and I wish you Godspeed.
A."

Rashid passed the note to Yusuf and studied the package; it carried Lufthansa tagging for Islamabad. "Very well," he said. "This should be easy to grow. It's an excellent idea to include another strain, particularly if it's new." He was amazed again by the clever strategy of the Hakim.

34
North Waziristan

Mahmoud was in the dining tent, instructing the cook about dinner preparation for the workers. It was to consist of cucumbers and tomatoes, yoghurt, lamb kebobs and naan. He had the cook prepare two separate servings laid out on trays and then ordered the cook to go back to the kitchen so he could do his work unseen. He consulted an instruction sheet and then broke the top off one of the vials that had sat outside all morning and used a small syringe and needle to draw up some of the material in the vial. He then drew up saline solution into the same syringe. He wore rubber gloves for this operation and was careful to squirt small amounts of the fluid on the cucumber and tomatoes and then also over the yoghurt.

The new schedule for meals for the workers was staggered so only two workers came into the dining tent at a time. The first two showed up promptly at five. The cook greeted them and gave them each a tray. One of the workers said, "Brother Cook, to what do we owe such a fancy meal today? We haven't had lamb and salad for a while now."

"Rashid is pleased with your progress, and since the end of your labors is in sight, he wanted to recognize your accomplishments."

The workers wolfed down their meals. The cook offered them some more food and they took up his offer, then thanked him and headed back to their jobs.

After the workers left, Mahmoud carried their plates and utensils to a large sink in the kitchen, again wearing rubber gloves. In the kitchen, the cook was bringing several large pots of water to boil, per

Mahmoud's instructions. When the water was boiling, Mahmoud had the cook pour it over the utensils in the sink. He instructed the cook to wash everything in the sink with soap and bleach when the dishes had cooled down.

Mahmoud told the cook the next group of workers was due to take dinner in another hour and the same foods should be served in the same manner. He would be back to inspect the food trays and do his special task with the food.

It took a day and a half to get all the selected infectious agents into the workers' foods in a way that would be undetected. Mahmoud smiled as he reflected on how well the "volunteer" program had gone. Now, they would have to wait and see.

35
Santa Fe

Salim was spent after a hard day at Nature's Harvest Foods. Nevertheless, he was looking forward to seeing his mentor Abdullah that evening, and he straightened up his messy apartment.

Nasir al Fakrah drove his rental car several times around the tree-lined block where Salim's apartment house was located before parking a block away. There were no suspicious looking cars or possible stakeouts that he could discern. He was dressed unremarkably—wearing a light blue windbreaker, blue jeans, a tan baseball hat and running shoes – and carried a small navy duffel bag. He walked slowly over to Salim's building and rang the apartment bell.

Salim greeted Abdullah enthusiastically. "Uncle Abdullah, how good to see you! Did you have a good trip here?" he asked while leading him upstairs to his apartment.

Nasir always had a difficult time connecting with the different names he used. "Yes, I had a nice trip here, thank you. My dear Salim, you are certainly looking well. Santa Fe seems to agree with you better than Detroit. How are you enjoying living here?"

"Things are going well, and I'm enjoying living in Santa Fe."

Nasir went over to a radio, and turned it on at a loud volume.

"Salim, tell me what you do in your new job?"

"My primary work is to help with bagging groceries. When things get slow, the manager has me helping in the back with stocking things that we sell out of. I haven't been asked to work as a cashier though. They probably don't trust kids with the registers. I've also helped to clean up spills when a customer breaks something."

"I see. Are you ever alone in the back of the store around the produce, meats and dairy products?"

"Yes, usually when I'm back in our kitchen eating lunch. It's tucked between the refrigerated rooms where the fresh stuff is kept."

"How long are you usually alone in the kitchen?"

"Oh, probably 20 to 30 minutes. We stagger our lunch breaks so I'm alone when I eat."

"Do you ever go into the refrigerated rooms as part of your work?"

"Yeah, from time to time when they need help with restocking produce, dairy stuff; you know, things like that."

"Do you think your co-workers like you, Salim?"

"I think so; they always tell me what a good worker I am. I try to be pleasant and a hard worker so that I'm accepted by everyone."

"That's good. We need to have your co-workers trust you, so if they see you in a place you don't belong they'll assume it's work-related. When we spoke on the phone, you said you would be working tomorrow, is that still correct?"

"Yes."

"Tomorrow I'd like you to conduct a trial run for your final mission. I have some things for you to use." Nasir unzipped his small duffel bag and unloaded its contents. "First of all, I have a nice new sports shirt for you; let's see how it looks on you."

Salim donned the new shirt and modeled it for his mentor. "It fits me just fine and I like the Hawaiian look. Thank you, Uncle. I really like it."

"Tomorrow you're to wear this shirt to work. Wear it tucked out of your trousers to better conceal this next item." Nasir held up a canvas belt with numerous little pockets that held at least a dozen plastic syringes. "This belt was tailored to your exact size. Hopefully, you haven't gained weight since you arrived here. Go ahead and try it on, but be careful with all the tubes. It latches in front."

"It's a perfect fit, Uncle, so I haven't gotten fat here in Santa Fe. Maybe it's because I'm working so hard."

"Ah, good. By keeping your shirt out of your pants you should be able to reach under your shirt easily to retrieve the tubes when you need them. You had told me earlier that you had a locker in the kitchen area; does it have a lock?"

"No, but nobody has had anything stolen since I've been there. The managers don't want any locks on the lockers to prevent employees from hiding and stealing things."

"I see. Tomorrow I want you to bring this belt to work in the small blue bag I have here. It's small enough to look like you're just carrying your lunch and a change of clothes. Leave it in your locker and when lunchtime comes, take the belt out and put it on. Before that, leave the bag unzipped with a pair of running shoes and a newspaper on top so they're visible. That way it looks like you have nothing of value in the bag and nothing to hide. Do you follow me?"

"Yes, Uncle."

"Good. In your belt there are two different types of syringes, one type with needles and the second with small plastic caps at the end. There's a piece of red tape on the syringes with needles so you can tell them apart quickly. Now listen carefully: The syringes without needles are for spraying over loose, unpackaged salad greens and supplies for salad bars or take-out food counters if they have any set up in the store. The syringes with needles are for injecting into packages of hamburger and containers of dairy products. Remember your training back home. The meat injections are done on the bottom of the package where there are several layers of shrink-wrapped plastic. After the injection, just rub the area to move some of the extra wrap over the hole. With containers of cottage cheese or yoghurt the injection is on the top at the junction between the rim and the flat top. If you can't inject all of these products, the fallback is prepackaged, washed salad greens. For this you will have to inject at the bottom central seam and then use a little bit of the glue we have in a tube in the belt. We trained you on this method and you know it's a last resort because it takes more time. Also, remember you can also use soft cheeses. Ingenuity should guide you. Just remember to avoid acid foods like pickles and also foods that require cooking.

Use the most expensive hamburger; it's more likely to be grilled and left rare in the center. Always put the empty syringes back into the belt holders. After you have injected or sprayed as many things as you think is reasonable in the time you have, go back to the lunchroom. If no one is around, take off your belt and put it back in the bag under the other stuff. Otherwise just wear the belt home. Just make sure your shirt stays fully buttoned and watch yourself when you bend over. Do you think you can do this tomorrow?"

"I think I can do it Uncle, Allah willing. As you taught me, there's always the chance someone will show up unexpectedly where I'm working, but I've rehearsed the lines I would use to explain my unexpected presence around the food storage areas."

"We have prepared you well and you have been an outstanding student, so we must pray for the best. I will come to your apartment again tomorrow night at about seven o'clock to collect your belt and used syringes. Also remember that if the operation seems to be in danger, wait for another day. Don't go ahead with the operation if you think it'll be discovered."

Nasir instructed Salim to store the belt in his refrigerator overnight. He then headed towards the door, and on the way out, informed Salim that his parents and siblings were well. After taking leave, Nasir drove to his motel room on Cerrillos Road for some rest after a hectic day. Sleep would be difficult as he waited for tomorrow's results.

36
Santa Fe

Salim was thrilled about this momentous day when he would at last become a true jihadi, a warrior to be feared. He could even become famous and show his heathen classmates how wrong they were about him. No one was going to call him "towel-head" or "camel-jockey" any more.

He was proud of the new shirt he was wearing and hummed one of his favorite tunes as he drove to work. His co-workers were getting things ready for opening as he went to leave his bag in the locker area. He unzipped it and arranged the newspaper inside, on top of his running shoes. Then he went up front to the check-out counters, where he was getting the shopping bags ready for the day, when one of the cashiers shouted, "Wow Sal, that's a nice shirt! You look like you belong on Waikiki Beach. Is it new?"

"Yeah, I just got it as a gift from my uncle and he has pretty loud taste."

"Well, we'll certainly be able to spot you in a crowd today."

That last remark registered hard with Salim, as this was a day for him to be unobtrusive. He kept his cool and retorted, "You know, one of the supermarket chains uses Hawaiian shirts to identify their managers for just that reason, so they can be spotted easily for help. Maybe my uncle was hinting that I should get promoted?"

"You should take that up with Management, Sal. It looks like the doors just opened."

It was a light day at the store, and when Herb, one of the Assistant Managers, took Sal off duty to help him restock some produce in back, Sal had to suppress a smile at this chance to scout the food in the storage rooms. Herb, too, noticed Salim's bright new shirt and teased him about it. He was standing out like a flag, he thought to himself, hoping that Uncle Abdullah hadn't messed up with this shirt.

It seemed like forever before his lunch break came. Finally, he walked back to the staff break area and withdrew his small duffle bag from the open locker. Nothing had been touched and no one was around, so he quickly withdrew his "jihad belt" and put it on under his shirt. He took out his prepared sandwich, put it on the table, and then took off for the refrigerated room that contained fruits, vegetables and salads. Seeing no one nearby, he let himself in. He had spotted the bulk salad greens earlier in the day, and that was his first stop. He quickly undid the twist-tie, opened the first bag, withdrew one of the uncolored syringes, and squirted the syringe contents over the lettuce mix. He resealed the bag and then lifted it to shake its contents. He repeated the operation twice more, using a fresh syringe for each bag of greens, making sure the used syringes were recapped and placed back in the "jihad belt," upside down to indicate they'd been used. He spotted bulk-packed olives in plastic vats. He pried open the lids of two vats and squirted the contents of one of the unmarked syringes into each vat. He resealed the vats and shook them vigorously. Time was running out, so he exited the room quietly, looked both ways and went to the refrigerated room where they kept packaged meats and dairy products. He quickly put on plastic gloves as he looked for the most expensive ground beef. He went for the ground sirloin first and withdrew fifteen packages from the cardboard box in which they were stored. He turned them over and carefully injected each with the blue syringes. He returned the packages to their container and then went over to a carton of cottage cheese. He withdrew ten packages, injected part of the contents of a blue syringe into each container and gave each a shake before returning them to their carton. He followed the same procedure with ten, quart-containers of yoghurt and then checked his watch. The whole procedure had taken less than fifteen minutes.

He removed his gloves, opened the refrigerator room door cautiously, looked both ways and walked calmly back to the lunchroom. First, he discarded the gloves at the bottom of a container of trash. Then he went to the sink and washed his hands thoroughly with soap. He was surprised his hands weren't shaking, as his heart was racing. He then wolfed down his sandwich to give the appearance he'd been eating for a while. He replaced his belt in the navy bag, got out his newspaper and read from it with feigned nonchalance, his heart still beating wildly. When his one-hour break was about up, he went to the water cooler and had a glass of water. He then went to the restroom, relieved himself, washed his hands, and checked his appearance carefully in the mirror. His loud new shirt looked neat, though a bit sweaty. He wiped his forehead with a paper towel and went back to work up front. As he walked back to the front of the store he suddenly felt a mixture of exhaustion and elation. The three hours remaining at work would seem endless until he could finally go home to relax and celebrate his new status.

37
Santa Fe

Salim collapsed on his bed when he returned to his apartment, still having a hard time believing how easily he'd completed his assignment and was startled when his cellphone rang.

"Good evening Salim. This is Uncle Abdullah."

"It went well, Uncle. I used…"

Abdullah interrupted, "I'll come by soon to hear what happened and to collect things."

When Abdullah arrived, Salim gave him a big hug and said, "I did it, I did it! It worked Uncle."

"Come; let's sit while you tell me everything. Don't get too excited or cocky about today; it could lead to mistakes."

But after Salim reported the day's activities in detail, Abdullah smiled and said, "You've done well my son. I'm proud of you and you have now become a soldier of Allah. You must wait patiently for the full delivery; it should come soon. Now give me your belt and its contents. I hope you didn't leave anything behind."

"No, Uncle. I was careful to collect everything, even the syringe caps, as you taught me during training."

Salim gave Abdullah the duffel bag that was given to him yesterday. Abdullah took the bag over to a table and inspected its contents. He had brought a brown paper shopping bag from which he took out a pair of latex gloves. He put on the gloves, removed the needles from the syringes and placed them in a plastic bag. He put the syringes in several paper bags and loaded everything in the shopping bag.

"I must go now, my son. You make me proud. Be patient." He hugged Salim and left.

Abdullah walked around the block before going to his car. He had checked out of his motel and headed straight to I-25 to drive to the Albuquerque airport. He donned latex gloves again and, along the way, he periodically threw needles out of the car window. When he reached Albuquerque, he stopped at a McDonalds for a quick dinner, then found a dumpster behind the restaurant where he scattered the small bags with syringes over the accumulated garbage. It was time for him to drop off his rental car and leave town, hoping for the best.

38
Santa Fe

Lucy Martinez was up to her ears in work at the Chamisa Mortgage Company, so she was having lunch at her desk. She was in the middle of a long call with a client when "Nature" called so suddenly that she had to interrupt her client. "Look, something really urgent just came up; can I call you right back? Thanks." She dashed off to the restroom and barely made it there before having terrible watery diarrhea.

Wow, that was strange, she thought, since she hadn't even had cramps. She decided to throw out her chicken salad sandwich. Then she called her client back, apologized for the interruption and wrapped up their transaction before heading to the kitchen to make a cup of tea to calm her stomach. She took a few sips, but before she could get back to her desk, she was overwhelmed by having to vomit, and she rushed again to the toilet. She felt light-headed, going back to her cubicle, when nature called again. As before, she was puzzled by the absence of cramps, fever, or any other symptoms preceding her diarrhea. This time she noticed her stool was watery and pale white. It was getting scary.

Heading back to her desk, she nearly collided with her boss, Jane, who stopped her and said, "Hey Lucy, you look terrible; are you okay?"

"Jane, I had a chicken salad sandwich for lunch and it's made me terribly sick. I never had this before outside of Mexico."

"Look Lucy, why don't you go home? The work will still be here when you feel better. Do you want me to drive you?"

"I guess you're right. I'll get my things and head on home. I think I can drive myself, but thanks for the offer."

Lucy had one more bout of vomiting before she got to her car and rushed home. She was light-headed and weak, but she slowly made it up the flight of steps to her apartment. There she made some more tea and took it to bed where she collapsed and dozed off into a deep sleep.

She was awakened when her husband Luis came home and turned on the lights. "What are you doing in bed? Are you okay?"

A groggy Lucy told him what had happened, but she thought she was feeling better as she offered to get up and fix him supper. But as she got out of bed, she realized she had been lying in a pool of diarrhea and collapsed like a rag doll. Luis rushed over and roused her by shaking her gently. She woke up and said, "I don't know what happened to me. I just felt woozy when I stood up and then every-thing went blank." She started to cry and said, "I'm scared Luis."

"Lucy, Honey, I think we need to get you seen by a doctor."

Before he could go on, Lucy rushed to the bathroom and had more watery diarrhea, again with no cramps. She emerged from the room and after a few steps collapsed again.

"That's it Lucy, we're going to the hospital." He helped Lucy down to the car, piled her into the back seat, and hotfooted it to the hospital.

Once they were in the ER, the staff helped Lucy into a wheelchair and he got her registered. Ten minutes later, Lucy's name was called and an attendant came to take her back while Luis was asked to remain in the waiting area. Lucy was wheeled into a small, brightly lit cubicle with a desk and lots of equipment.

"Hi, Ms. Martinez. I'm Jody Maguire. I'm the triage nurse this evening and I need to ask you some questions before the doctor sees you. Do you understand English?"

"Yeah, I was born in the U.S."

"Sorry about that; it's a legal requirement that I ask. What brings you to the hospital tonight?"

Lucy explained what had happened to her that day, and the nurse asked if she'd had similar episodes before?"

"No. This is the first time. I just got light-headed and crumped."

"Okay. Let me get your blood pressure before we go on. Do you have any history of high or low blood pressure?"

"No. I'm pretty healthy in general."

The nurse called out to an attendant in the hallway, "Sam, would you come in here for a second? I'm going to have Lucy stand up while I measure her blood pressure and I need you to steady her if she gets light-headed. She may have orthostatic hypotension." She asked Lucy to stand up with Sam behind her and took her blood pressure while Lucy stood.

Lucy suddenly complained, "Uh, oh; I'm going to pass out again," as she slumped into the wheelchair guided by Sam.,

Lucy was out of it while they got her onto a gurney, drew some blood for the laboratory and started an intravenous drip on the back of her hand. The next thing she knew, she was being awakened by a doctor shaking her. "Lucy, I'm Doctor Anderson. Can you hear me?'

She was in some sort of examining room behind green curtains, and Luis was sitting in a chair at the side of the room. "Yeah; I hear you. Sorry; I must have dozed off."

Dr. Anderson proceeded to ask her the same set of questions as the nurse. He seemed interested in her sandwich and asked where and when she bought it, how it tasted, how long after eating it she got sick and things like that. "Lucy, have you had any cramps or stomach pain at all with your diarrhea."

"No; there was nothing. When I had diarrhea like this in Mexico, I remember having terrible cramps, but not with this."

"Pardon me for asking, but what did your diarrhea look like?"

"It was really strange. It wasn't brown or yellow, but like grayish-white water."

"I see. Now did you have a sensation of nausea before you vomited?"

"Come to think of it, no. That's so strange. What do you think's going on Doctor?"

"Well, you passed out because you're severely dehydrated from the diarrhea and vomiting. On a simple probability basis, your most likely diagnosis is staphylococcal food poisoning from your sandwich. But what doesn't add up is that typically, it's two to eight hours after ingesting the staph toxin that you'd get sick. There are other diagnoses that could give you similar signs and symptoms, but they're far-fetched. When I was in medical school, one of our professors always used to say that whenever you hear hoof-beats, you should think of horses before you think of zebras. So, we'll go with the staph poisoning diagnosis for now.

Here's what we need to do. We need to replace your lost fluids and electrolytes and correct your acidosis by IV here in the hospital. I think we should keep you overnight, mainly because you passed out. Typically, with staph poisoning, you should be feeling fine by midmorning and we can discharge you. I don't usually get stool cultures done on cases like yours, but your symptoms are unusual and I recently attended a course on infectious diseases, so now I'm being more attentive to oddball causes of GI infections. In any event, you're looking much better already after the IV fluids and electrolytes."

Luis, who'd been silent, chimed in "Doc, is she going to be all right?"

"I'm pretty sure she'll be back to normal in 24 hours."

Luis went over to Lucy and said, "You see Honey? The doctor will get you well in no time flat."

39
Eldorado at Santa Fe, New Mexico

Mary Hernandez was grocery shopping with her three-year-old son, Ramon, when he suddenly grabbed her blouse and tugged. "Mommy, Mommy. Need to go poo-poo."

"Ramon, can't you wait?"

"No, Mommy. Big poo-poo coming."

Mary looked for a toilet in the store and rushed Ramon over just in time, as he had voluminous diarrhea. She asked, "Are you all right Baby?"

"No Mommy. Tummy hurts bad."

"Okay, Honey. Let's check out and take you home, you poor thing."

On the way home he again complained of his tummy hurting and a big poo-poo coming. He was still wearing diapers, so Mary didn't rush. He really stank up the car as he let go. When they got home, Mary changed his diaper and was startled when she saw a lot of blood in his stool. "Baby, this doesn't look right," she said, "I'm going to call the doctor."

Mary called their pediatrician in Eldorado, just outside the City of Santa Fe, and his nurse insisted she bring Ramon right in. She cleaned up Ramon, called her husband, and grabbed a supply of disposable diapers as she rushed out the door.

The doctor's waiting room was crowded. Mary parked Ramon on a seat in the corner and went to the desk to register. The receptionist was expecting them and told Mary that the doctor would see them shortly. Mary cradled Ramon on her lap as he continued to complain of tummy pain. He didn't feel warm to her, but he did appear pale. They only had to wait 5 minutes before the nurse called them back to the examination area. She sat Ramon on an examining table and checked his vital signs—pulse rate, blood pressure, oxygen saturation and temperature. She looked concerned as she told Mary that Ramon's blood pressure was low and his heart rate was rapid.

"Mommy, big poo-poo coming," Ramon cried. The nurse undid his diaper to see a mostly bloody, unformed stool. She placed the diaper on a stainless steel instrument table and hurried to fetch the pediatrician.

After placing the bloody sample in two glass tubes, Dr. Greene took a careful history from Mary as he gently examined Ramon. He learned Ramon hadn't been exposed to anyone with the same symptoms recently and they'd eaten rare grilled hamburgers a few days before. Dr. Greene sat down at the desk in the room and asked Mary to have a seat. "Mary, I don't like what I see in our little tiger," he began. "This could be the sign of a telescoping of one section of the bowel into another, or a bad infection like dysentery or pathogenic E. coli. Any of these should be treated at a specialized pediatric center. I think we need to get you to the University of New Mexico Children's Hospital in Albuquerque immediately. Can you drive there now?"

Mary nodded yes as she began sobbing. "How sick is he, Dr. Greene?"

"I don't know, but he needs to be evaluated. I'll call my friends at UNM so they'll be expecting you. Go to the admitting area in the new Children's Hospital just off Lomas; it's east off I-25. Just pull up in front of the hospital and tell them it's an emergency." He fetched the two tubes with stool samples and gave these to Mary to bring to the hospital.

40

Santa Fe

Win was startled when his BSAC pager went off. It was after dinner and he was in his study surfing the web when the beeping started. He had almost given up on wearing the pager, since no one ever paged him, so it sat on the credenza behind his desk. He retrieved the number and dialed it, reaching the BSAC nurse on call.

"Dr. Sage, This is Monica Ramirez." She sounded relieved. "I'm so glad I was able to reach you. I just got a report of a patient with one of the diseases on our watch list. The patient is a 27 year-old woman seen at Santa Fe Community Hospital with probable cholera. She came in severely dehydrated and almost in shock. Her lab report came back as positive for Vibrio cholerae, but they didn't report any typing of the strain. I just stopped at our office at the Health Department to check for messages and to pick up my paycheck, and I found the message."

"Is the patient okay now?"

"I have no idea and I'm not sure whom we might call at this hour."

"Do you have John Grant's home telephone number?"

She found it and read it to Win.

"Was there mention of any other cases in the note?" he asked.

"No, just the information I gave you."

"Well, why don't you brief the morning nurse when you sign off tomorrow? I'll call Grant and set up a meeting for tomorrow. Thanks for the heads up, Monica. Have a good night."

Win dialed Grant's number; he was home and answered the phone himself. Win told him about the call.

"That's interesting; we haven't seen a case of cholera here in Santa Fe for years, if ever. Did anyone ask the patient about a recent visit to Haiti?"

"I don't know. Someone took a message from the Hospital and left it in Monica's mailbox. I think we should meet tomorrow to plan an investigation along the lines the Committee developed."

"Unfortunately, I can't make it tomorrow. I have budget meetings at the Governor's office."

Win hit his head with his palm and said, "I thought we were going to have a rapid response time for outbreak investigations."

"We could do it the day after tomorrow or better yet, next week. That'll give our nurses more time to conduct an investigation. They can also check the accuracy of the diagnosis; it could be a lab error. I've been at this business a long time and reports like this usually turn out to be false alarms. I'll have my staff set up a meeting and we'll call you when it's all set. Thanks for your diligent input Win."

Win got up and went looking for Julia. He found her asleep on the living room couch with a book on her lap. When he woke her up, she asked him what was wrong.

"Oh Julia, you won't believe this; there's been a case of cholera in Santa Fe and the bonehead bureaucrat who runs the BSAC isn't concerned about it at all."

"Are you freaking out over one case of cholera? It's probably a mistaken diagnosis. Win, I think you've gone off the deep end with your infectious disease and bioterrorism obsession. Why don't you lie down next to me, I could use a hug."

41
Santa Fe

Late the next week, Judy Smith called—she was the nurse who seemed to be running the Committee—to see if Win could make an afternoon meeting the next day. While the first woman treated for cholera was doing fine, a second case had been reported by Community Hospital, in a 47 year-old, male scientist over at Los Alamos.

"When was the second case reported?" Win asked.

"It was late last week; Friday I think."

Win rolled his eyes and said through clenched teeth, "Do you think meeting tomorrow gives you enough time to investigate the cases?"

"We really haven't had enough time, but we thought we should get the team involved now, even though we have incomplete information."

Win covered the mouthpiece and said to Julia, "I don't believe what I'm hearing. The State people are totally incompetent. They have no idea of what a rapid response system might be." He uncovered the mouthpiece and asked Judy, "What have you found out so far?"

"Well, both cases have confirmed cholera; we don't know the type. Neither of the cases knew each other or ate at the same places, had any recent foreign travel or ate raw shellfish. One lives in Santa Fe and the other in Española. "

"Is someone looking into the cholera types involved in the two cases?"

"I'm not sure. I think maybe we had the hospital forward the bugs to the Air Force lady at Kirtland and maybe the CDC as well. I'll find out for you."

"Okay, that's great. I'll see you tomorrow."

Win hung up and cradled his head in his hands. "Julia, we've had two cases of cholera in the Santa Fe area and the State people have no appreciation of this representing an epidemic. Like government flunkies the world over, their investigation is proceeding at a snail's pace. We could have a lot more cases in the meantime. These people use calendars instead of watches."

Julia smirked and said, "I told you not to get involved with this dumb project."

Win kissed her and said, "You're right once again, Babe."

42
Santa Fe

Win spent the next morning at his computer checking on the incidence of cholera in the US. He was surprised to learn that there were only six to eight cases per year on average in the whole US, most due to foreign travel or consumption of contaminated raw seafood. There had been a spike in US cases after the hurricane disaster in Haiti, when US relief workers came back with the infection following an epidemic over there. But the infections in the US weren't spread to others, probably because of America's good medical treatment and sanitation systems. Win couldn't find any statistics on cholera in New Mexico, so he decided that two cases in the small Santa Fe area should be investigated promptly. He checked and found that all of Santa Fe County had a population of only 141,000.

He arrived at the meeting early, hoping to chat privately with John Grant, but only Tom Shaw was there. "Well, well; what's the illustrious Doctor Sage up to?" Shaw asked with a thin grin.

"Nothing good. I think we have an epidemic of cholera here in Santa Fe that demands an investigation."

"Two cases is hardly an epidemic! I think you're getting a bit carried away."

Win clenched his teeth. "Tom, the definition of an epidemic is the occurrence of a disease clearly in excess of normal expectation. The expected number of cases in all of New Mexico is zero, so two cases constitute an epidemic and the CDC recommends vigorous investigation of any case of cholera in the US, epidemic or not.

There likely was a common source of infection and other people could have been exposed."

Tom waved his hand and said, "There you go again Sage – seeing problems where none exist."

"Yeah. Just like the spy at Los Alamos that you guys never discovered until I tumbled to him."

The entrance of Grant and his bureaucratic retinue interrupted their conversation. "I'm glad you could make it today," he said to Win and Tom.

They were joined by Nancy Thomas—the Air Force microbiologist—and Bill Applegate, and took seats around the conference table. Grant began, "As you know, we've had two cases of cholera diagnosed in the Santa Fe area. They're both adults, with no contact between them, and no history of foreign travel. Nancy, have you been able to type the strains of cholera?"

"Yes. They're the same strain; both are Vibrio cholerae of the O139 Bengal serogroup, so it's likely due to a common-source exposure. Since neither patient had a history of recent overseas travel, they had no interaction, and they lived far apart with different water sources, how the hell did they both get these infections?"

"We haven't seen any epidemic strains of V. cholerae in New Mexico during my time here," Applegate added. "The only cases of cholera I know of in the State were due to non-O1 and non-O139 strains. These were mild cases linked to eating contaminated seafood—raw oysters, to be specific."

"I agree, it's a curious occurrence," Grant said. "But there's no need to panic; there's probably a simple explanation we've missed. Maybe they both were exposed to a foreign visitor."

"John, there's no direct person-to-person transmission of cholera. It's more likely they consumed some contaminated food or drink in common." Win said. "Nancy, why's the serogroup termed 'Bengal'?"

"That's because it was first identified in Bengal, the area of India and Bangladesh near the Bay of Bengal. It's one of the most densely populated regions in the world and includes two huge cities, Calcutta and Dhaka. The organism was first identified in the early 1990s and has since spread all around that region. It still occurs primarily in India and Bangladesh and it's rare outside the region."

"I guess with this new information, we'll need to interview the two patients again and focus on visits from foreigners or any undisclosed international travel," John said.

"So both of our cases are likely to have interacted with an Asian visitor with cholera who didn't wash his hands well or pooped in their water sources. Or maybe they both have amnesia about recent travels to Asia," Win retorted.

"There you go again Win," Tom interjected. "As John said, there's probably a simple explanation. Two cases don't constitute a big deal."

"Well, we should definitely interview the two cases again regarding risk factors," John said. "Maybe Bill and Win can come up with additional questions to ask the victims. I'll have Judy call you in a few days for your ideas."

Win wondered how quickly John would act on re-interviewing the patients. Would it be days or weeks?

They covered some minor points such as making sure the cholera typing was repeated by the CDC and then adjourned until after another field investigation. Win left the meeting dejected by the indifference of the group, or was it denial? This Committee was supposed to pounce on unusual infectious disease outbreaks and none of them understood that two cases of cholera constituted an epidemic. Grant also seemed to have forgotten that cholera was on his PowerPoint slide as a CDC Category B bioterrorism agent.

Jesus Christ! Win thought. These jackasses either weren't listening or didn't understand what he was saying. Or maybe they didn't respect his opinion. He grimaced and drove home with the radio blaring.

43
Santa Fe

After dinner, Win retreated to his sanctuary—his home office. After years of being a desk jockey in his work, he felt most comfortable and did his best work seated at a desk. Win surveyed the room. His desk was in the center of a maple-paneled office. Win was an avid collector of Japanese pottery, which typically came in light-colored wooden boxes, and the architect who'd designed their new house had the bright idea of fashioning Win's study as such a box, with Win at his desk in the center like a piece of fine pottery.

But that evening he didn't feel like a piece of fine anything as he mulled over the cholera cases in Santa Fe. He retrieved a bottle of calvados and a brandy snifter from the credenza behind his desk and poured himself a glass. He got up and went to a bookcase to retrieve an outdated textbook of tropical medicine from his student days. Just as he thought, the primary route of transmission of cholera was fecal-oral transmission. So the patients had to have eaten or drunk something contaminated by cholera organisms from the feces of an infected person. The two local cases had the same strain of cholera, which pointed to a common-source exposure.

Win pulled out a calculator from a desk drawer. If there were normally 10 cases per year in the US, that would amount to an annual rate of 0.032 cases per million based on the US population being 310 million. Applying that rate to the New Mexico 2010 census population of 2.06 million would give an expected number of 0.066 cases per year. Had there been only one case, he might have chalked it up to a chance occurrence related to foreign travel or seafood consumption. But they had observed two cases in only one month, which was 30.1 times that expected for an entire year in the whole state. Win took a sip of his drink and concluded this was a big-time epidemic. He leaned back and thought about what to do. They really needed to see the two cholera victims again and ask more questions. They had to have ingested something in common. Their geographic proximity made it a disease cluster; not only was there an excess, but they were close together in time and place at diagnosis.

Before he called it a night, he thought he'd surf the web to see if there were any other cholera cases diagnosed recently that had been picked up by the media. Just as he thought, there were no recent cases in the US, at least that were detected and reported. The two Santa Fe cases hadn't hit the media yet. He was well aware of the lag time in cases of infectious diseases getting reported and tallied and most never were picked up. He wrote on his pad in large letters, "VERY STRANGE! CHANCE?" He then crossed out chance. The odds were against it, and cholera doesn't occur by chance anyway.

44
Santa Fe

Judy Smith called Win two days after the Committee meeting to solicit questions to ask the cholera victims, and it was another week before Win heard back from her, inviting him to attend the next day's BSAC meeting when they would report the latest findings. Being retired, Win was free, though he was getting more and more irritated by the bureaucratic inertia and the short notices.

John began the meeting. "Well, the good news is that we haven't had any new cholera cases. The bad news is we haven't been able to find a source, let alone a common source, for the two cases. I guess we have to chalk up the occurrences to chance."

"I think you're right on this," Bill said.

While everyone else nodded in agreement, Win sat there astonished and proclaimed, "Cholera doesn't occur by chance, particularly in the United States! Two cases in the US within a week and in a small area represent an epidemic."

"There you go again Sage," Tom piped up.

Win fixed Shaw with an icy glare and resisted the urge to call him an idiot. Instead, he took a deep breath and asked, "Have there been cases of other diarrheal diseases that could be mild cholera infections or missed diagnoses?"

"No. Unless they're clear-cut cases of cholera they wouldn't get reported to us," John answered. "There was a case of enterohemorrhagic E. coli in a child from Eldorado, but nothing else unusual. The child's doing well and the CDC is investigating that case. I think we just have to attribute the two cholera cases to chance or some flukey introduction of organisms into a batch of food or drink."

Bill Applegate chimed in, "You know, this observation and quick reporting of the cholera cases demonstrates our surveillance system is working well." The others nodded in agreement.

Win couldn't believe how self-serving and congratulatory these bureaucratic wonks could be. The cases may have been reported promptly, but the investigation of this epidemic had been glacially slow and grossly inadequate.

John droned on with some bureaucratic details about record keeping and concluded by saying, "We'll certainly be on the look-out for further cholera cases and act accordingly if we find another." He looked at Win as he said this. "Why don't we break and have some refreshments. Our next meeting will be on our regular monthly basis."

The group meandered down the hall to the staff break room. Everyone else seemed pleased. Win ate a chocolate-covered dough-nut and didn't say a thing, as he contemplated whether to resign from this joke of a Committee.

45
Santa Fe

Julia had cooked a special dinner to cheer up Win. The main course was coq au vin, a throwback to their early days of marriage when they were dirt poor, chicken and wine were cheap, and traditional French cooking was in vogue. The winey smell of the dish brought back a lot of memories. After dinner, Win went over and kissed Julia who complained that he reeked of alcohol, which wasn't surprising since he'd consumed half a bottle of wine.

"Julia, I'm going to my study to do some research on cholera in the US."

"Win, don't obsess over this outbreak."

"I'll just do a cursory web search," Win mumbled as he walked off.

He found that between 1995 and 2000, in the US, there had been an average of 10.2 cases of cholera per year, 61% of which were travel related. Two cases got it by eating sliced cantaloupe, which made him realize that they hadn't asked the two Santa Fe cases whether they had consumed any prepared fruits. Another CDC site reported 12 cases in the US during 2009, eight of which had a recent history of travel to East Asia, mostly to India. None of the cases occurred in New Mexico. Interestingly, there was no secondary transmission of cholera to other people in the US during this period.

Win reached into the credenza behind his desk and retrieved his favorite calvados and a snifter. He poured a short one and sniffed its appley aroma as he realized the US incidence of the disease was probably higher than he had thought previously. Even so, two cases in New Mexico still represented an epidemic. The lack of evidence of secondary transmission suggested the two cases were independently exposed to some source. He decided he should look again for recent reports of cholera and did a search under "cholera cases in the US + newspapers," mostly pulling up sites from Latin American newspapers.

He eventually found an article in the Knoxville Journal that reported a single case of cholera in an adult from Oliver Springs, Tennessee. The case was a 37-year-old man and the date of the report was about the same time as the Santa Fe cases. Win took a swig of his drink and went on with his search. He said "Holy Shinola!" out loud when he found another newspaper report of cholera, this one in Livermore, California. It was an article in the Livermore Independent about an elderly woman who "mysteriously" came down with cholera, again at the same time as the Tennessee and New Mexico cases. "What the heck is going on here," he muttered. Was the US in the midst of a generalized cholera epidemic?

Win took another sip of calvados as he reflected on his findings. Because the close temporal occurrence of the cases suggested a particular batch of food or drink, the best explanation was a contaminated food source marketed nationally. Out of curiosity, he looked up Oliver Springs; it was near Knoxville and Oak Ridge Tennessee. He decided to call it a night and think about whether he should contact the CDC about his findings. There was no point in bringing it to the attention of the BSAC; they'd just blow him off again.

46
Santa Fe

The next morning, Win was up early; he hadn't slept well and he had a hangover. He picked up the newspaper, walked the dogs and prepared breakfast in a trance, preoccupied by last night's discovery. When Julia, who was not a morning person, finally appeared, Win served breakfast and discussed what he had found on the Internet. She listened carefully and finally said, "This could be a big public health problem. If it's a real epidemic, it'll become apparent to the authorities pretty quickly."

"I'm not so sure about that, after working with the State Health Department. Their preference is to sweep things under the rug and hope it'll go away. I'll hold off on doing anything for a while at least."

"Isn't today your day in town with creepy Herky? Maybe it'll get your mind off the topic"

"Herky isn't creepy; he's just different."

"I don't think the guy has had a single thought that wasn't related to his diet and physical fitness. He's a modern-day Narcissus. That makes him a creep."

Win excused himself and went to his study where he worked on his latest T-shirt design to bring to Morris. It was one of his favorite quotes for teaching medical students about scientific investigation, and his latest Internet searches had reminded him of it. Morris will love this one, he thought.

It wasn't long before Herky silently materialized at Win's study, dressed in a too large, red jacket and tan riding pants, like something you'd dress a scarecrow in.

"Hi, Herk. Are you riding to the hounds today?"

"No; but you're sharp Win. I wasn't fox hunting; I went riding with a friend who keeps horses. You know, I don't think we have foxes around here." He walked over to Win's desk scanned the items on it and asked, "Are you working on another T-shirt project?"

"What does it look like to you, Herk?"

"Well aren't you snippy today, Dr. Sage?"

"Well, I'm frustrated with my work on infectious diseases. I think the US is in the midst of a cholera epidemic that's probably food-borne, but the authorities won't take me seriously."

"Hmm. How many victims are there in this epidemic?"

"We have two cases here in Santa Fe and I found two more on the web so far.

"If you ask me, four cases ain't any epidemic," Herky said with a scowl.

"Herk, did you know there are typically eight to ten cholera cases in the whole US per year, and these four cases all occurred in the same month."

"So how'd you find these cases?"

"I found them on the Internet. There was one case in Tennessee, near Knoxville, and another in Livermore, California."

Herky nodded his head a couple of times and said, "I've been to Livermore. I have a cousin who's a nuclear physicist at the Government's nuclear lab there. It's a nice town and real yuppie with good natural food stores."

Win closed his eyes and thought for a while, but suddenly something Herky had said caused him to have an epiphany. "OMG! All of these cases live near Government nuclear facilities. Maybe they're working on biologic weapons at these facilities, and there was leakage of cholera organisms? Years ago, I think it was in the late 70s, the Russians had a leak of anthrax spores at one of their secret germ warfare labs and it killed a bunch of local people and animals. One of the Santa Fe cases worked at LANL. Holy Shinola!"

Herky frowned. "Is there any chance I could catch cholera? Maybe I should get immunized."

"About the same chance as your winning the grand prize in a lottery. You don't need cholera immunization, Herk. I'm going to have to report these observations to some Government agency, but I don't know which one."

"I think you're getting carried away. It's probably just coincidence."

"You're starting to sound like the idiots at the State Health Department. I've got to think things out differently now. Let's get going to town. Where are we going to dine today?"

"I don't think I'd call it 'dining,' but I've picked a dive with the best red chili in town. It's called 'Chili Heaven' and it's on Cerrillos Road."

"Can we drive over to my T-shirt maker on the way?"

"Sure; it's not too far out of the way."

Win gathered up his T-shirt design, patted the dogs on their heads and kissed Julia on the cheek on the way out. They drove off in Herky's beat-up truck at high speed. Herky was silent, except to ask, "Are you sure I don't need to get shots for cholera?"

47
Santa Fe

Herky pulled up to Sam's Tees and waited in the truck while Win went inside. Morris was sitting on a stool behind the counter, smoking a joint. "Yo, Doc, I've been waiting to see your latest design. How you been?'

"I've been fine, except trouble seems to seek me out."

"You're not in trouble with the cops?"

"No. I think I just uncovered an epidemic of a tropical disease and there's something odd about it."

"Are you doing detective work again, Doc? You nearly got yourself killed the last time!"

"I guess I'm a risk-taker and a sucker for puzzles. Anyway, let me show you what I've got for you."

"Let me know if I can help. My buddies can find out a lotta things for you – a lot more than the fuzz can."

"Thanks for the offer. I'll do things above board for now," Win said as he unrolled his sketches.

Morris took a puff of his joint and inhaled deeply. He held up the joint and said. "Smoking this stuff gets my creative juices going. This project looks interesting. Is it from another of your DWEMs?"

"This one is from a scientist DWEM, not a literary figure."

"This could be awesome."

Win gave Morris some details on the quote and its source and they agreed on the number of shirts, sizes and price. Win always left the details of color and design to the Grand Wallah of Tees. He agreed to come back for them later before rejoining Herky and off they went to Chili Heaven for lunch. The restaurant was a hole-in-the-wall next to a gas station. It didn't look too clean, the clientele was shabby and the paper menus were covered with food stains. "Are you sure this place has good, let alone safe, food? "Win asked.

"I've eaten here many times and I'm still alive," Herky said.

"All right, what do you recommend?" Win asked, knowing full well that Herky always went for the high-fat, high-calorie dishes.

"Their tamales are good; they're made the real way—with lard. Also, their gorditas are great."

Win ordered some pork enchiladas with Christmas sauces, the local term for both red and green chili sauces. Herky ordered gorditas with extra cheese on top and red sauce. Win didn't know what a gordita was, but assumed it was something big since "gordo" is Spanish for "fat." It turned out to be a large, deep-fried corn cake stuffed with meat and cheese.

"Okay, hot-shot sleuth, do you really think we've got an epidemic in the US?" Herky asked around the corn chips filling his mouth and salsa dribbling down his chin.

"Unfortunately I think we do, or maybe these cases are due to some biologic weapons program. Neither possibility is good."

"I thought your field was cancer research. Aren't you out of your league?"

Win smirked and said, "Absolutely not! Remember, I had a lot of training in public health, I worked in Ethiopia and saw a lot of tropical diseases, and my early research was on whether there could be person-to-person transmission of cancers."

"Whoa. Don't get huffy," Herky said as he held up his salsa-stained hands. "I'm just suggesting you should leave it to specialists on cholera to investigate what's going on." Their meals arrived and the conversation ended with Herky tearing into his lunch. At the end of their meal, Win headed off to the new History Museum, and Herky promised to pick him up and take him back to the T-shirt shop afterwards.

"Try to walk around the Plaza several times," Herky advised him. "You need to burn off some calories after your lunch."

Julia was right. He was food and exercise obsessed. But he was also lovable.

48
Santa Fe

This was Win's first visit to the History Museum and he started at the gift shop, where he thumbed through some books on the history of Los Alamos and the Manhattan Project during World War II. This got his obsessive gears rolling again over the cholera outbreak. His imagination was stoked by the museum's exhibit on the history of the Manhattan Project. He was intrigued by the fact that everyone working on the Project had the same mail address— P.O. Box 1663, Santa Fe, N.M. Even birth certificates and marriage certificates listed that box number as their address.

He strolled on through the museum, but wasn't really looking at anything so he decided to leave and get some fresh air. He turned the corner and walked down the street under the portal for the Palace of the Governors where many famous Indian artists got their start selling jewelry, pottery and souvenirs. Win observed that many of the artists were now making jewelry in copper, probably due to the high price of silver. He started to do a count of the proportion of jewelry artists now working in copper, but stopped when he realized this was another obsessive behavior. He chatted with several artists and almost bought a bracelet for Julia. He continued east on Palace and looked for 109 East Palace, the place where all newcomers to the Manhattan Project were met before being transported to the then-secret Site Y at Los Alamos. There was now an Indian art gallery, The Rainbow Man, at the site. This historic place got Win thinking again about the three nuclear facilities and why the cholera cases occurred in proximity to them. He turned back to the Plaza and found an empty park bench.

Win sat down, closed his eyes and began ruminating about the odd distribution of cases. He was coming to doubt his theory that the nuclear facilities could be producing biologic weapons. He remembered that the US signed a treaty promising to give up production of biologic agents of warfare. Also, it would be a really big deal to reequip three nuclear weapons production facilities to produce contagious infectious agents and do it secretly. So why were the cases near nuclear labs? He was aroused by a tugging on his pants leg and sat up with a start. There was a puppy at his feet. The owner came over and apologized for his puppy being off a leash. "De nada," Win responded. "He's cute." Win wondered why he'd used Spanish; was he getting senile?

Win got up and decided to kill time at some of the shops and galleries on the Plaza before ambling over to the history Museum entrance and waiting for Herky. Herky was on time and Win hopped into his truck. "Did you have a good afternoon?" Herky asked.

"No. I spent most of my time thinking about the cholera cases and why they occurred near Government nuclear facilities."

"So did you get any brilliant ideas?"

"I keep coming back to the idea that this could be the work of some crackpot anti-nuke character or group."

"I gotta hand it to you, Win, you've got one helluva rich imagination. Should we head over to get your T-shirts?"

"Let's go. You can have one if you like it."

"Why wouldn't I like it?"

At Sam's Tees, Herky stayed in the truck and Win was greeted by a smiling Morris, who picked up a shirt from the counter and ceremoniously unfurled it. It was a navy shirt that proclaimed, in red print:

In the fields of observation,
chance favors only the prepared mind.
(Louis Pasteur, December 7, 1854)

"It's perfect, Morris."

"I found out where he said this and got the original French quote. Let me show you my version; if you don't like it, you don't have to pay." Morris held up his version; the front was the same as Win's design, but the back read:

**Dans les champs de l'observation
le hasard ne favorise que
les esprits prepares
(Louis Pasteur, University of Lille
December 7, 1854)**

"You know, I should get a degree in history or literature after reading the background material for your tees."

"Morris, did you ever see the movie The Wizard of Oz?"

"I think I saw it as a kid, but I don't remember much about it."

"Well, in the movie there's a Scarecrow that goes off to ask the Wizard of Oz for a brain. The Wizard, who was a fake, tells the Scarecrow that anyone can have a brain, but what he needs is a diploma. Morris you have a brain and a good one. You don't need a diploma."

"Thanks Doc; you make me want to learn new things. I'm even reading books now. It's changing my life."

Win's eyes teared up as he paid for the shirts and gave Morris a bear hug.

He went out and got into Herky's truck, where his mood was broken by Herky's curiosity. "Okay, Win. Show me your latest creation."

"Here goes." Win held up a shirt and watched Herky's face.

Herky stared and asked, "What does this mean?'

"It means that in science, chance findings are more likely to be recognized as important by an investigator with a prepared mind."

"That's an interesting concept. Is this guy Pasteur related to pasteurization?"

"He invented it, Herk."

"Sometimes there's a positive side to your academic background, Win. You taught me something today. Let's head home."

49
North Waziristan

Yusuf and Rashid met over breakfast to check on final details of the packaging program and the closing of the facility. The plan was to pack all the equipment in their original cases, which had been saved. They would be carried out as they had been delivered, by camels. The Quonset buildings would be left behind and camouflaged. The top personnel would leave first and the rank and file would leave last. The large and the less valuable equipment needed to be buried for a month.

"Where do you think would be best to bury the equipment?" Yusuf asked.

"Why not in the assembly area near the kitchen? It's the most level ground in the camp and we won't need it for assemblies in a few days."

Yusuf agreed. "I don't believe we'll use this camp again, so it really doesn't matter where we bury the equipment. Besides, we'll dig it up in a few weeks. Why don't you round up some men soon so we can avoid the afternoon heat."

Within an hour, five of Rashid's men showed up with picks and shovels. They joined a like number of tribal guards and got to work. Yusuf wanted the trench to be at least six feet deep, five feet wide and fifteen feet long to accommodate the crates. They would have to check the actual sizes of the boxes to make sure they would fit. It was hard, sweaty work, but at least it was morning and the cook brought out cool tea for the workers. The ground was rock-hard and it took three hours to dig the trench. One of Rashid's men went off to find him to identify one of the crates selected for burial to see if it would fit the hole. He and another worker came back with an empty large crate to try out. Unfortunately, they needed to enlarge the hole and this time overdid it slightly so further excavation wouldn't be necessary. It was early afternoon when they finished. They would have to see if the selected crates would fit, but for now the hole seemed adequate. The men put up some stakes around the hole with white cloth ties to warn people. They were then sent back to their usual jobs.

It was good they did the digging then, because on the second day after the feeding of the infectious agents to the workers, one of the men fell ill with severe diarrhea and weakness. Rashid instructed his men to bring the sick worker to a makeshift infirmary near the kitchen and then rushed to find Mahmoud, the nurse, who was talking in the kitchen tent with Yusuf.

Rashid announced, "Well, it looks like the cholera agents are viable; one of my men has developed severe diarrhea. I ordered him brought to the infirmary."

Yusuf answered, "Well done Rashid! The nurse will treat him and he should be fine. We first need to observe him for a bit to confirm the diagnosis. Mahmoud, how many men were given cholera agents?"

"Four. The incubation period is a bit variable, usually 2 to 3 days. We might see other cases soon, but not everyone that ingests cholera organisms will contract the disease."

Yusuf asked, "When might we begin to see symptoms of typhoid and hepatitis?"

"The typical incubation period for typhoid is 8 to 14 days," the nurse responded. "If we see any cases, it'll be just before we leave. We gave the men a heavy dose, so the incubation period could be a bit shorter. Hepatitis is another matter. The incubation period is usually 28 to 30 days but in a few days we'll do blood tests on the men who ingested the virus. We can detect early infection this way before any symptoms develop, and my little lab is equipped to do the tests. I will summon these men in a few more days for testing. Those are the only agents we tried on the men."

As Rashid listened to the casual nature of the two men's conversation, he began sobbing.

It was the nurse who tried to comfort Rashid. "Rashid my brother, jihad is difficult and we must make great sacrifices. Our men will be rewarded for their struggles in Paradise. We must defeat the American infidel.

Yusuf put his arm around Rashid's shoulder and whispered, "Come my brother, let's have some tea. Will you be able to get everything wrapped up in the next few days?"

"Almost certainly. When will the first camel caravan arrive?"

"In about four to five days, God willing. The Hakim will be pleased with your work and you shall be rewarded."

Rashid muttered, "Inshallah."

50
North Waziristan

Everyone was on edge awaiting the first caravan to carry out the equipment and the packaged infectious agents. The men had awakened before dawn to begin assembling the crates in neat piles, sorted by size, near the central assembly area. A separate pile was made for the crates that would be buried. After the work was done they all went into the dining tent for breakfast.

Yusuf stood to make an announcement. "Men, you have done the impossible in completing this project in amazing time. Our leaders had doubts that you could succeed with such limited equipment, but you've done it! Today, we hope to receive the first camel caravan to move things out. Only two of you will leave today, Rashid and his assistant Jalal; they will be needed to accompany the products to their next phase for further processing. We'll need to load the equipment rapidly so the caravan can get going quickly and disperse to avoid being seen by American drones and satellites. We'll be receiving caravans every other day to finish moving the equipment and get you back home. Let us praise Allah for guiding us in our jihad!"

The men responded loudly, "Allahu akbar!"

Yusuf took a seat next to Rashid. "Well my brother, you'll be the first to leave. We'll need you to supervise the packing of your agents into shipping containers. I have no idea where you will be taken or what happens after that. It is bad for any of us to know too much. I hope we meet again; you are a great scientist and a fine, devout man."

Rashid's face flushed at the compliment from this hard man. "We've worked hard under impossible conditions and have been lucky. Unfortunately, we still have a way to go in completing our goal."

"Rashid, I am becoming optimistic about the success of our mission."

They got back to their steaming porridge and naan that was deliciously smoky from the tandoor oven. Rashid had mixed feelings about leaving this camp he had built and heading back to civilization. He found being so intensely focused on his project exhilarating, and completing it successfully would probably be his greatest achievement in life. He was awakened from his reflections by a ruckus outside.

The caravan had arrived with its noisy camels. Outside, Yusuf's guards were armed and already loading the boxes onto the surly camels.

Rashid went back to his hut to gather his duffel bag and tightly rolled prayer rug. He looked around the hut and realized he would miss this place. He sighed and headed back to the loading area. There were horses for Rashid and Jalal and the guards tied their baggage to the horses' sides. Rashid shouted out to his men, "My dear comrades, thank you for your help with this important project. You have done well and I'll miss you. The Hakim has assured me you'll be well rewarded for your hard work. Until we meet again. Allahu akbar!" He then went off to the infirmary to bid goodbye to his men with the tested diseases.

Tears streamed down his face as they left the compound and rode off. He looked over at Jalal, who was also tearful. They had been through so much together. Jalal was the first to speak. "I'm really looking forward to getting home. I should be a father now and I hope I have a son. We worked hard and I trust the rest of the operation will go as well as our part."

Rashid wiped his eyes and said "Inshallah, my son."

51
North Waziristan

Shortly after the camel caravan left the camp, Yusuf called for an assembly of all the workers in the center of the compound. The healthy men lined up around the hole in the center; the sick remained in the infirmary. The armed guards stood on the periphery and listened in. Yusuf got up on a small stool to the side and began, "My devout brothers, you have done an outstanding job in advancing our jihad against the Great Satan. You've accomplished a miracle here in our harsh, but beautiful, mountains. The Brotherhood and Allah shall reward you well for your deeds"

One of the guards brought out a large cardboard box that he set down next to Yusuf. He handed an envelope to Yusuf, who withdrew a sheath of Pakistani rupees that he waved to the men. "The Brotherhood has been generous. Please come around and stand up tall in front of the ditch so I can present our gifts to you."

The men proudly took their places in front of the hole and stood at attention. The guards casually lined up behind the lab workers.

"First, I must read you a letter from our great leader." He withdrew a sheet of paper from a vest pocket and began reading. "My dear comrades in Jihad, You have completed an impossible and great task to help us win the war against the infidels. You've worked tirelessly and skillfully. The Brotherhood and I congratulate you on a job exceptionally done. For such a great deed, your reward shall be entry to paradise."

Yusuf nodded to the guards, who quickly raised their rifles and opened fire on the workers. Almost simultaneously, there were the sounds of shots from the infirmary. The guards inspected the downed men and put bullets in the heads of those not yet dead. They were experienced executioners.

Yusuf smiled crookedly and addressed the guards, "Well done, men! You've helped speed these men to Paradise. They were righteous jihadis and shall reap their just rewards. Push the bodies into the hole and get the others from the infirmary. Let's get them covered with earth immediately. We have another caravan arriving tomorrow to remove the remaining equipment. They will also return our horses. We'll load the camels and then leave to join our families. Everything you've seen here is never to be mentioned to anyone. It's a matter of honor that we should never be responsible for the leaking of secret information. You are a credit to our tribe and the Brotherhood."

Yusuf reached into the cardboard box that had been brought out to him and retrieved thick envelopes that he distributed to the men. "The Brothers have been generous in rewarding your work," he said as the men examined the wads of bills in the envelopes.

Yusuf went off to join the nurse in the kitchen. The nurse boiled water for tea as they discussed the next steps in dismantling the compound.

"Well Mahmoud, things have gone according to plan. It's now up to others to bring things to a conclusion. But we're one step closer to striking a major blow against the infidels." Yusuf stroked his scar and went on, "Allah willing, I shall avenge the deaths of my wife and daughter by a stupid drone aimed at the wrong target, and you the loss of your father to another drone. He was a great Taliban leader."

After a pause, he continued. "I'll have the men take down the fencing for storage or for salvage if we have enough camels to transport it. We'll take down the tents in the morning, but leave the Quonset huts in place. Our aim is to make this place look like a deserted army compound. We'll put some signs on the buildings tomorrow morning."

Yusuf reached under the table to retrieve a burlap sack of signs. He pulled out a weather-beaten sign that read in Urdu, "Commandant's Office," and another that said, "ISI Liaison Office."

"We'll nail these and others at the entrance to the remaining buildings; they will suggest this was an abandoned, secret military base. The Brothers thought this would be better than burning everything down and attracting the enemy's attention with fire and smoke. Also, if agents of the Great Satan find this place and connect it to our jihad, they'll blame it on the Pakistani Army or Pakistan's Inter-Services Intelligence. The ISI is notorious for playing both sides of any game."

Mahmoud agreed, "Yes, the Brothers are clever strategists."

52
North Waziristan

The caravan worked its way slowly over the steep, rocky terrain. After an hour, the camel train broke into three parts that headed off in different directions. Rashid and Jalal were brusquely instructed by a sullen camel driver to stay with one of the columns. Being inexperienced riders, they found the trip difficult, particularly when crossing rapid streams that spooked the horses. These harrowing streams were surrounded by lush greenery that smelled of wild mint. Rashid would have found the scenery beautiful if he wasn't so scared.

After another three hours, they came to a dirt road where a truck was waiting. At long last, Rashid and Jalal were able to dismount from their horses. Rashid was a bit shaky after the ride, but wasted no time in getting the camel drivers busy unloading the crates next to the truck. Before dismissing the drivers, he checked the crates against a list he carried and made sure everything was there. Their horses were tied to one of the camels at the end of the column, wishes for a safe journey were exchanged, and the camel train went off.

Two Waziris in the truck got out and greeted them with big smiles. They introduced themselves using first names only and went to the back of the truck where two fierce-looking men sat guard, armed with Kalashnikovs.

The younger of the two men up front said, "We'll nestle these containers into special chests that are shock-proof and insulated. Do they require air conditioning?"

Rashid thought for a moment and answered, "Probably not, unless the day turns sunny."

The younger of the two men, who were obviously brothers, seemed to be the mouthpiece for the team. "We're expecting rain today so I think we'll be all right without the air conditioning. We'll cover the crates with a waterproof tarp."

Jalal carefully supervised the stowing of the boxes in back. He was instructed to sit in back while Rashid sat up front. The brothers were cheerful and kept offering Rashid cigarettes and dried dates.

They drove slowly over the potholed and wash-boarded road until dark. They were still in a desolate area when they stopped. The men got out from the rear of the truck and assembled two tents. Rashid felt he was still vibrating from the ride after he got out. They made no fire but served a cold meal of deliciously prepared food and lukewarm tea from a vacuum bottle.

"Tomorrow, we'll blindfold you as we near our destination," the younger man said. "You mustn't know where you are being taken."

Rashid and Jalal were exhausted and slept soundly. They were awakened at dawn the next day and served a light breakfast before being blindfolded and led back into the truck. Several hours later, the truck pulled up at a characterless, yellow stucco house on the outskirts of Islamabad, and the two men were led out of the truck and into the house. The brothers gingerly unloaded the crates and brought them inside, where the Waziris removed their blindfolds and left. The building was dimly lit and they were greeted by a small, lean man wearing a black suit with a white shirt and red paisley tie. He looked professorial in his wire-rim glasses.

"Welcome my comrades-in-arms," he said. I trust the trip here went well. Come, wash up and let us have a meal; you must be hungry." He didn't introduce himself, and when Rashid began to do so, he stopped him by saying, "It is best we remain anonymous."

After eating, the "Professor," as Rashid began to think of him, brought them into a brightly lit room without windows where the crates had been moved and the transfer packaging laid out on three long metal tables. Rashid and Jalal carefully took apart the shipping crates to extract their precious cargo. A quick inspection revealed no breakage.

The professor took out a can from its nest in a box and said, "These have been made to precisely fit your vials and ampoules and the cans have been made to look like aerosol sprayers. The tops screw off and the cans contain Styrofoam blocks that will snugly hold your glass containers. The boxes are cushioned and insulated as well."

Jalal pointed to the Chanel, Louis Vuitton and Hermes labels on the cans.

"We need these to look like expensive products to justify their being shipped by air. We have five different labels."

Rashid picked up one of the cans and unscrewed the top to inspect the inside. He went to one of the unpacked crates and withdrew a glass vial about three inches in length and an inch in diameter. He tried fitting it into the machined Styrofoam block and smiled when it snuggly fit the hole. "This is well done, my brother; well done."

"You're probably in need of rest, so why don't we call it a night and you can complete the packaging in the morning? Shall we have some tea and sweets before bed?"

Rashid replied, "That would be nice." All the windows in the house were covered and he had no idea whether it was day or night. The Waziris had taken their watches—to be returned later.

Rashid hardly slept in anticipation of completing his end of the operation, which had started as a pipe dream with the Sheikh. His thoughts shifted back and forth between marveling at their success and worrying about the next phases of the operation. He also worried about his men, who had served as guinea pigs for testing the infectious agents. He had so much at stake—his reputation, his monetary reward, and maybe his life. He woke up exhausted, but a hot shower and an elaborate breakfast restored him. The Professor then escorted Rashid and Jalal to the packaging room and left. They were surprised by the sound of a key turning in the door. "It looks like the Professor doesn't trust us or maybe we're now prisoners,"

Rashid quipped. "He never said how we're to contact him when we're done. Well, let's get going and finish our work; I'll be glad when it's over!"

They had printed instructions for which agent was to be packed in each of the brands. Luckily, all of the vials and ampoules fit perfectly into the Styrofoam blocks. They tightly screwed on the can tops and then loaded each container into the appropriate labeled cases. When they were done, they sat on an old couch and waited to be fetched by the Professor.

53
Islamabad

They didn't wait long before their host came to fetch them. He locked the door behind them and ushered them to a lunch of biryani chicken and curried vegetables, followed by thick, sweet coffee and sweets. They rested a while after lunch waiting to be transported once again. They were to leave the packages and instructions behind and go off with their drivers. After this, their role in the project was finished and they could rejoin their families. Rashid's youngest son was about to go to university and he was most anxious to see him off. Jalal's wife had presumably given birth and he had no knowledge of whether he was now the father of a boy or girl. A newborn son would be a just reward for his work.

The Waziris arrived and gave Rashid an envelope with his name in Arabic on the front. The talking Waziri brother announced that Rashid was to open and read the letter now because he would be blindfolded before they left the house. He opened it and read:

"My esteemed brothers,
    Please go with these men. We have decided that for your safety and the secrecy of our operation, you should spend the next few months in one of our secure mountain camps. If the Great Satan's agents trace the project to Pakistan, the two of you would become likely suspects as a bacteriologist and chemical engineer suddenly taking leave from their universities and disappearing as you did. It would be a red flag. We can't risk that and need you for future operations.

So bear with us for a while longer and we will get you back to your families safely. You have both performed extremely well and, Allah willing, the project will be a great success.

The Brotherhood"

Rashid recognized the handwriting as the Hakim's. He walked over to Jalal and whispered, "Well Jalal, we won't be going home yet. The Brothers think we need to remain under cover for a while longer until after the operation unfolds. They have a good point there." A frowning Rashid handed the letter to Jalal.

Jalal read the letter and shook his head as tears rolled down his cheeks. "No. I'm going home now to see my child and wife!"

Rashid tried to pull Jalal off to the side, but he resisted, going over to the Professor and shouting, "I'm leaving right now. I want the money promised to me and I want to go home. I need the money to buy a house for my family; I earned it. If you don't release me now, I'll go to the newspapers when I get out and tell them all about this plot!"

Rashid said under his breath, "Oh, my innocent Jalal. Don't be a fool."

The "Professor" calmly said to Jalal, "Unfortunately you will not be allowed to leave. It's for your own safety. The doors and windows are locked and there are guards outside."

"I want to go," Jalal persisted.

The Professor went off to make a phone call, and then he and the Waziris had their own whispered conversation outside the dining room.

Rashid understood Jalal's feelings, but he knew these men were nasty players. He finally convinced Jalal the delay wouldn't be too long and was for his safety. He also would try to get Jalal extra pay. He didn't tell him he feared for Jalal's life if he refused to go along with the Waziris. "Okay, we're ready to go. Shall we put on our blindfolds?" Rashid announced.

"Yes brothers, we have a long journey ahead."

The two men were blindfolded and escorted out to a waiting Land Rover. They were seated in the back and helped with their seat belts. A second Land Rover followed them.

The road was smooth, so they thought they were on some highway rather than one of the dirt roads of the past days. Jalal was sobbing and muttering to himself how he must get home as they drove on. After about 45 minutes, the car slowed and pulled off the road. The verbal Waziri brother asked them to get out. He informed them this was a stop to relieve themselves as they wouldn't be stopping for a long time after this.

"Come Jalal; let's do as they suggest," Rashid said as he put his arm round Jalal.

One of the brothers led them away from the road through some trees. As the men were peeing, a man from the second car came up behind them, quickly put a large pistol to Jalal's head and fired. The sound was deafening. Jalal pitched forward and Rashid, whose ears were ringing, fell to his knees. The shooter lowered his gun and said, "This had to be done to protect the operation. He will go to Paradise for his deeds. My men will take care of his body. Come; let us get you to safety."

Rashid was led back to the car. He was in a daze, nearly deaf, and shedding tears that were absorbed by his blindfold. "What have I done?" he muttered to himself. Why did he ever consent to take on this job? Would they kill him too? How would he deal with Jalal's wife? Would she receive Jalal's pay? Was this the righteous Jihad he and the Sheikh had discussed at length? He let out a long sigh and shook his head as he wondered where his righteousness was leading him.

The car started up and Rashid began beating on his thighs and reciting the Qur'an, searching for answers.

54
Islamabad

The Tarkani brothers returned to the "Professor's" house late the next day to pick up the loaded cartons for transport to the Islamabad airport and their family's freight-forwarding warehouse. The cartons were stored in an air-conditioned room and had been tied with jute rope, but not sealed.

They briefed the Professor, who listened silently and then said, "It had to be done. How did the old man handle this outcome?"

"He cried for a while. He had grown attached to his assistant and had treated him as his son. He's a hafiz and found solace in reciting the Qur'an all the way to our destination. He's a true believer in Islam and our cause and put it behind him. He's now tucked away safely in a secure village. I understand he's a valuable resource."

The Professor held up his hand and said, "Don't tell me any more; it's safer that way."

The three men loaded the unmarked van outside and said goodbye. The Professor said under his breath, "Allahu akbar," as the van drove off. His work was done.

55

Frankfurt am Main Airport, Germany

Gerhard Tarkani was hanging around the harshly lit freight terminal of the Frankfurt airport, waiting for a PIA flight from Islamabad. His father had sent him to receive a shipment from his uncle's shipping company. Gerhard knew most of the customs people and was joking with them about the sad state of local football. He had grown up in Frankfurt am Main and was more German than Pakistani. He did most of the airfreight pick-ups for his father's company and this was routine for him. The flight was late, so he went off to get a cup of coffee and brought back an extra two cups for the customs officers on duty.

One of them said, "Thank you Gerhard, you're always so thoughtful. Your father should be proud of you."

"Unfortunately, he's old-fashioned, and I can never be polite enough to please him. Pakistani fathers are hard to please."

The other officer quipped, "You Pakistanis have real manners and are well educated, unlike our Turkish gastarbeiter."

Gerhard stayed away from the Turk-bashing so prevalent in Germany. "I suspect there are many Pakistanis who have bad manners like any ethnic group. At least our little community here tries to be good Germans."

"Ja, ja," the guards responded.

His father did not want these cartons to go to their bonded warehouse for direct forwarding to the US. He insisted they be brought to their regular warehouse and then reshipped so it appeared the packages had originated in Frankfurt.

It was another half hour before the PIA plane arrived and the cargo was off-loaded. Gerhard had the shipping documents and claimed the ten cartons. His guard friends studied the shipping manifest and signed the forms without any inspection. One of them handed the papers to Gerhard and said, "Here you go, Gerhard. Don't go betting on our football teams. Auf wiedersehen."

Gerhard loaded the boxes carefully on a large cart he had brought with him and headed outside to find the company van waiting. His brother came out from behind the wheel to help load the cargo. He said, "Father will be pleased his precious cargo finally arrived. He told me I'm to deliver the packages for shipment on the Lufthansa flight to Newark tomorrow."

Neither of the brothers had the faintest idea what was in the packages and neither cared. Judging by the weight of the packages, it certainly wasn't gold. Smuggling is common among Waziris, and their father taught them it was always best to look the other way. Besides, this was a task for their beloved Uncle Ahmed in Pakistan, so no questions would be asked.

56
Santa Fe

Win decided to go on a hike with the dogs to deal with his frustration with the stupid BSAC. They took one of the densely forested trails near the Santa Fe Ski Basin; it was steep and a good antidote for too many doughnuts. The dogs looked concerned as Win huffed and puffed. "Hey doggos, don't worry about me, it's just the altitude," Win said. He estimated they were about 9,500 feet above sea level. After two hours, Win and the dogs were bushed, so they headed home to their usual 6,600-foot altitude.

Win found Julia presiding over a mess on the kitchen island, with flour all over her apron and face. "Whatcha doing. Babe?" he asked.

"I'm using my new pasta machine to make ravioli; it's challenging."

"It sure looks it. I need to get to my computer to do some more sleuthing about cholera in the US. I got some new ideas on my hike."

"Just don't get carried away by your nutty ideas. I'll have dinner ready in about an hour."

Win patted Julia on the butt, the only part of her not covered with flour, and headed off to his study. Back at his desk, the first search he did was a check on whether any additional cases of cholera had been reported. There was nothing new. He then searched to see if any of the three involved nuclear facilities had ever produced biological weapons; there was nothing there. He discovered that in 1969, President Nixon banned all offensive, not defensive, aspects of the US bio-weapons program, and in 1975, the US ratified the

Biological Weapons Convention, an international treaty that outlawed all biological warfare.

If the current cases were related to common-source exposure from foods or drinks that were distributed across the country, why were cases only reported near US nuclear facilities? Had someone released cholera organisms near nuclear facilities for some reason? He remembered that John Grant had mentioned a case of pathogenic E. coli infection near Santa Fe. That was not one of the likely bioterrorism agents, but then neither was cholera, so he started to look for information on E. coli infections in the US.

The incidence of infections with E. coli O157:H7, the strain of E coli that causes severe disease, was on a far different order of magnitude than cholera infections in the US. So the Eldorado case was not rare and could be a sporadic case. Just for the heck of it, Win searched for any reports of pathogenic E. coli in Kentucky. He jerked up when he found a report in the Knoxville Journal of an outbreak of O157:H7 E. coli infections in the Oak Ridge area; it occurred around the same time as the Santa Fe case. There were five cases reported. The Kentucky Health Department thought it was due to consumption of undercooked ground beef and they were investigating possible sources. He pursed his lips when he found a newspaper account of a second cholera case in the area.

Win quickly looked for reported cases in the Livermore, California area. It didn't take long to find a newspaper article on an outbreak of E. coli infections in the area of Livermore. This outbreak consisted of three cases; one was a child that died of hemolytic-uremic syndrome. This seemed an incredible coincidence, particularly when he found an article on two more cholera cases in Livermore. He pounded his fist on his desk and exclaimed out loud, "Holy Shinola!"

To be on the safe side, Win searched for other US nuclear facilities and chose two to investigate—the Savannah River and Pantex facilities. He tried all permutations of possible nearby towns and came up with no reports of E. coli outbreaks.

The occurrence of both cholera and E. coli outbreaks near three nuclear facilities was unlikely to be due to chance and smelled very fishy. As a last search he entered several terms looking for any recent occurrence of cholera and E. coli outbreaks in the same community. No matter what and how he searched, only the three communities, Livermore, Oak Ridge and Santa Fe, were doubly affected. Win's guess was these were due to bioterrorist acts committed by some anti-nuke fanatics. He wondered how they got their hands on cholera organisms and how they coordinated and carried out the attacks. It dawned on him that he needed to report these findings to some authority ASAP, but to which agency? Win was tempted to pour himself some calvados, but decided to have wine instead with Julia's pasta. She struck a loud gong and shouted, "Come and get it!" They had bought the brass gong in Korea years ago. Legend had it that these gongs were used for scaring tigers away. Their new house was big and the gong became their intercom system.

Julia had set the dining room table with candles and flowers, but Win barely noticed. "Julia, you won't believe what I found on the Web. There's something scary going on with potential bioterrorist attacks in three communities near US Government nuclear facilities."

"Can't it wait until after dinner, Win?   I made a nice supper; let's not spoil it with your bioterrorism obsession."

"I'm sorry, Honey. Dinner smells really wonderful, so I'll open a nice bottle of red wine." Win finally appreciated the table setting and the rich aroma of Julia's special Bolognese sauce. "Boy, Julia, you went all out for this dinner. Little did I imagine when I married my zany, brainy doctor, I'd get a talented chef to boot!"

They had a lively discussion about making perfect pasta dough and ravioli. The red wine, a Chianti classico riserva, went well with the food and Win drank half the bottle.

"Okay Julia, what's with all the fancy meals?" Win asked. "Are you preparing for a cooking contest or auditioning for a cooking show?"

Julia shook her head and said, "Neither. Food is love and you need some love for what looks like depression to me. And you're also drinking too much."

"I'm not depressed! I'm just frustrated by the incompetence of government seat-warmers."

Win pushed aside his wine glass as Julia served desert, managing to get through Julia's zabaglione before breaking his terrorism-silence to tell Julia what he'd found. She listened carefully and said nothing.

"So, what do you think, Julia?"

"What I think is that your idiotic hypothesis about the cholera cases is valid and you've tumbled onto something big. I was trying to come up with a probability estimate for the concordance of these events. This is way, way beyond chance. So what are you going to do?"

"I've got to report it to some government agency and not to the cockamamie State Committee. I'm not sure the CDC would investigate things quickly, and besides this probably involves criminal activity and should go to a law enforcement group like the FBI. I don't think the CIA handles investigations on US soil. It's a relief to be finally taken seriously by the one person whose opinion really matters to me."

"You know Win, you've developed a new branch of epidemiology—cyber-epidemiology. You're detecting epidemics on the Web. I should make a new T-shirt for you that reads, 'Winston Sage, MD, Cyber Sleuth.' Anyway, maybe you should contact your buddy, Fat Boy, at the FBI. Isn't he in their counter-intelligence program?"

"Do you mean Dan Tilikso?"

"Yeah; fat Dan."

"He and I didn't get along too well in that investigation of the spy at Los Alamos. I don't know if he'll listen to me. Let me think about it. You know Julia, the first atomic bomb tested here in New Mexico as part of the Manhattan Project, was named 'Fat Boy' and this cluster of diseases is somehow related to our nuclear programs. So, intuitively you came up with a great pun."

"Win, have you been reading encyclopedias again?"

"Nobody reads encyclopedias anymore; everyone uses the Internet and there's a trove of material on the history of our atomic weapons programs."

"Well either your memory or whatever you read is dead wrong. Everybody knows that the bomb tested in 1945 in the Jornada del Muerto desert in New Mexico was called 'The Gadget.' You're conflating the names of the two bombs dropped on Japan—Fat Man and Little Boy."

"You never cease to amaze me, Julia."

"C'mon, let's go to bed Lover Boy."

57
Astoria

Win wasn't the only one scouring the Internet for reports of cholera and E. coli infections. When Nasir al Fakrah hit pay dirt in his Internet searches, he promptly set up a meeting with his beloved Imam, to break the good news.

"Our test worked! The shipment survived the trip and the delivery system worked in all three test sites." Nasir briefed the Imam on what he had found on the Internet.

"So your idea paid off. I will inform the Shura of this," the Imam said.

Nasir went on, "The boys reported that the placing of the documents at work went well and was quite easy."

"So it looks like we are on track to deliver the documents on the chosen date. Inshallah! You will soon be going home, my son. Come let us have tea."

58
Santa Fe

Win was glad that he'd saved the business card of Dan Tilikso, head of the Counter-Intelligence Division of the FBI, with whom he'd worked when he'd uncovered a high-level spy at Los Alamos. They mixed like oil and water, but Dan had listened carefully to Win's hunches and opinions, so Win hoped he could get Dan to hear him out again. He rummaged through his desk and found the card. He sat back and drummed his fingers on the desk for a while before screwing up the nerve to call. It was before 5:00 PM in Washington.

He dialed and a female voice answered, "Counter-Intelligence Division, Director's Office. How may I help you?"

Win took a deep breath, and said, "I'd like to speak to Mr. Dan Tilikso. My name is Dr. Winston Sage. I worked with Mr. Tilikso on a case involving a nuclear scientist at Los Alamos National Laboratory a year ago. Please tell him I've uncovered a probable bioterrorist plot related to US nuclear facilities and I need to discuss it with him. There's strong evidence in support of this being a terrorist operation." Win was sure she thought he was a nut-case, but she was well-trained, asking for his name and number, and politely promising to get back to him.

After hanging up, Win felt stupid. He was sure he'd never hear back from the FBI. He tried to make himself busy reading a medical journal but couldn't concentrate. This was too much of a mess and time was running out. He was about to go for a hike with the dogs when the phone rang.

He picked up the phone; it was the same female voice from his earlier call to Washington. "Is this Dr. Sage?"

"Yes, this is he."

"Let me transfer you to Mr. Tilikso."

A loud voice boomed at Win. "Well, if it isn't my old buddy Win Sage. How're you doing?"

"I'm fine, except I keep getting into trouble. I'm frustrated by my inability to persuade any of the local authorities that there may be acts of bioterrorism in towns near our Department of Energy nuclear facilities."

Dan guffawed. "You know Win, if anyone else had called me about some off-the-wall terrorist plot, I'd just blow it off or refer the call to the local police, but I remember your hunches in the Los Alamos affair and they were damn good. So tell me what you're on to."

Win related the findings and the results of his investigation. It was a convoluted tale and he tried to be succinct.

Dan listened and asked. "So you found two cases of cholera in the Santa Fe area, two near Oak Ridge, and three near Lawrence Livermore Lab, and then you found pathogenic E. coli cases in the same areas. That is suspicious. Did you contact our local New Mexico FBI office?"

"I didn't have to. Your buddy, Agent Tom Shaw from Albuquerque, is a member of the New Mexico Committee on Bioterrorism. He blew my information off, saying it was chance and I was being paranoid. He's a good agent but totally unable to think outside the box and so is the rest of the Committee."

Dan paused for a moment. "Sage, Can you come to Washington?"

"Sure. I'm retired."

"Can you come tomorrow? We'll arrange transportation for you. We'll get back to you soon. In the meantime, please don't say anything about this to your beautiful wife, or anyone else. I need to get you a quick security clearance so I'll need your date of birth and social security number. If you have a recent resume or CV could

166

you E-mail me a copy? My E-mail address is on my card, if you still have it."

Win gave him the information and quipped, "So how am I to take off for Washington, with no prior notice, and not tell my wife why I'm going?"

"We'll think of some cover. Get yourself packed for a several day visit. I'll talk to you again soon. Thanks for the heads-up. I hope you're wrong this time."

Win realized he could be all wet and make a fool of himself in Washington. But the probabilities were in his favor. He smiled and punched the air with his fist. At last, someone other than Julia took him seriously.

He sought out Julia who was at her desk typing. "Hey, guess what Julia? Tilikso buys my story and wants me to come to Washington. He expects me to say nothing about it to my 'beautiful wife' or anyone else."

"What a creep Fat Boy is. At least he's got enough sense to take you seriously, unlike those local morons. I guess when you're a spook, you can leave your wife and tell her nothing. When does he want you there?"

"Tomorrow."

59
Santa Fe

Win lucked out. There were no commercial airline seats available that would get him to D.C. in time for an afternoon meeting, so the Bureau had to send an executive jet to pick him up. That was the good news; the bad news was that he was scheduled to leave from the Santa Fe Airport at 5:00 AM Since he'd retired, Win never got up early, rebelling against years of 7:00 AM meetings when he was a medical school department chair. Since Win was an inveterate night owl, he was always sleep-deprived during those years.

It was dark when Win got out of bed to prepare for the trip. Win was haunted by memories of his dreary "dark-to-dark" days as an administrator, leaving for his high-sounding job too early and getting home too late, having spent too many hours away from his beloved research and his family. He made some coffee and a peanut butter and jelly sandwich for the trip; nothing highfalutin nowadays.

Win drove the 12 miles to the airport, parked in the small un-paved lot in front of the private aircraft service building and went inside. A tall guy in civilian clothes, coffee cup in hand, came over and introduced himself as the pilot. They walked out to the small jet that was waiting. Win's larger bag was stowed underneath the plane and he took his backpack on board, to work on a PowerPoint presentation for the meeting. There was a second pilot in the cockpit and they started up the engines and taxied out to the runway. Win had only flown on private planes a handful of times and was still amazed by the concept of departure time being whenever you

168

showed up. He was the only passenger and had his choice of oversized, plush leather seats; he chose one that faced rearward. The interior was pretty posh for a government plane with lots of wood trim, unlike the stripped down, small Air Force jets he had flown on years before. There was no flight attendant and no sign of food or drink, but they did have a toilet.

The flight was pleasant and relatively quick. Win was glad he'd packed a sandwich as they only had coffee on board. He put the finishing touches on his presentation and snoozed until the pilot announced they'd be landing. Win buckled up and watched as they landed at Reagan National Airport. He had expected they would land at a government airport like Andrews Air Force Base, now Joint Base Andrews. They taxied over to the private side of the airport and it wasn't long before steps were rolled up to the plane and the door opened. Win thanked the pilots as he left.

A man in a black suit and dark sunglasses waited for him at the foot of the stairs, introducing himself as Roberto. He pointed to a black sedan parked nearby and said, "Why don't you go over and wait in the car while I get your bag." The car had tinted black windows. Black was a big color with the FBI. Maybe they all bought their clothes at Barney's in New York.

It was a quick ride into the District and to FBI Headquarters. This FBI building was a lot more posh than the local field office in Albuquerque. There was no institutional green here. Tilikso's well-furnished reception area looked like it belonged in an upscale D.C. law firm, except for the government flags. The receptionist greeted him warmly. "Welcome, Dr. Sage. We spoke on the phone yesterday."

Win smiled and said, "I'm so glad you didn't blow me off as a kook."

"We never know which calls are for real, so we take everything seriously. Have a seat. Mr. Tilikso will be out shortly."

Win sat down and noticed his stomach was grumbling. He didn't have a chance to get lunch at the airport.

169

It wasn't long before Tilikso came out to greet Win. Tilikso was a huge bear of a man, over 6 feet tall and at least 250 pounds. With a paw-like hand, he shook Win's hand firmly, to say the least. "Well, if it isn't my old buddy and antagonist Win Sage. Welcome to Washington and to FBI Headquarters. You once were a special agent for us and it worked out well; so I'm going to enlist you again."

"I thought that might be coming." Win retorted. "Am I on salary this time?"

"Nope; it'll be the same arrangement again, with some free meals."

"Dan, you know as well as I there ain't no free lunches."

"That reminds me; you left early and probably haven't had lunch. We have a good deli nearby, so how about a pastrami or corned beef sandwich?"

"If you can vouch for the safety of the food, I'll take corned beef on rye and a Diet Coke."

"You haven't changed, Win. Do you think delis are the source of your supposed outbreaks? Remember your theory; we're not near a nuclear facility."

They moved to a sleekly furnished, windowless conference room, where Dan had him sign a confidentiality agreement and a contract to serve as an unpaid consultant to the Bureau.

Win signed them and said, "Here we go again."

Dan took the papers and said, "Welcome aboard, Win.

60
Washington, DC

Win was left alone in the conference room to eat his lunch. His corned beef sandwich was delicious and the side of potato salad some of the best he'd ever had. Leave it to Dan to know where to find good food. Win wiped some spilled mustard off the shiny mahogany table and was interrupted by the entry of Dan and another man who looked remarkably non-descript in a gray suit, white shirt and plain blue tie.

"Winston Sage, I'd like you to meet Herb Armitage. Herb, this is Win." Dan said.

"It's nice to meet you, Herb." Win said, as they shook hands. He thought a better name for Herb would be Herb Bland.

"Herb works in the Bureau's Counterterrorism Division," Dan said. "We're expecting two more people and then we can begin. Do you have a flash drive of your talk, so can we get you set up for your slide show?"

"Here it is. Can I use your landline? I should call home to let Julia know I arrived safely. My cell phone doesn't work in here."

Dan chuckled and said, "It's not supposed to. The walls of this room are lined with copper to prevent electronic eavesdropping. We need to get down to work, so I'll have my secretary call home for you." Dan used an intercom to instruct his secretary to place the call and told her to send his warm regards to Win's "charming wife."

At that point, two more men knocked and entered. One was Bill Huntington from the FBI's Weapons of Mass Destruction Directorate, and the second was Roger Salay from "another agency."

171

They were all dressed in "power suits," with ties and shiny, lace-up shoes, except Win, who was wearing an old navy blazer, silver bolo tie and loafers. Win took an instant dislike to Salay's shiny bald head, bushy dark eyebrows and his bright green bowtie. He noticed that Salay in turn was glaring at his bolo.

After Dan called the meeting to order, he turned on the projector, dimmed the lights and turned the floor over to Win, who spent the next 15 minutes outlining why he suspected some party made a bioterrorist attack on the US, albeit on a small scale. Once he finished, Salay was the first to comment. "Okay, how can you be sure this isn't all coincidence?"

"In my business we call it chance, and of course, that was the first explanation I considered. However, these cases all lived close to Department of Energy nuclear facilities. I could find no reports on the web of any other joint occurrences of these two diseases in any town or region. Remember, only 8-10 cases of cholera are normally seen in a year in the whole US, but we've seen seven cases in a month and that's why I called Dan."

Huntington, a somber-looking guy, asked, "Couldn't this all be due to the cases having consumed some food or drink product that had been contaminated and then was distributed nationally?"

Win shrugged. "I've thought about that. Cholera is most often transmitted via contaminated water. In this country, most cases are traced to having eaten raw shellfish. The entero-hemorrhagic E. coli in the US is often related to consumption of contaminated beef. So it would be unlikely that the same food or beverage product would transmit both. We need to check this angle out by taking careful histories from the affected people regarding their travel, diet, and water sources and where they bought their food and drinks—stuff like that. Our two New Mexican cholera case had little in common on these factors. Also, why were only these three sites affected?"

"What kind of security clearance does Sage have?" Salay asked.

"We're getting him approved for a Top Secret clearance. He worked with us a year ago on an espionage case at Los Alamos and did a bang-up job. It was top secret and he's kept his mouth shut, even though he was pissed off at us afterwards. I'll vouch for him," Dan replied.

"Okay, Dan, it's on your shoulders. Here's why I'm concerned about security: Several months ago, we heard that Al-Qaeda was plotting another attack on US soil. It was to involve some weapon of mass destruction. Our source didn't know if it would be nukes, bugs, chemicals or conventional explosives. Al-Qaeda is believed to be going all out on this one and they're more tight-lipped than usual. We couldn't learn anything to confirm or refute this report. The question now is whether Sage's theory is related to this supposed Al-Qaeda plot. If it is, why are the numbers of cases so low and why would they target civilians around DOE facilities? Why these diseases and not more conventional agents like anthrax?"

"Our Directorate has been informed of this report and we're on full alert for a possible WMD attack," Huntington piped up. "This story of Sage's doesn't fit our gamed scenarios, so I'm skeptical."

"What I just reported to you isn't from some game," Win spoke up. "It's real, and way beyond chance. Also, don't forget that these cases could be the work of a domestic anti-nuke group, which would account for the sites of the outbreaks."

"I agree with Win," Dan said. "This is a curious and alarming set of concordant events. We have little to lose by mounting an investigation and a lot to lose if Win is right and we do nothing. I think we need a full-court press. I've worked with Sage before and his hunches were uncannily right. Win, how do you explain the small number of cases if this is a terrorist attack?"

Win raised his eyebrows, sighed and replied, "That question has bothered me a lot. It could be the inocula, the mixes of bacteria that the terrorists used, weren't completely viable and thus not effective. It could be that the wrong vehicles for transmission were used, for example foods that were acidic, which could neutralize some agents. But anybody sophisticated enough to mount such an attack should know this. It could be an attack by anti-nuke crackpots who aren't particularly skilled in how to isolate and spread the infectious agents. Maybe this was a test on a small scale. Who knows? I do think we need to move quickly and find out the sources of these cases' illnesses. I'm sure your groups have the resources to find things out quickly."

"You make a convincing argument, Win," Dan concluded. "We need to get you over to your hotel and settled for the night. Our group needs to discuss this situation further and consult with colleagues in other Departments before making any decisions. We'll meet here again tomorrow morning at 8:30. A driver will take you to your hotel and pick you up at 8:00 AM. You're not to discuss the substance of this meeting with your lovely wife or anyone else. I suggest you have dinner in the hotel dining room; they have a good Italian chef and I recommend you try his zampone and lentils. Splurge and have a good meal on us."

"Should I pack and check out tomorrow morning, Dan?"

"I don't know yet. Just tell your charming wife you might have to spend a second night here."

Dan escorted Win out to his secretary and had her page a driver. It sounded like Dan wanted him to stay in the hotel, but if Dan thought the hotel had good food in their restaurant, it was probably outstanding. Win probably wouldn't notice what he ate for dinner, but he would try the zampone. This had been an incredible day for Win. The trip was exciting; it was nice to be believed finally, give a scientific lecture again and to spar with some intelligent people. Yup, he was back in the saddle again.

61
Washington

Win fell into a sound sleep after his dinner with the recommended wine pairings; it took about ten rings of his wake up call to rouse him. He packed his things in case he ended up catching a late flight home, and called Julia, who was getting irritated by Win's not sharing any details of his meeting. Win stuck to his line that the he'd been pledged to secrecy and they were talking over an insecure line, and no, he wasn't shacked up with another woman. He felt flattered that Julia was jealous after so many years of marriage and thought other women might find him attractive.

Win waited outside the hotel to be picked up and had a nice chat with the Ethiopian doorman who laughed at his limited Amharic. Having lived in Ethiopia, Win could recognize the accents of immigrants to the US, and would throw them off-guard by greeting them with the Amharic "Tinastelling." He would then use the opportunity to catch up on news from Ethiopia.

It was Roberto who came to pick Win up. Win said goodbye to the bellman in Amharic, leaned over to say something in his ear, and shook hands. He got into the car and Roberto looked puzzled. Win picked up on Roberto's expression and said with a smile, "He's an Ethiopian secret service agent I worked with when I lived in Ethiopia."

Win wasn't sure Roberto realized he was joking since he drove on silently. They pulled into the FBI's underground garage and Roberto escorted Win up to Tilikso's office. Dan wasn't ready yet, so Win took a seat in the waiting area. He picked up a Washington

Post and noticed Roberto had written something down that he passed to the secretary. Win raised the newspaper to hide his smile.

It wasn't long before Tilikso came out to greet Win. "You jack-ass," he said while shaking his head. "Come back to my office before we go to the meeting." He led Win back to a posh office with fancy wood furniture, pictures on the wall of Dan with leading dignitaries, from the President on down, an American flag and a Bureau flag.

"Nice digs," Win said.

"Don't change the subject, Sage. This is Washington D.C., not Santa Fe."

"I was just pulling Roberto's leg and he took the bait. He's observant."

"Look Sage, we take things seriously here and we're in the midst of obtaining a Top Secret security clearance for you. So don't screw it up. Capice?"

"Okay, Boss."

"You're hopeless, Sage, but at least you're smart. Let's go down the hall to our meeting and watch what you say. I hope your input justifies putting up with you again."

"Hey, that restaurant you recommended was superb," Win said as they walked down the hall. "I got top grades from the servers too; the waitress said my appetizer choice was 'perfect' and my main course was 'excellent' and the sommelier said my wine choices were 'like awesome.' Anyway, the food was like totally epic and life-changing."

Dan waved his arm and winced as he led Win into the same con-ference room as yesterday; there were some new characters today. Dan sat at the head of the table and Win beside him. "Our meeting today is to plan an investigation of the disease outbreaks near our DOE nuclear facilities," Dan began. "Dr. Sage has been invited, since he stumbled upon the coincidental disease occurrences and he's a first-rate investigator."

Dan went around the room and identified the new people from the Bureau, Departments of Agriculture and Energy, and the

CDC, who would put the investigation together. He looked at Bill Huntington and suggested that he begin.

"Dan and others met with the Director, who decided this investigation would be run out of my division. It's going to require a broad range of expertise, which is why we created a Task Force and you're all here. Dr. Sage met with some of us yesterday and laid out a plan for how we might proceed. It has several prongs. First, we need to interview the people infected to learn about possible common-source exposures, you know, common foods eaten, drinks, restaurants; things like that." He looked at the lady from the CDC. "You people do that all the time. Second, we need to find out if these people drank bottled liquids or ate seafood or ground beef from the same distributors. The Agriculture people can help us with this. Third, we need to question the victims about foreign travel or travel within the US, particularly to other DOE sites. Fourth, we need to look for any 'Typhoid Marys' that could have handled the food or drinks they consumed. Fifth, we need to know if any of the victims worked at our nuclear facilities."

They spent the entire morning fleshing out the details of their planned investigation until they were interrupted by the arrival of a lavish lunch Dan had ordered. It came from the same deli as yesterday, so Win made a beeline for the potato salad.

After lunch, some different players as well as Roger Salay joined them. The three newcomers were FBI agents who were from the WMD Directorate and would lead the investigations at the three outbreak sites. Huntington kicked off the reconvened meeting. "We need to cover the elements of our field investigations in Tennessee, California, and New Mexico. We envision that the field teams will be comprised of a Bureau WMD Agent and a CDC Epidemic Intelligence Service Officer. We don't want to get local officials involved yet. We'll start tomorrow."

Dan picked up, "Since Dr. Sage got us started on this investigation and has thought about the implications of his findings longest, I'd like him to share his thoughts with us."

Win was still picking at some potato salad. He wiped his mouth and said. "Dan's right; I've been thinking about this for a while and I think we have a big-time problem, except nobody in New Mexico would listen. That's why I contacted Dan." He took a sip of Diet Coke and continued. "Here's why I'm worried. We have three geographically dispersed outbreaks of the same two diseases, cholera and enterohemorrhagic E. coli. As you know, cholera is an extremely rare disease in the US. From the little we know at this time, none of the cholera patients had a history of foreign travel. Pathogenic E. coli isn't that rare, but it's rare enough to get the health department people investigating. When you see the occurrence of the same two diseases, one exceptionally rare and the second uncommon, together in three separate places and close in time, that's way beyond chance in my opinion. It's hard to compute a probability, but the expectation of these occurrences would be close to zero."

"It still might be chance or there could be some simple explanation like they all ate a batch of contaminated shellfish from the same distributor," one of the Agents said.

Win shook his head and answered, "That's unlikely. But here's the real kicker; why are the three outbreaks of paired diseases only in sites adjacent to DOE nuclear facilities?"

"That's why you're all here and there's urgency," Dan interjected. "So what do you think is going on Sage?"

"Before jumping to the conclusion of some plot to attack personnel at our nuclear facilities, we have to rule out the remote chance there was a common food or beverage distributor that supplied all three markets and that the affected people used those products. Although I think it's an exercise in futility, we gotta do it before launching a big response."

"How long should that take, Sage?" Salay asked.

"I don't know what your capabilities are, but if we send out three separate skilled teams it shouldn't take more than two days," Sage answered.

"I think we could do it in that time frame," one of the WMD Agents piped up.

"Okay, let's say we rule out any common vehicle spread of the two diseases, what should we do next, Sage?" a smirking Salay asked.

Win paused before answering. "You might think me crazy, but we should start looking for disease vectors, human vectors. We look for suspicious characters among food handlers in restaurants and supermarkets, or people lingering around restaurant salad bars or bulk salad bins in supermarkets. Each site would require a separate vector. I know it's not politically correct, but I'd look for people of Middle Eastern background or home-grown converts to radical Islam."

Salay sneered at Win and said, "Hey fella, I think you're getting way ahead of yourself. If this were a concerted attack, why couldn't it be a homegrown terrorist group or some disaffected US radical group?"

"It's just a hunch I have, but you're right, it could just as well be some US radical group," Win answered.

"Since you're on a roll, do you think there might be other attacks?" Dan asked.

"If we just witnessed a trial run, and these three outbreaks are just the beginning of attacks on a wider scale, we're in for big trouble," Win answered.

The rest of the afternoon was spent deciding on the specific questions to be asked and how they would collect the information. Win offered to help with the Santa Fe arm of the investigation and was politely turned down. He was miffed at his exclusion; he always wanted to be a field epidemiologist, not a desk jockey. So he sulked.

It was late, so Huntington summed things up. "It looks like our first priority is to assess whether the occurrences could be due to some common-source exposure. If we rule that possibility out, we'll regroup and mount intelligence and counter-terrorism operations. I agree with Dr. Sage that this is unlikely to be due to common food suppliers. To avoid losing precious time, the Bureau and the

CIA should immediately begin investigating these outbreaks. Does anybody have anything else to add?"

It had been a long day and everybody was talked out, so they adjourned. The meeting ended too late for Win to catch a flight back to Santa Fe, so he was sentenced to another evening of gluttony at the hotel. Dan said goodbye and recommended Win try the risotto with beef marrow this time; he could always be relied upon to choose the worst foods for your health.

Roberto drove Win back to the hotel while avoiding Win's gaze. Win couldn't resist saying, "Hey Roberto, you're a good observer and agent, but you gotta get a sense of humor. I was pulling your leg, Buddy." But Roberto drove on in silence. They agreed on a pick-up time tomorrow morning to get Win to the airport. Another Ethiopian doorman on duty at the hotel opened the car door for Win. "Jeez, another Ethiopian secret service agent," Win said as he exited.

62
Oak Ridge, Tennessee

FBI Agent Jim Greene was amazed that the small town of Oak Ridge, population 27,000, had 24 groceries. He had worked halfway down the list by the time he parked his car at the Sundance Supermarket. It was a small independent grocery and didn't look promising, except that both of the cholera victims and one E. coli victim shopped there when they were in a hurry or didn't want to make the longer trip to the supermarkets in nearby Knoxville. He was accompanied by Judith Tobin, a physician and an Epidemic Intelligence Service Officer from the CDC, which had been an elite corps of epidemiologists back in the days of the Vietnam War. It had lost some of its cachet, but its officers remained well trained in investigating disease outbreaks.

"Judy, you do the talking this time," Greene said. "Introduce yourself to the manager as an EIS Officer investigating an outbreak of an exotic disease in the community. Show him your official ID. Tell him it's routine to investigate all possible food sources in the community when these diseases are found. Introduce me as a local health department official. I'll remain quiet while you run down the list of questions."

At the service desk, Judy asked if she could speak to the manager, and when he appeared, she extended a hand and introduced herself. "We're here as part of an investigation of an outbreak of unusual disease in your town," she told him. We have reason to believe it's from contaminated food or water. When we see an outbreak of this exotic disease, we routinely make inquiries at all stores and shops selling food and drinks in the area."

The manager scratched his head. "Well I'll be darned. I'm George Demopoulos, the store manager. Are you implying my store was the cause of some disease? You know, people living here buy most of their food in the big chain stores or in the big city nearby."

"As I said, we do routine checks of all possible food sources in a case like this. We're particularly interested in your suppliers of seafood, ground beef and bottled water. Also we need to know if any of your workers has been ill recently with severe diarrhea or fever or any other unusual illness."

"While I think about any of our workers being out sick, let me send someone back to get my order book. We keep our order receipts in a ring-binder in the back office." He took some steps toward the checkout counters and called out, "Hey Abe, could you come over here please?"

A scrawny, teen-age boy with a dark complexion came over and asked, "Do you need help, boss?"

"Yes. Would you go back to my office and bring me the large, black, loose-leaf binder on my desk that says 'Orders' on the front. It's usually up against the wall behind my desk."

"Yes, Sir," Abe replied as he headed off.

"That young kid is one of the best workers I've ever had. He's always willing to do more than he's asked to and there's never any backtalk," the manager said. "You know, beyond a couple of people being out for a day or so with colds, we haven't seen anything unusual here."

"Were any of these butchers or handlers of seafood?" Judy asked.

"No; they were cashiers. They come into contact with a lot of people," George said.

Judy next asked if any employees were known carriers of things like Salmonella.

George thought for a moment and said, "I don't know. We don't have routine testing of grocery food handlers in this neck of the woods."

"Do you sell much fish or shellfish here?" Judy asked next.

George answered, "We don't sell much shellfish beyond shrimp and we carry only frozen fish. Our volume isn't heavy enough to carry too many perishable items."

They were interrupted by Abe coming back with a huge ring binder. "Is this what you needed Mr. Demopoulos?"

"Yup, that's it. Thanks Abe."

"I'm here to help anytime, sir."

As Abe walked off to his bagging station, Greene followed him with his eyes. "That is one very polite young man," Greene said.

"As I said, he's almost too good to be true. His parents are naturalized citizens and they brought him up the old-fashioned way."

"Where's the family from?" Greene asked.

"They're originally from the Middle East. His real name is Abdullah, but he prefers to go by Abe. His father is a physicist at the Oak Ridge Labs. They moved here from Illinois and must be one mighty fine family."

"How long has he worked here?" Greene asked.

"About two months now. He learned his job real quick and we've been training him in restocking food."

"Was he born in the US?" Jim asked.

"Yeah, he was born in Illinois and is a flag-waving American."

"I wish my teenage boy was half as well-mannered as your Abe." Greene said. "That reminds me, I need to call home about my unruly son. Judy, why don't you go on, I'll be right back."

Greene had to force himself to walk out slowly. He got in his car and placed a call. He waited and asked, "Is Mr. Huntington available? This is agent Jim Greene. Please tell him I'm in Tennessee and I think I may have stumbled onto something important."

63
Oak Ridge

It was getting close to the end of Abe's shift at the Sundance Market. He sought out George, the manager, told him he was ready to leave and asked if there was anything he should do first.

"No, Abe. We're in good shape with stocking, the new shipment is unloaded and shelved, and the checkout lines are short. Why don't you go on home?"

"Thanks Boss. I hope you're not in any trouble. It looked like those people earlier today were investigating the store's records."

"We're okay. There've been some cases of an exotic disease in town and they're doing a routine check of all food suppliers and restaurants."

"They looked like police to me," Abe responded.

"Oh no. The lady said they were from some government center in Atlanta and were sent here to investigate the sick people. They wanted to know where we purchased our supplies and looked at our purchase receipts. I'm not sure what they were looking for and I'm not concerned."

"That's good. I'll see you tomorrow, Boss."

Abe got his lunch bag from his locker in back and left. He was in a hurry to get home to call Uncle Abdullah who had told him explicitly that if anyone at his job seemed suspicious or asking questions, especially anyone who might be police, Abe was to let him know immediately. Abe drove home quickly, went into his apartment and sat down to catch his breath. He took out his cell phone and dialed the number.

A voice at the other end said, "Ibrahim's Halal Grocery. Can I help you?"

"Yes, I'm trying to reach my Uncle Abdullah. This is his nephew in Tennessee."

"He's not here. I'll have him call you," the man said and hung up.

Abe changed his clothes and sat on his bed as he waited. He sipped a soft drink as he studied the Qur'an Uncle Abdullah had given him. In about thirty minutes his cell phone rang.

Abe answered, "Hello."

"How's my nephew Abe doing? I'm glad you called. Is there anything you need, my righteous nephew?"

"No, Uncle. Do you remember you asked me to call you if any police or others came into the supermarket and began asking questions? Well today, two people came to talk to the manager, a man and a woman. They told the manager there was an exotic disease in town and they were doing a check of all restaurants and food suppliers. She told him she was from some government center in Atlanta. The manager sent me back to his office to get the order book he keeps. The woman seemed interested in it."

"Did the manager give a name to the center in Atlanta?"

"No."

"Did he actually use the term 'exotic disease' and did he say what the disease was?"

"He did say 'exotic disease' but didn't give it a name. Is there something wrong?"

"No. You've done well my son. This is important information. Keep up your good work and be patient. The time is coming soon for your real work. Be good." Uncle Abdullah hung up and said a prayer for this good fortune.

64
Santa Fe

Win arrived home late in the afternoon. Traveling to Santa Fe was a drag. There were far fewer flights than to nearby Albuquerque and no direct flights from the East Coast. Then there was the two-hour time zone difference. But he liked the feel of a small-town airport and the fact it was only 12 miles from home, while Albuquerque was 70 miles away.

Win was assaulted with licks from his two exuberant dogs as he entered the house. They had missed him and the treats he would surreptitiously pass them. Julia was another matter.

Win gave Julia a big hug and a kiss and she glowered at him. "Okay Win. What the hell is going on in Washington?"

"Julia, I'm not supposed to tell you, but the FBI and some other Government agencies have taken my story about the disease out-breaks seriously. They've mounted a big investigation."

"I don't know what to do with you, Win; you've developed a knack for stumbling into trouble in your old age."

"I'm beat, Julia. I'm going to take a snooze if that's okay with you."

"Okay. I'll get you a cup of tea."

Win settled into his recliner in the den and promptly fell asleep. It felt like no time had passed before Julia shook his arm to wake him. "It's your fat friend from Washington on the phone," she said, as she handed Win the cordless phone.

"Hello Dan. What's up?"

"Your hunch turned out to be right, Win. I can't say any more over an unsecure phone but we need you back in Washington right away and you may have to stay for a while. Your buddy Salay even wants you here. He said to get that damned Sage with his crystal ball back here ASAP. Coming from him, that's a compliment. We'll send a plane for you early this evening."

"Dan, are you nuts? I just got home and my wife is about to throw me out because of my top-secret disappearing act. I don't think I have any more to add."

"Win, let me talk to your charming wife for a minute."

"Dan, you used that tactic before when you were here in Santa Fe with the Los Alamos business. She doesn't trust you." Julia was looking daggers at Win.

"Just put her on please."

Win cocked his head and said to Julia, "Your bosom buddy Tilikso wants to talk to you."

"Here we go again," she said. She took the phone and asked, "Okay Dan, what con line are you going to feed me this time?" She rolled her eyes and listened for a full five minutes saying nothing. Finally she said, "All right, you can have him. Win, Dan thinks you're brilliant and indispensable and I'm charming and understanding. What a phony. He wants to talk to you again."

Win and Tilikso discussed travel arrangements and Win hung up.

Julia, who was glaring at Win, said, "You know Win; I'm getting fed up with your crazy adventures. We worked our butts off all our lives and we came to Santa Fe to relax, enjoy the cultural activities here, and spend time together in a beautiful place, but instead of taking peaceful sunset walks, you keep gallivanting off playing detective. I want a happy retirement with you. You almost got yourself killed the last time and I'm too young to be a widow!"

"I'm sorry Honey, but trouble just has a way of finding me."

"Baloney!" Julia said as she stormed off.

65
Washington

This time they had sandwiches on board Win's flight to Washington. Win had two sandwiches and a Diet Coke and promptly dozed off in his comfortable seat. He was awakened by the pilot just before their approach to Reagan Airport, where Roberto picked him up again.

"How's my old friend Roberto doing? I see they've got you working the night-shift now," Win said as he descended from the plane.

"I was doing fine until I was asked to pick you up."

Roberto dropped Win off at the same hotel as before. "I'll pick you up at 7:00 AM tomorrow morning for a 7:30 meeting at Headquarters," he said as he left.

The next morning, Roberto drove a groggy Win to FBI Headquarters in silence. They parked and Win was escorted to Tilikso's office where Dan was waiting. He began with an overdone apology for bringing Win back on such short notice. "Let's head down to the situation room where this meeting is being held," he said as he led Win out.

"What's with a situation room?" Win asked.

"You'll see. Our investigation has moved up several notches in priority. I'll brief you when we're in a secure room."

The nondescript room contained all sorts of audiovisual devices and computers and had bare, wood-paneled walls. The usual suspects were there plus some new faces. Salay, Armitage, and Huntington were huddled at one end of a large mahogany conference table that occupied the middle of the room. There was also the woman from the CDC and another woman in a Navy uniform whom he hadn't met before.

As soon as the door was locked behind Win and Dan, Huntington began. "Well, Dr. Sage, your hunch has paid off." He told him how their field agent checking out food sources in Tennessee had noticed an employee named Abe, short for Abdullah. "He's American-born, his father recently relocated to take a position at Oak Ridge, and he's an exemplary worker. The manager raved about young Abe. You had cautioned us about suspicious store workers of Middle Eastern background."

Win was puzzled as to where this was leading.

"We've been worried for a long time about terrorist groups like Al-Qaeda recruiting American-born jihadists, and Abe turned on a light bulb for our Agent," Salay interrupted. He was wearing a crimson bowtie with neat shields on it today.

"You guys have been accusing me of drawing strong conclusions from weak data, and this finding looks flimsy," Win said.

"Let's talk to Agent Greene in Tennessee and get more information; he's waiting for us," Huntington said. He pressed a button that brought down a screen on one of the walls. A face appeared on the screen.

Win spoke up: "What made you think this guy could be an agent for a terrorist group?"

"First off, it was the name Abdullah. Second, this kid was 'too good to be true' as the manager said. He was hired as a bagboy and the manager was training him to do restocking. I've got a teenage boy at home, so I knew this kid was too straight to be believable. It's all about hunches in this business and I had a hunch. I'd like to go back and get some more information on this lad."

Win smiled as he realized that government agents too relied on hunches.

"If he's the manager's pet, we don't want him to tip off the kid about our interest in him," Huntington said.

"I have an idea," Win interjected. "Agent Greene, how did you and your team introduce yourselves to the manager?"

"The doctor from the CDC introduced herself as being from the CDC. She introduced me as being from the State Health Department."

"That's good," Win said. "Why don't you go back and request all employee records to search for identified carriers of transmissible diseases; you know, to check names against a 'Typhoid Mary' registry. Some states have such lists, but he won't know whether what you say is true or not. He should bow to authority since he's afraid of his store being the source of some awful disease. Tell him you need to go over the records in private since the identities on your list are confidential. This is Thursday, and I'm willing to bet your Abdullah won't be working on Friday, the Muslim Holy Day. What do you think?"

"I think it'll work, except I don't like waiting until tomorrow," Greene said.

"I like Win's idea and think it's worth waiting another day. This kid's been in place several months now, so what's another day?" Huntington said. "Is everybody on board with this approach?"

All heads in the room nodded in approval. "Good thinking Sage," Salay added.

"I have another suggestion," Win said. "Why not look for potential home-grown terrorists in the other two towns where cases occurred? I'd look for other workers like Abe: hard working, overly polite and with Middle Eastern names or who are devout Muslims."

"Good idea," Dan piped in. "You're on a roll, Win; do you have any other ideas?"

Win thought for a moment before answering. "While we're at it, why not check grocery stores in towns around all the other DOE defense nuclear facilities? I think most of them are near small cities so it shouldn't involve many stores. Albuquerque might be the largest nearby city and you could start with stores near where Sandia Labs personnel are most likely to live."

No one responded for a while. Bill Huntington was the first to react. "That could be a major undertaking that's not justified by our flimsy finding. There are a lot of groceries out there, even in small towns. I think we should proceed in step-wise fashion. Let's check out the suspect Abe and stores in the other two cluster sites first."

Win shrugged. "I'm only making suggestions and they might not be feasible or justified. If this proves to be some sort of intentional bioterrorism attack, speed is essential. So maybe you ought to ready a plan to mount a full-court press if Agent Greene's hunch proves correct?"

"Jim what do you think of the discussion?" Bill asked.

"A lot rides on my hunch and whether it proves right, so I think we should proceed in a sequential manner. I think the Doctor's ideas are good and we should be ready to roll if Abe turns out to be a bad-guy. If everyone agrees, I'll go back to the Oak Ridge store tomorrow morning and use the Typhoid Mary scheme."

"Okay. I think we all agree that's the way to go," Bill replied. "You can go now. We'd like you to report what you find tomorrow morning ASAP. Don't forget to finish checking out all the groceries in Oak Ridge. Good luck Jim."

The screen turned blank and someone raised it remotely. "There are a couple of nagging questions left," Win ruminated out loud. "If this is a concerted attack and not just a common-source exposure scenario, why did they pick these three towns and why were there so few cases? We raised these questions before and I have some better hypotheses now. Could this be the start of an attack on our personnel at US nuclear defense facilities? I've been thinking that maybe these limited outbreaks are field tests of biologic weapons to see if they work and the organisms remained infectious after they processed them. If this is true, will a full-scale attack follow?"

Salay shook his bald head and said, "There's been a lot of intel chatter in Pakistan the past few months that we haven't been able to piece together. Our analysts suggest this could be the harbinger of another Al-Qaeda attack on the US. Al-Qaeda security has suddenly gotten extra tight following Bin Laden's death. I'll have our intel teams scrutinize our intercepts to see if there's any suggestion of biologic weapons."

Herb Armitage interjected, "Win raises an important question about why these three towns. I've been thinking, I wonder if it isn't because these towns are so small. In a small town you won't have lots of hospitals; all the patients would go to the same place. Three cases at one hospital are more likely to be noticed than one case at three hospitals. Also, in small towns an apparent epidemic would be more likely to make it into the newspapers. The terrorists, if they were doing a test, wouldn't have access right away to health department and CDC reports. They would need to rely on the media."

"That's brilliant!" Win blurted out. "You're a natural epidemiologist. That makes sense to me. I think you're right."

"Lunch is here," Dan announced, and they took a break.

66
Astoria

Nasir al Fakrah walked warily from the subway station to visit the Imam. He was a little more cautious this time, checking that he wasn't being followed. As he walked past the decadent Greek restaurant below the Imam's apartment he wondered if this would be his last visit there. He raced up the steps and knocked on the unmarked door.

The Imam opened the door and said. "Come in my son. You look happy today. Do you have news for me?"

"Yes."

The Imam led Nasir into the living room and led him to one of the cushions on the floor. He went through his usual routine of turning on the fan and radio, then took a seat near Nasir and asked of this news.

"Yesterday, a team of investigators came into one of our test sites to inquire about possible food sources of an exotic disease in that town. One of our bright students observed this, and also learned that they were from a government center in Atlanta. That is almost certainly the Centers for Disease Control—that's the agency that would investigate outbreaks like the one we caused. The newspaper reports of cases in that town proved correct. I am fully confident now that we're ready to launch our educational program."

"Is there any chance our student will be suspected?"

"I think it's unlikely. They were doing a standard epidemiologic investigation looking at food sources. It certainly didn't sound like they were looking for any suspects."

"But they came to the store where one of our boys worked."

"I suspect they were surveying all stores where the affected heathens might have shopped. I wouldn't worry."

"I trust that you are right." The Imam closed his eyes and his lips moved silently in prayer. He kept rocking his head as he sat there mute. Finally he said, "I have news too. The full documents have been shipped and just picked up by the Druze. We will be able to start the program on the chosen date. Can your students do it?"

"Yes. We're all set. I'll arrange the deliveries of the holy texts to arrive precisely on time."

"I will inform the Brothers of this new confirmation; they will be pleased. Now, Nasir, you will proceed according to plan and turn over last minute details to your deputies. You must go back to your family before the target date. I have the papers for your trip here. You must first repackage the texts and complete all shipment and delivery arrangements. Today, I will also give you the travel documents and instructions for our young scholars to disappear before they return home. They should be delivered with the holy books. Now, let's take some tea."

"You know, I've always felt uneasy about leaving the deliveries of the precious texts to people the boys don't know. I've also been concerned they might not remember their training for using the texts. If I did the deliveries, I could review the procedures with each of them," Nasir said.

"No, my son. The scholars are well trained and too dispersed for one man to visit. You should have no more contact with the boys. You know too much and need to disappear. You must go home."

Nasir grimaced in acceptance.

The Imam got up and led Nasir by the arm to the kitchen. As they walked to the tiny kitchen, the Imam stopped at a closet, took out a bulging, large leather briefcase that he handed to Nasir. They made small talk about their health and their families as they sipped tea. Nasir said goodbye and the Imam embraced him as if this might be the last time they met.

"You have done well, my son. We shall not forget."

Nasir rushed down the steps and headed to the subway station where he knew there was a payphone. He dialed a number, deposited the right amount of coins, and left a brief message. "The special class is on. Pick up the textbooks and move them to my place." He hung up and waited for the next train to Manhattan, giddy from the realization that the program would work.

67
Washington

Bill began the afternoon session by reminding everybody that they still needed to evaluate the information on the distributors used by the local groceries. There were a lot of food stores in the three towns affected, which meant a lot of data to sift through. He pointed to the unidentified woman in the room and said, "This is Dr. Mary Carpenter of the CDC. She's been supervising the analysis of the data collected by our field agents. Mary's a great addition to the team. She has an MD-PhD from Johns Hopkins and is board-certified in infectious diseases. Her PhD dissertation was on bio-terrorism." She was wearing a Navy uniform with rear admiral's insignia, so she was a high-ranking Public Health Service Officer. Win thought she was very attractive.

"We've been looking at commonalities in the food and beverage distributors serving the three clusters," Mary began. "Our main areas of interest are sources of seafood, beverages and ground beef. I'm sorry to report that while within areas there were consumption commonalities, there were none between areas. So there don't appear to be common-source exposures covering all three sites. Several groceries at the three sites carried common brands of beverages, but these were bottled at different plants. We're not fully done with our investigation, but at this point we're left thinking that Dr. Sage's ideas are valid. Our investigation raises the probability of this being an intentional contamination."

"It's starting to look like Agent Greene's investigation tomorrow is becoming more and more important," Bill commented. "Maybe we should spend some time planning an extension of our grocery investigation to areas around all of our nuclear facilities, so we can move rapidly if indicated."

Win hadn't noticed another man sitting at the table. He introduced himself, "I'm Sam Oberdorf with the DOE Security Division. Let me outline where our defense nuclear facilities are located." He walked over to a large white-board and began writing. He listed 14 facilities, four of which were in closure status, spread all over the country. "Investigating supermarkets in all of these towns is going to be one helluva job. I Googled the towns where our facilities are located and it's amazing how many food stores these towns have. Do the Bureau and CDC have enough field resources?"

"We're going to have to marshal resources in a hurry," Dan commented. "Mary can you handle this at the CDC?"

"We've been preparing for years now. We have a plan to mobilize personnel in the event of a bioterrorism attack and it's about time we put it to a test," Mary said.

There was intense discussion of how the massive investigation would be designed and a plan was worked out. The big problem was how to mobilize field personnel rapidly, while keeping the investigation under tight wraps. They didn't want to alert any terrorists to the fact that they were under scrutiny, or create public panic.

They worked till late and decided to call it a day. Everything hinged on tomorrow's findings in Tennessee.

Dan came up to Win and said, "You've done a great job, Win. I'm going to take you out to dinner at a special restaurant as a reward. Do you like sushi?"

"Yes. Remember, I lived in Japan when I was in the Air Force."

"I bet you never had sushi as good as you'll have tonight. Their omakase dinner is mind-boggling."

Leave it to Dan to use food as a reward, Win thought, as they left.

68
Washington

Dan drove to the sushi restaurant in his car, a Lexus with soft leather seats. "Tell me about Roger Salay," Win asked on the ride. "For some reason, he doesn't seem to like me. What gives with him?"

"Salay's a complicated piece of work," Dan replied. "He's with the CIA, as you probably figured out—in their Terrorism Analysis Group and in charge of their new section on Radical Islamic Terrorism. He was the first appointee to our Task Force. Ever since the Agency was blind-sided by the 9/11 attacks, he's become obsessed with destroying al-Qaeda. You know, you and he have a lot in common; for starters, you're both obsessive creatures. Maybe that rubs him the wrong way?"

"I don't think that's it," Win said. "Wait a minute. Did you say that Salay was involved from the beginning of your Task Force, before there was any evidence of Middle Eastern involvement in the disease outbreaks?"

"Damn it! I hadn't thought about that. You're on to something there. When we were setting up the Task Force, our Director suggested we include someone from the CIA. So I called the Deputy CIA Director and he picked Salay. Shit! They knew from the get-go that these attacks were related to Islamic terrorists and they've been keeping us in the dark! Those bastard spooks!"

"Sounds to me like one big happy government family," Win replied.

"Well, we're at the restaurant. To be continued. It's helpful to have an outsider like you look at the situation."

The restaurant was in a strip mall with lots of parking. Dan hefted his body out of the car and led the way into what looked like a dive. They were greeted by a loud "Irasshai masen," as they entered. When the chef at the sushi bar saw Dan, he called out, "Dan-san, konbanwa."

"Ah, Hiro-san, I'm so glad you're here tonight. This is my friend Win; he lived in Japan for three years."

"Ah, good. I will prepare a real Japanese menu. I have very good fish tonight."

The sashimi, sushi, and grilled fish were every bit as excellent as Dan had promised. In addition, after too much sake, Win learned that Dan's excellent high school grades and skills as an offensive lineman got him into Princeton. Because he came from a poor family, he qualified for financial aid so he could attend. He was a top student at Princeton and a football Academic All-American, which earned him a scholarship to Yale Law School. He passed up job offers from top law firms to join the FBI, where he worked his way up the ranks pretty quickly. Dan had three teenage kids and was a doting father who required no prompting to whip out his iPhone to show Win endless pictures of his family and dogs. As Dan put it, "It's because of my wife and kids that I work so damn hard to keep our country safe." It was an impressive story, and as they say in North Carolina, where Win had taught at Duke, he thought he might could get to like Dan. They were both too slushed to talk any more about Salay on the way back.

69
Washington

Win woke up with a big-time hangover, the head-throbbing kind. Since he needed to be sharp for the next meeting, he ordered a room-service breakfast with extra coffee, but it didn't do much to stop his headache. It was 9:00 AM when he went downstairs. Because of the one-hour time zone difference in Tennessee, they would start their meeting late.

The handsome Ethiopian bellman was on duty again this morning. He recognized Win and said, "Tinastelling, Dr. Winston

"Tinastelling, Ato Aklilu. Endemin allu?" Win replied.

Out of the corner of his eye, Win caught an impatient Roberto sitting in the black car glaring at him.

"Looks like I've gotta go, Aklilu. I'll see you later."

Win entered the car gingerly, his head still hurting. "Good morning Roberto.

Did you enjoy your eavesdropping?"

Roberto dismissed Win with a wave of the hand and drove to Tilikso's office, where he left without any goodbye. Dan was on the phone, but he waved Win in and gestured for him to take a seat. Win picked up an outdated magazine and waited. "Did you enjoy last night's feast?" Dan bellowed when he got off the phone.

"It was great, but my head feels like a cement block this morning," Win answered.

"My head isn't feeling too great either. Let's mosey on down to our meeting. Today we need to get you photographed for your

Bureau ID badge. Congratulations, you have a Top Secret clearance now and you're one of us!"

Win didn't know how to react. He was an unpaid consultant, which he hoped still made him an outsider. Win had an aversion to being part of any government bureaucracy and was turned off by the Bureau's self-serving ways.

They entered the situation room, which was crowded and buzzing. Everybody was pre-occupied, so Win got some coffee and a croissant and went through some notes until Bill Huntington called everyone to order. A button turned on the monitor to reveal Greene's big-screen face. Bill greeted Greene. "Good morning Jim. How did your investigation go?"

"It was very interesting. I think we've got a *bona fide*, homegrown terrorist in Tennessee." Jim hesitated for effect, and everyone in the situation room sat transfixed.

Bill sighed and asked, "What'd you find Jim?"

"To begin, my job was made easier by both the manager and Earnest Abe being off today. I was able to photocopy Abe's employment application. He claimed to have come here from Champaign, Illinois and graduated from high school there. But when our office checked with that high school, they had no record of any attendee by Abe's name. We have a photocopy of his Tennessee driver's license, and the State Motor Vehicle Division people tell us that Abe got a new license here two months ago by exchanging his out-of-state license. Guess what? His previous license was from Michigan. He lists his father, one Farid Khan as next of kin. He had told the manager they relocated to Tennessee for his father to take a job at the Oak Ridge operation. We checked that too. No one of his father's name ever worked at Oak Ridge. His entire record is Swiss cheese. We're working on the Michigan connection."

"Jim, I want this Abe under surveillance and I want you to get a court order for a wiretap on him ASAP."

"We're setting everything up as we speak. We know where he lives and have his phone number; it's a cell phone."

"Jim, exercise extreme caution. We don't want to tip Abe off before we have a complete picture of the operation. Use your best people for this surveillance," Bill cautioned. "We'll let you get back to work now. Don't forget to finish checking all stores in the town to make sure there aren't any more Earnest Abes. Do you need more personnel?"

"Yeah, I could use another two experienced surveillance operatives."

"We'll get two people out to you ASAP," Bill said.

Greene's face disappeared and the monitor cabinet was closed.

"Well, it looks like this could be the real deal. We need to hear from our agents at the other two cluster sites ASAP. It looks like we need to search for suspicious workers as well as investigate food sources. If they find another Earnest Abe, we'll mobilize big time. For now, why don't we take a break, "Bill concluded.

Win had believed for a long time this could be a terrorist attack, but the realization he was right left him dumbfounded by his speed-of-light journey from a snooze in his den to the inner sanctum of the FBI.

70
Washington

Lunch was another splendid Tilikso repast, except no one commented on it. They were all ruminating about the reports from the other two towns. The atmosphere was becoming funereal.

It occurred to Win that this cloak and dagger stuff was a lot like conducting a scientific research project. You design it, plan how the research would be done and then you turn it over to your research assistants, in this case FBI investigators. Then there was the long, impatient wait for the collection of data and analysis. He hoped this investigation took less time than his research. He was bracing himself for a boring afternoon, so he helped himself to another fortifying portion of Greek salad and a bowl of blueberries.

"While we're waiting," Bill resumed, "is there anything else we should be doing?"

"We're still analyzing the results of our food source investigation with no success," Mary, the CDC official, said.

"Have you looked at the dietary histories taken from the victims?" Win asked. "I mean not just where they ate or bought their food, but the actual foods consumed, like loose salad mixes, ground beef, or open, serve-yourself foods?"

"We focused on ground beef for the E. coli cases. All of those cases had consumed hamburgers; most of it was grilled. We focused on drinks consumed by the cholera patients and didn't find any commonalities," Mary replied.

A phone rang and was answered by an aide at the back of the room. He looked at Huntington. "I think you need to take this call, Sir."

Bill picked up the phone, introduced himself and listened intently. "It's Agent Bob Forsyth in Livermore, California," he informed the group. "I'll put this on speaker phone so you can all get the news. Bob, why don't you tell our group what you've found?"

"Well, Sir, we investigated several food stores around Livermore looking for recently hired personnel. We finally found a small store that hired a young man as a bagboy about two and a half months ago. Surprise, surprise; he has a Middle Eastern name. As instructed, we became circumspect on learning this. I did get a copy of his job application form and personnel records, but I don't think we alerted anybody at the store unduly. Our local office is doing a check on his data and we'll report to you as soon as it's completed."

"Well done, Bob. Is this young man an exemplary worker?"

"Yeah, everyone at the store raves about this kid."

"That fits the emerging profile," Bill said. "Stay away from the store for now and all inquiries should be made by secure methods."

"Will do! Any more questions before I get back to work?"

Bill scanned the group and saw that Win had raised his hand. "Bob, we have a question from one of our consultants, Dr. Sage. He's the one who tipped us off to this problem."

"What type of grocery store is this bagboy working at?" Win asked.

"It's a small-to-medium size, family-owned grocery. They sell fresh fruits and vegetables, packaged products and have a small butcher shop. It's a pretty ordinary small-town grocery," Bob answered.

"Do they emphasize organic foods and fresh produce?" Win asked.

"Yeah, they do, come to think of it."

Win thought for a moment and went on, "Did you see any bulk salad greens or sprouts for sale? You know, the open bins of greens that get sold by weight."

"I think so, but I'll have to go back to check."

"I think it's best to stay away from the store presently," Bill interrupted. "Does anyone else have questions for Bob?" No one did, so Bill thanked Bob and told him to keep them informed.

"What were you getting at with your questions, Win?" Mary asked.

"I've been thinking that an excellent vehicle for transmitting cholera might be open piles of salad greens. It'd be real easy to inoculate a pile of greens. They're usually kept moist, and they would be eaten raw, probably even unwashed." Win pointed at the food in front of him and said, "I got the idea from looking at my salad and berries and the thought passed my mind that maybe the sites selected for the bagboys were stores that sell organic products. You know, catering to the nuts, berries and sprouts crowd. A lot of the products they consume would be eaten uncooked. Did we ask Jim in Tennessee about the store where Earnest Abe works?"

"That's an interesting question and we should check it out ASAP," Bill said as he nodded to one of the people in the back of the room who got up and left.

"Along these same lines, I wonder if the mastermind behind this plot didn't select mom-and-pop groceries since they would probably have fewer resources to do security checks on personnel than big chains. They also might be apt to have looser work rules and more lax control of stored foods," Win added.

"Yeah. You've got some good points there," Mary piped up. "Now I'm curious too about the grocery in Oak Ridge."

"If I'm right, we could narrow our searches to small, privately-owned health food stores. That could speed things up."

They sat silently while Win's ideas sunk in. It wasn't long before the agent dispatched to inquire about the Tennessee grocery came back with a smile on his face. "It looks like Dr. Sage has tumbled to something significant again," he reported. "The Kentucky store is a small, privately-owned grocery that specializes in natural and organic products and has a large vegetable section with bulk salad for sale."

"Okay. That does it! We'll narrow our searches to stores catering to the granola and sprouts crowd," Bill said. "Hopefully it'll speed up finding other bagboys if they're out there. If we're wrong, we can go back and check all groceries in the cluster towns. All of our findings are pointing to a terrorist plot. I think it's time to brief the Director and the President. I don't want them to get blindsided by an attack."

71
Washington

Things were accelerating. The FBI Task Force was on full alert as they awaited updates from Tennessee, New Mexico and California.

The first agenda item was a review of the findings from an evaluation of the bacteriologic specimens. Bill turned the meeting over to Mary and a new face, Jim Marburg, M.D., an associate of hers from the CDC. He was dressed in civilian clothes. "We've completed the typing of the organisms isolated from the cluster victims and have surprising results," Mary began. "The cholera organisms from the victims are all the same strain, O139, and Bengal serogroup which is the most prevalent strain in Southern India, Bangladesh and other Asian countries. It's not the O1 El Tor Inaba strain we've typically isolated from the sporadic cases in the US. The pathogenic E. coli isolates are a different story. We found two different types: one is the common enterohemorrhagic strain O157:H7 and the second is the O104:H4 Shiga-toxin-producing strain. The latter strain is the one found in a recent German outbreak linked to contaminated sprouts consumption. We found the O157:H7 type in the cases from Santa Fe and Livermore and the German strain in the case from Tennessee. That makes it less likely for the three E. coli infections to be from a common source or means of transmission."

"We haven't seen much infection with the German strain in the US, so it argues for malicious introduction or foreign travel by the victims," Jim Marburg added. "But the two different strains also argue against a terrorist introduction."

"No!" Win interrupted. "What alerted us to these outbreaks as a possible terrorist attack in the first place was the concordance of reports of two different diseases, cholera and pathogenic E. coli infections. The outbreaks were all near DOE nuclear facilities. The likelihood of these events being due to chance is almost nil. If they used two different microorganisms, why couldn't they also use two different strains? Maybe the terrorists are using a mix of microorganisms to throw us off in any investigation or to spread greater terror. We've got to think outside the box. I think we're up against a clever adversary."

"What makes you think that, Win?" Bill asked. "What we've seen so far is pretty low-tech with organisms easy to collect and propagate, a primitive delivery system, and an easily detected and controlled set of infections."

"Bill, it's a damn clever plot in my humble opinion. First, I believe what we've seen so far is a test in preparation for a larger attack. There may be more sites and even more infectious agents. Since they're going for the mixture approach, why not throw in other food-borne infections like shigellosis, that's bacillary dysentery, or even parasitic diseases like trichinosis that would serve us pork-eating heathens right."

"That's all pie-in-the sky, Dr. Sage," Marburg said.

"Let him go on," Dan intervened.

Well, well. Dan Tilikso was coming to his defense, Win thought. He smiled and went on. "So far they've used agents widely available in third-world countries, but rare in our country and likely to scare the hell out of people here. Most Americans don't know what cholera is all about and would be totally panicked by an outbreak of an ancient pestilence in their back yards. Third, they've used a simple, but sure, delivery system that gets the agents directly to the means of ingestion. It serves a double purpose in showing us we're vulnerable to attacks by homegrown US jihadists."

Salay perked up and added, "That's been a big concern of ours for a long time now, and so it makes sense."

"Fourth and most important is that this is more than a terror attack; it could have a potentially devastating economic impact," Win resumed. "Just think of what would happen to food distribution and sales in the US if the attack or attacks succeed. Who would want to buy loose greens or sprouts or even packaged salads? No one is going to want to eat any uncooked foods. The FDA and Department of Agriculture are going to have to develop expensive food safety and surveillance systems in a hurry. Natural food stores may go out of business. Food handlers are going to require registration and supervision. Our beefing up of airline security after 9/11 will seem like small potatoes after a successful bioterrorist attack on our food distribution system. Our politicians are going to face the wrath of a lot of angry constituents. Even the Department of Energy is going to have to beef up their security. If I'm right and the terrorists are targeting sites near our nuclear facilities, they're sending a message—we know where your nukes are and they're next in line for an attack. Remember, there are a lot of unaccounted-for rocket-propelled grenades out there after the Libyan revolution. This is a clever and cunning plot, if you ask me."

"I hope you're dead wrong Win, but I think you're right, unfortunately," Bill added. "Let's take a break. Coffee has arrived."

Jim Marburg came over to Win and introduced himself. "You know, trichinosis would only be transmitted to humans by ingestion of live encysted larvae from infected animal tissues and not by eggs. So it's unlikely to be used as a mass bioterrorism agent."

"Jim, please pardon the forgetfulness of an aging epidemiologist. I was trying to make a point. Where did you get your training?"

It turned out that Jim had also received his MPH degree at Harvard, and they had a nice conversation reminiscing about their experiences in Boston. Win noticed out of the corner of his eye that the CIA spook Salay was trying to get his attention. Win excused himself and ambled over to Salay.

"You're pretty good as an intelligence analyst, Win, and original in your ideas. How do you do it?" Salay asked.

"All I do is read the papers, search the web, and try to think creatively. It's a lot easier to think outside the box when you're not in lockstep with insider group-think."

"You've got a good point there. Keep up the good work and thanks," Salay said.

Win noticed that the little shields on Salay's crimson bowtie said "Veritas." It was beginning to look like a mini Harvard Club here.

72
Cambridge, England

Mostafa Aziz tidied up his tiny office after his last tutorial of the day. Aziz was a rising star on the faculty of Computer Science and Technology at the University of Cambridge. He came from a prominent family in Egypt, had come to the UK to take his degree at Cambridge, and was recognized as a brilliant theorist soon after he arrived at Trinity College.

He rushed downstairs and unlocked his bicycle. Running late for an important meeting, he cycled rapidly over to his destination, a coffee house on Trinity Street, across from Heffers Bookshop. At the coffee house, he scanned the crowded room for the man he was to meet and found him at a small wooden table in a corner, staring at his laptop. His friend was dressed punk style with a shaved head, an earring, nose ring and beat-up, studded, black leather jacket. One would never know he was an honors graduate of Cambridge with mathematical tripos. Under Aziz's tutelage he had developed into a brilliant software engineer. He now worked as a highly sought after freelance software developer.

Aziz went over and sat down. "Great to see you, Nigel. Can I get you a cuppa?"

"Thanks, Mo. I'll have some cappuccino."

Mostafa wended his way over to the counter and flirted with the attractive barista in a tight sweater as he waited for their drinks. He barely made it back to Nigel through the crowd without spilling the coffees.

"I'm excited that you think you've got the perfect software for the job," Mostafa said, after adding sugar to his coffee.

Nigel raised his hands in surrender. "This was one of the toughest jobs I've ever undertaken. I'm sure this worm will evade any anti-malware out there. I stayed up several nights until the solution just hit me one morning." He went over some technical details with Aziz, who listened carefully and shook his head between exclamations of "Brilliant!"

"That's amazing, Nigel. I think you nailed it. It's a shame we can't patent it."

"Are you sure this has to be kept secret, Mo?" Nigel whispered.

"That's what our client wants. I'm not sure how this will be used or by whom, but they're paying us mega-money for it, so I'll go along. Which reminds me: here's your share." Mostafa reached into his backpack and extracted a large thick manila envelope. "There's money in there for you and all your assistants. This was a heavy-duty programming effort."

Nigel opened the thick envelope and thumbed through the crisp, purple 20-pound notes. "This is nice, Mo. It'll fund a lot of parties." Nigel extracted a CD from his computer case, a flash drive from his pocket, and an envelope from his backpack. He lowered his voice and said, "Here's the material in the format you wanted. I've spelled out on the disc exactly how the worm is to be embedded in attachments. I wrote it for O-level types, so it should be easy. I've also returned the specs on the operating system to be attacked."

Mostafa thanked Nigel profusely and left. Back at his apartment, he inserted Nigel's CD, and reviewed the program as a music lover might read his favorite score. Mostafa kept shaking his head from side to side as he read and occasionally said out loud, "Absolutely brilliant!"

He got up and went to his closet to retrieve a clean disc and a new flash drive. He unpacked a pair of polyethylene gloves and retrieved a CD from a brand new box. He used scissors to cut open the plastic container for a new flash drive. He then burned a copy of the program and instructions on the new disc and downloaded a copy to the flash drive. He shut down his computer and sat staring ahead. The protégé had outperformed his teacher and Mostafa beamed with pride. He went over to his bookcase and retrieved the thickest volume, a text on computer theory. He opened it, slid the fingerprint-contaminated disc between some middle pages, and returned the book to the shelf. He put Nigel's flash drive in a locked metal box in his closet, inserted the new disc and flash drive in a brown envelope, and then sealed it in a second larger envelope. Mostafa stowed the envelope in his backpack and then discarded the gloves in a wastebasket. He tore the pages with the specs into small pieces and took them to the fireplace in the room. He opened the damper, set the pieces on fire with a match and then swept up the ashes and flushed them down the toilet.

It had been quite a day, and Mostafa decided to reward himself with a nice dinner in the College dining hall and a movie afterwards. He would deliver Nigel's work to London tomorrow.

73
Cambridge and London, England

Mostafa had shifted his student tutorials to early morning so he could catch the 10:15 AM train to London. He was in a cheerful mood as he bicycled to the train station. He checked his bike and purchased a day return ticket to King's Cross station. He was proud of the product he was about to deliver to his uncle. He became engrossed in a book and, before he realized it, was at King's Cross. It was a beautiful, sunny day so he decided to hike over to his uncle's office near Russell Square. He reached Guilford Street and rang the bell beneath a shiny brass plaque that read, "Samuel M. Aziz, Financial Consultancy." His uncle owned this three-story, white brick building. He leased the first floor to a solicitor and used the third floor as his London pied-à-terre. Mostafa was buzzed in and climbed the creaking, carpeted stairs to his uncle's office on the second floor. The receptionist recognized him and invited him to have a cup of tea, but he declined.

It wasn't long before his uncle came out to greet Mostafa. "How's the brilliant professor?"

"Oh, I'm doing well, Uncle Samir."

"Come into my office before we go off to lunch." He put his arm around Mostafa to lead him inside and said, "Your mother keeps asking me to keep a keen eye on you. She's been looking for a suitable wife for you, so don't you take up with a British woman."

Mostafa took a seat and withdrew the special envelope from his backpack. "Uncle, this is the project you requested and paid for. It's a magnificent piece of work by a brilliant programmer. He knows

214

nothing about its intended use, nor do I. I've included instructions for mounting and deploying it. Please deliver it unopened; I don't want your fingerprints on any of it."

"I understand, Mostafa. Why don't you wait outside while I make a call?"

After Mostafa left, Samir dialed a number he knew by heart. He said, "This is Mr. Aziz. I have the new financial projections for this year and will deliver them to the Imam this evening after prayers, if that's all right." After a pause he said, "Very well. I'll be at the mosque at 8:30 PM." He placed the envelope in the center drawer of his ornate mahogany desk, withdrew a set of keys from his pocket and locked the drawer.

He checked the drawer to make sure it was locked and went out to fetch Mostafa. "I thought we'd have lunch at my club. They have your favorite desert on the menu today, treacle tart with clotted cream." He took Mostafa by the arm and led him out.

"You never forget anything, Uncle Samir." Mostafa had fond memories of his meals with his uncle when he was a student at Cambridge. He had enjoyed the very British atmosphere at the club and their long scholarly conversations over lunch. His cultured uncle would frequently take him to the nearby British Museum after lunch to teach him about the great history of Egypt and the tragedy of its plundered art.

As they walked to the club, Mostafa recalled how he was taken aback several months ago, when his uncle hesitantly made an unusual request. He asked if Mostafa would take on the task of creating a computer virus directed at destroying a computer operating system. Apparently an important Iranian client of his uncle knew of Mostafa's computer skills, and threatened withdrawal of their vast holdings unless he would recruit Mostafa. He remembered the tears in his uncle's eyes when he brought the subject up and how he put his arm around his uncle's shoulder to comfort him. He owed so much to him, and the family's fortune was at stake. How could he refuse to help his beloved uncle? His uncle assured him nothing could be linked back to Mostafa and the client would make a substantial, non-traceable contribution to Mostafa's trust fund in addition to a hefty cash payment to Mostafa and his assistants.

74
Washington

It was a beautiful day in Washington as Win was driven from his hotel to FBI Headquarters. On the way, Roberto, who must have softened towards him, wound around the Tidal Basin to show Win what was left of the Japanese cherry blossoms. Win was reminded suddenly of some lines by the German poet Heinrich Heine, "Im wunderschönen Monat Mai, Als alle Knospen sprangen…"—in the wonderfully beautiful month of May, when all the buds are bursting open… He forgot the subsequent lines that had something to do with singing birds. Not having thought of those lines since a college course in German literature decades ago, he worried that this sudden recall could be an early sign of senility. He shrugged. Nothing he could do about it, and anyway this was April, not May, and it was a gorgeous day. Win had no desire to spend the day locked in a windowless room.

There was an air of urgency in the situation room this morning. Both Bill Huntington and Dan looked unshaven and rumpled.

"We have nothing new to report," Bill began. "This is going to be a slog. We've mobilized our search teams in the other seven potential DOE nuclear facility sites and we're holding off on the four closure sites for now. We have nothing from Santa Fe yet."

"While we're waiting, we can go over some important issues," Dan picked up. "We're trying to develop mobile diagnosis and treatment teams, to get to outbreaks quickly to diagnose and treat victims. The Air Force will supply us with Medevac planes and choppers. As part of this effort, we'll have trained experts to quarantine involved grocery stores and patients. We've also been accumulating stockpiles of antibiotics, particularly ciprofloxacin. We'll use local Bureau agents and police for protection of our teams; panicked crowds can be dangerous. Now let me turn the discussion over to our CDC colleagues."

"We know the terrorists have used V. cholera and two strains of pathogenic E. coli," Mary Carpenter began. "Both diseases require proper rehydration. We have some contractors making up large quantities of oral rehydration solutions using the latest WHO formula, although things are moving more slowly than we'd like. The severe cholera patients may require IV replacement fluid and electrolytes and manufacturers have reasonable inventories of solutions we can use. Antibiotic therapy is less important, but we're gathering large amounts of doxycycline and ciprofloxacin in case. We're assembling supplies of drugs to cover a wide spectrum of infections. Based on our knowledge that they're using food as the means of spreading infections, I bet they'll also include Shigella organisms that cause dysentery. Only a small inoculum is needed to cause infection, and having hordes of people rushing to emergency rooms with bloody diarrhea would create mass panic."

She stopped there and Win asked, "What about protection of health care personnel and prophylaxis for the general population?"

"You always ask tough questions," she replied. "The good news is that quarantine isn't necessary for either infection; good hygiene should suffice. There is no vaccine available for pathogenic E. coli. There's a pretty good oral vaccine for cholera, but we don't have much of it on hand. However, with careful hygiene, we don't think we need to immunize health workers. The real problem is the question of whether to use prophylactic antibiotics in health personnel and for case contacts. If we have a massive attack, everyone is going to demand cipro prophylaxis and Congress will be all over us about it. We don't have large enough supplies on hand and we worry about the dangers of overuse of antibiotics—emergence of resistant strains, superinfections and the like. We've been debating this issue in Atlanta and our recommendation is to use antibiotic prophylaxis on a limited basis for exposed health workers and close contacts of cases of cholera, but not for E. coli infections."

Over a break for coffee and pastries, everyone looked grim. Win said to Mary, "This isn't a pretty situation."

"Yeah. We talk a good game but we're unprepared," she answered. "With limited budgets, preventive measures don't get the money they should. We've got to stop this plot!"

They reconvened and Bill announced, "Our field team in Santa Fe thinks they've found another suspicious bagboy. He's a teenager, of Middle Eastern descent but born in the US, and a clone of Earnest Abe—an exemplary worker who's too good to be true. He too was working at a smaller store that specialized in health foods and fresh fruits and vegetables. They're checking him out and we should hear back soon. Let's turn the floor over to Roger, who'll give us an update on the CIA's efforts to trace the source of this plot."

"This has been a hard area for us to get information on," Salay began. "From what we've discovered, this looks like a complex operation and an expensive one that's not home-grown. The involvement of American-born Muslim boys suggests the group behind this is either Al-Qaeda or a splinter faction based in Yemen or Pakistan. But the darned thing is we haven't picked up a single communication between members of such groups. A lot of things about this operation are puzzling. Who's paying for all of this, and how? It's likely the cholera bacteria came from Asia and one of the E. coli strains from Germany. The terrorists needed a laboratory to grow the bugs and that's likely to be overseas. They would then have to smuggle them into the US. We're talking big bucks for an international operation of this size and complexity. This and the superb planning all point to Al-Qaeda. We constantly monitor large flows of money to suspected affiliates of Al-Qaeda and other terrorist groups. We haven't found any unusual money transfers in recent months. They may well have used the ancient hawala system of money transfer common in many Asian and African countries. The hawala brokers are pledged to secrecy, particularly when they're working for a terrorist group. We want to get the mastermind behind this plot and we're stuck investigating the tail end of their attack. We need to proceed up the leadership chain in our investigation, so we can't tip our hand too early."

Salay went on and presented a brief history of bin Laden, al Zawahiri and Al-Qaeda. "You know, their current head, al Zawahiri, was a physician. Maybe this is his idea."

Following this, lunch was served and then Bill suggested they adjourn until there was further news. Since it was such a pleasant day, Win decided he'd walk back to his hotel. It was a long walk, but he needed the exercise and some fresh air.

He heard nothing more from Bill or Dan so he caught up with calls home and watched some television. Feeling beat, he ordered a room-service dinner and a beer and decided to do some Internet searches on Al-Qaeda. It was interesting to read about the group and how they got their name—it literally meant "The Base," and was named after the camp at which they trained mujahedeen to fight Russians in Afghanistan. He read about the early roles of bin Laden and his physician buddy, al Zawahiri. He clicked on bin Laden's name and was delivered to another website to learn more about this strange but charismatic figure. As he read, he suddenly stared at the screen and said, "Oh my God!" Bin Laden had been killed on May 2nd. He thought back on his bizarre recalling of the lines about May from Heine that morning. Why had he dredged that up from his subconscious? May 2nd could be the date of a revenge attack, he realized. It was only eight days away. Win needed to sleep on his hunch, but he knew he was right. He didn't have Dan's cell phone or home telephone numbers, so it would have to wait till morning, but he didn't think he'd sleep soundly that night.

75
Washington

Win was finishing breakfast when Dan Tilikso called. They wanted Win at the situation room ASAP and would send Roberto over to fetch him. Roberto drove quickly and took Win directly to the Situation Room, where the meeting was already in progress. Win found an empty seat and unloaded his stuff.

Before listening to what the others had to say, Win told them what he'd figured out: about how the timing of Bin Laden's death was approaching on May 2nd, eight days away. "I'm willing to bet a full-scale bioterrorist attack is scheduled to be launched on the anniversary of bin Laden's death," he predicted.

"I think Win raises an excellent point here," a smirking Salay piped up. "Al-Qaeda has a record of taking actions on symbolic dates. The closeness of the bin Laden termination date and of the probably imminent bioterrorist attack makes me agree with Win. If Win is right, we now know the date of the planned attack."

Win raised his hand and said, "It may not be so easy to pinpoint. The attack could be planned for a few days before bin Laden's an-niversary. Three days would accommodate the incubation periods for cholera and E. coli infections after eating contaminated foods. I imagine they'd like to see hordes of Americans getting sick on bin Laden's death day. If they add some other infectious agents to their mix, that could change the incubation period and may lead them to attack earlier; we just don't know. In any event, we need to wrap things up."

"I'm afraid Win's right," Bill said. "Let's get back to what we were discussing earlier. Before you joined us, Win, I reported that we found three other suspicious bagboys near the Idaho, Savannah River and Sandia nuclear lab sites. One bagboy had a Middle Eastern name, one was a North African with an Arabic name and the third's family was of Indonesian origin. All are native-born US citizens. We also learned the Santa Fe bagboy's story was full of holes, just like the others. So we decided to go ahead and investigate the four DOE nuclear closure sites as well. We were about to discuss the actions we should take at this point. I'll turn the discussion over to Dan, as he'll be running this aspect of our counter-terrorism plan."

Dan, who was munching on a jelly doughnut, cleared his mouth and said, "Our first actions are to place the six bagboys under close surveillance and get court-ordered wiretaps in place. We have search warrants approved for the six boys' apartments and vehicles, should we need them. We need to identify their contacts so we can trace the attack back to its source. We'll nail these bastards and teach them a lesson they'll never forget."

Bill took over. "Right now, we don't know whether the boys have the infectious agents in their possession or not. We don't want to arrest them prematurely without the incriminating evidence. They haven't been talking to anyone since we started our phone taps, so the germs may already be with them. We're planning a break-in of one or more of the boys' apartments to search for evidence and get some fingerprints. We'll do this when they're at work and under surveillance there. We'll start with one of the three boys at the previous attack sites. We don't think the boys are storing the agents in their cars; the high temperatures in a car or trunk would inactivate the agents. We'll also do a search of their workplaces and their lockers at work. We're proceeding with great caution so we don't tip off the boys. Beyond that, we just sit back and wait."

Dan picked up and said, "We're trying to run down the billing addresses for their cell phones, now that we got their numbers from employment records. We've dispatched agents to interview landlords and managers of their apartments to learn how they've been paying their rents. We think they all have personal vehicles and we're running the vehicle registrations and insurance to ground for those cars we've identified. All of this is being done with circumspection and that slows us down."

Mary Carpenter raised her hand and said, "My thinking is that the infectious materials will be delivered to the bagboys at the last minute. I suspect the agents have been lyophilized and may have to be reconstituted before use. This would make them more subject to temperature damage and would require refrigeration. The boys may not be able to provide stable refrigeration. On the other hand, they could use the lyophilized materials directly on foods containing moisture. That still would require stable, temperature-controlled storage before use. I may be wrong on this, but that's my hunch."

"Let's break now," Bill announced.

76
Washington

The topic for discussion that afternoon was planning for the worst-case scenario of the bagboys launching a successful attack. The featured speaker was Herb Armitage from the Bureau's Counterterrorism Division, who looked and sounded like an undertaker.

Armitage went over to an easel holding large sheets of paper for presentations and used a marker pen to write down a single word: TERROR. He began: "A major goal of terrorist attacks is to create just that, terror. So far, we know they've used cholera and pathogenic E. coli. They may have other agents in store. If there are large numbers of cases, particularly of diseases uncommon to the US, the public is going to panic. Think of parents' reactions if their kids suddenly become ill with a severe or life-threatening new disease. They're going to swarm our health care facilities and rail at their congressmen. There'd be chaos and anger and a lot of difficult questions from the media."

He wrote the word "Communications" beneath "TERROR" and said, "How we handle informing the public about these attacks is critical for calming the public and permitting us to deal with the outbreaks effectively. In our preparations, we assumed the Secretary of Homeland Security would be the major mouthpiece. The content of what the Secretary says will have to be determined by the President. If things go really bad, we may need the President to address the public directly. We probably should have the Director brief POTUS to begin thinking about this with his advisors. Let's hope we don't need to make any statements."

Armitage went back to the easel and wrote "Command and control" next on his list. Another priority is the need to deal with command and control. We need to establish command centers to control the situations at hospital emergency departments and other first response centers. People are going to flock to emergency rooms and mayhem can occur if there are delays. Pharmacies will be deluged with patients. If we're dealing with highly contagious diseases, we may need to restrict people's travel outside the affected zone. We'll need police trained in crowd control. If the primary site of the infection source is identified, we'll immediately shut down the store and provide security there. That site should be treated as a crime scene, and could be a danger if booby traps were left behind. If we don't know the specific store involved, we'll close down all groceries and supermarkets in the affected areas. The success of that would hinge on whether they'll stick to the same MO of using foods as the means for agent introduction. Most police and fire departments provide training for their personnel in crowd control and the protection of important sites and we'll have them work with us. Some have had training in terrorism response methods, except most have been trained to deal with different agents and modalities. We'll need FBI agents to supervise the most problematic sites. We also may have to pull in the National Guard."

Win sat there, puzzled. Although he'd been immersed in bioterrorism for weeks, he hadn't thought about the impact of a successful attack and how law enforcement groups and the country's political leadership might handle it. He was a victim of scientific gun-barrel vision. He poked fun at government operatives who couldn't think "outside the box," and yet he'd been doing the same thing.

Armitage went back to his list and wrote the word "Aftermath." He resumed his talk: "The aftermath of a successful attack is where the terrorists can have their greatest impact. Aside from beefing up security and screening of food-handling personnel, the ways in which we sell food are going to have to change and that will have a major economic impact. After 9/11 we changed the way we screen airplane passengers and developed our Department of Homeland Security. There is no equivalent of metal detectors or body imaging when it comes to searching for biologic or chemical agents. We'll probably have to stop the sale of bulk salads and other foods. I'm not so sure our mom-and-pop food stores can survive in the new security era. I could go on, but you get the picture."

After a short break, everyone looked even more disheartened than before. They took their seats and Bill began. "We've identified suspicious bagboys at two more sites. So now we have bagboys located near eight of the ten sites. So far, we've only found one bagboy per site. The big question is: what to do now? We've gotten wiretaps approved for the first six boys' cell phones. None of them has a landline, as far as we can tell. We'll do the same for the two new ones and any others we find. We have some of the boys already under surveillance and we'll extend it to all of them. We're rushing break-in specialists to two sites—Santa Fe and Oak Ridge. We chose those sites since the bagboys there have already mounted one attack and might have some residual infectious materials in their apartments."

"Let's say the weapons haven't been delivered yet," Dan said. "Then what?"

Herb Armitage replied, "Then we have a great opportunity to uncover another link in the terrorist chain, the delivery source. We've instructed our surveillance teams to be on the lookout for any deliveries and to follow the delivery persons rather than apprehend them. If the deliveries are from FedEx or UPS, we can trace them."

Salay said, "I don't know how much these boys know about the plot and its organization, but my guess is they know only about their single task. We've still picked up nothing from overseas about the operation. This is a complex operation with a lot of actors, but eventually, one of them will screw up and provide us with a lead."

A phone rang at the back of the room and one of the agents answered and took notes. All eyes in the room turned to him. He got up and came over to Bill, handed him the notes, and whispered something in his ear. Bill said to the group, "One of our agents already got to Oak Ridge and entered Earnest Abe's apartment while Abe was at work. He found nothing that looked like it could contain infectious agents. It was a pretty bleak apartment; minimal cheap furniture, a radio but no TV, a Qur'an and a bunch of books in Arabic, a porn magazine, and a lot of soft drinks and junk food. Nothing was hidden and there were few places to hide anything. If our agent in Santa Fe finds the same scenario, we can make a good guess that the agents haven't been delivered yet."

"All right, why don't we break for the day," Bill said.

As Win was packing his stuff, Dan came over and suggested that he and Win go out for dinner since Dan had to stay near Headquarters. So off they went to Dan's favorite pizzeria.

77
Washington

The Task Force started promptly at 8:00 the next morning. Win was told they'd have breakfast at the situation room, so he slept a bit later than usual, but the pedestrian food made him regret having missed breakfast at his fancy hotel. He fixed himself a plate of fruit, a bagel with cream cheese and some coffee and took his usual seat. He remembered from his days as a peer reviewer at NIH the remarkable consistency of Washington-area buffet breakfasts. It probably wasn't easy to always select cantaloupe and honeydew melons that had the taste and consistency of cucumbers. Win was brought back from feeling sorry for himself when the meeting began.

"Let's get started," Bill said. "We have some more news. We were able to speed things up by focusing on health food stores and adding more personnel to the search. So now we have ten suspicious bagboys spread across the country, all under surveillance and with wiretaps in place. We just have to wait to see what happens and that will determine when we apprehend the boys."

"Have we gotten anything useful from watching the boys or listening in to their phone conversations Bill?" Dan asked.

Colorless Herb who was running the surveillance operation said, "These boys just go to work and stay home afterwards. There are no other activities, not even a movie or a trip to get some pizza. They shop at the stores where they work and at Walmart. They're all using prepaid phones so we can't get any billing records. If they're using SIM cards, we should be able to get a record of their calls after we confiscate their phones. What's even more interesting is that none of them have used their phones since we started our taps. I bet they're waiting for orders."

"What about checking out how the boys pay their rent?" Dan asked.

"We've checked out four boys so far. All rents were paid three months in advance, in cash, by their uncles. We've gotten varying descriptions of these uncles, but they all looked and sounded like foreign-born men. We instructed the rental office people to keep mum and put the fear of God in them."

Win was listening carefully and also was doodling on a pad. He suddenly scribbled "Eureka" and shot up his hand like an anxious kid in grade school.

"What is it now, Sage?" Bill asked.

"You know, the DOE also has nuclear research laboratories spread around the country, many associated with Universities. Maybe we need to check out those sites."

"They don't make any weapons, but they do conduct research related to materials that go into weapons," Sam Oberdorf answered. "Our Office of Science funds 10 facilities, many near big cities, and most people don't think of them as related to our weapons pro-grams. They're more into high-powered physics research. I hadn't thought of these labs as possible attack candidates and none of them was among the three outbreak sites. What do you think; should we investigate these sites as well?"

Before anyone could say anything, Win said, "Why don't we sample a few sites to be safe? We could check out 2 or 3 of the DOE-supported laboratories to be thorough. If none of these turn up any suspicious bagboys, than you could assume they're only aiming at nuclear weapons facilities."

"Bill, do you have the personnel to investigate a few more towns?" Oberdorf asked.

"Not really, but I think we need to do it. We'll round up some ad-ditional troops. Mary, can you recruit some of your people to help?"

"We're getting stretched thin too, but I agree, we need to do it," Mary replied.

Most of the people in the room were glaring at Win for making additional work for them. It bothered Win that even when the safety of the US population was at stake, expediency mattered most to these bureaucrats.

During the break, Sam wrote the names of the ten other DOE laboratories on small pieces of paper that he folded and placed in a coffee mug. When they reconvened, Bill announced there would be a random drawing of three laboratory names from the mug as the additional surveillance sites. "Okay Win, this was your idea, so you get to choose the three sites." He passed the mug to Win.

Win shook the papers in the mug and then chose three that he passed to Oberdorf. Sam unfolded them and laid them out on the table. "All right, the sites are the Ames Lab in Ames, Iowa, the Fermi Lab in Batavia, Illinois, that's a Chicago suburb, and the Princeton Plasma Physics Lab in Princeton, New Jersey. There's going to be a lot of stores to check out in Princeton, and a lot of work."

"So be it," Bill said. "We'll mobilize our troops and get going ASAP."

78
Jersey City, New Jersey

It was a watershed day for Nasir al Fakrah. He had two large work-tables set up in his apartment living room, one of which was covered with the products of an elaborate and great enterprise. It was the shipment from Pakistan, and his task was to repackage and reconstitute the contents for use in the planned attacks. The window shades were drawn and bright lamps aimed at the two tables. Heavy cardboard boxes on the floor had contained the original shipping boxes from Pakistan and their Styrofoam blocks. Nasir had removed the metal aerosol cans from the blocks and disassembled them to remove the glass containers inside. He discarded the empty Chanel, Vuitton and Hermes labeled spray cans into two large, green trash bags.

Nasir donned a green operating room gown, surgical cap and mask, stamped, "Property of King's County Hospital." He then put on a pair of safety glasses and rubber gloves. In preparation, Nasir had unpacked the carefully labeled vials and ampoules alongside bottles of saline on one table and the color-coded syringes and carrying belts for them on the second table. The large volume of infectious agents surprised him. The cloth belts resembled bandoliers for carrying cartridges, except these were designed to be worn around the waist. The belts all were stamped with the notice, "Property of the ISI," in Urdu—a nice touch, he thought, to divert attention to the wrong source.

He sorted the containers by organism using a guide list and laid them out on the white sheet covering the table. The belts had been set out on the second table with the site for each one marked on a sheet of paper under it. He had worked out the combinations of organisms to be the most confusing to any investigators and had his directions typed out on two sheets of paper.

He said a prayer and got to work. When he finished, Nasir placed all of the now empty glassware in roasting pans and placed them in the oven. He carefully collected the needles and plastic syringes he had used and dumped them into a bucket of bleach in the sink. He turned the oven control to the "broil" setting and went back to work. Next, he carefully removed his gloves and gown and placed them in one of the large, green, plastic garbage bags. He then went to the bathroom and carefully washed his face and hands and his glasses.

He went back to the living room and donned a fresh operating gown, mask and gloves. The arranged belts looked impressive with their neatly lined up, color-coded syringes, some with plastic sheathed needles for injection into products and others covered by a plastic cap that would be removed for spraying. He had an array of cardboard boxes on the floor against one of the walls. Each box was unsealed and addressed for shipment. He checked to verify that each box contained two envelopes, one labeled "Student Instructions," containing instructions for use of the belt contents, and travel instructions and documents for leaving the country after completing the mission, and the second marked "Delivery Instructions" for the delivery person. He made sure the numbers on the envelopes matched the numbers on the boxes. Nasir carefully rolled up each belt, placed it in a plastic bubble-wrap envelope and then in a plastic bag and fit it snugly into the appropriate box. He then sealed the boxes with plastic tape and loaded them into large, black plastic lawn bags. He went to the kitchen, turned off the oven and poured off the bleach from the bucket. Then he went back to the tables and removed the covering sheets and added them to the garbage bags. He let out a sigh and took off his operating room outfit, which he also added to one of the green bags.

While he washed again, he noticed his hands were trembling. He went to the living room and collapsed into an armchair. The enormous responsibilities he had assumed were taking a toll. If his segment of the operation failed, it would be all over for the entire scheme. The Brothers were most concerned by chokepoints like this, where a single failure could abort the whole project. There were several such points and they assigned their best operatives to them. Nevertheless, Nasir couldn't believe that things had gone so well. The goal was in sight and that made him feel jubilant but also anxious. As he sat, he recalled how badly he'd been treated as a student at Johns Hopkins, how they looked down on him and his Pakistani medical training. Yes, he'd show them who was smart and who was dumb!

After a short while, he took out his cell phone and dialed a number. He waited and then asked, "Is that you Hassan?" He went on and said, "The materials are ready for you to pick up. Good. Thirty minutes would be fine. I'll be expecting you."

Nasir got up and emptied the needles and syringes and the now cool, sterilized glassware into a box, which he then put into a green garbage bag in the living room. He took his typed instruction sheets, tore them into small pieces and flushed them down the toilet. Finally, he collapsed in the easy chair, exhausted. He dozed off and was roused by the sound of his doorbell. He buzzed his visitor in and it wasn't long before there was a knock on the apartment door. Nasir checked through the peephole before letting him in. He greeted the visitor with an embrace. "Welcome Brother Hassan! Let me show you what I have here for you to take care of." He pointed at the lawn bags and said, "These black bags are to be delivered to my brother Ibrahim. He'll take care of them. There are three of them and you must count to make sure all are delivered. Put them in the front of your van." He next pointed to the large green garbage bags and empty boxes. "This is the material to be taken to the incinerator and burned." He walked over to one of the green bags and said, "Handle this one by the top only; there's broken glass inside."

Hassan said, "I haven't forgotten my assignments, Sir."

"I also have an envelope for you to give to Ibrahim." He picked up a bulky manila envelope and handed it to Hassan. He got up and said, "I'll help you load your van."

After several trips, Nasir watched Hassan drive off and then went upstairs to finish packing. Tomorrow he'd leave for Pakistan. It would be a long journey since he wouldn't fly directly home and would use different airlines to confound anyone trying to track his movements. Ibrahim would have the keys and documents for disposing of Nasir's car and belongings and for terminating his apartment lease; they were in the manila envelope. Nasir felt conflicted as he went about his packing. He was anxious to get home and see his family, but he also felt sad that he wouldn't get to witness first-hand the panic and chaos in the heathens. The Brothers were right that he should leave America before the attack—he knew too much and his services might be needed again. He would visit his family in Pakistan briefly and then disappear for a while.

79
Newark

Ibrahim Nasrulla drove Nasir's car to Newark to deliver the packages to the Cedars of Lebanon Freight Forwarding Company. The old car was slated to be donated to a local charity tomorrow. He circled the block where the Company was located and there were no suspicious vehicles parked nearby, so he pulled into their driveway and drove around to the shipping dock at the rear. He honked and waited. Soon the metal shipping door was rolled up and the same tall bearded assistant he'd met at earlier visits came down to help unload.

When they were done, the tall, silent assistant indicated that Ibrahim was to follow him into the cozy sitting room where they had met before. Jumblatt, the owner, was waiting, nattily dressed and once again looking every bit the banker. He gestured for Ibrahim to sit on an upholstered chair and the bearded assistant left to fetch tea.

"The materials arrived in excellent condition and are now ready for shipment to their destinations," Ibrahim began. "The new packages are addressed to the same destinations as we had planned."

Jumblatt nodded and said, "Good. I presume the delivery date will remain the same and all are to be delivered on the same day."

"Yes. Some of the packages will likely have to be shipped by air. They now contain medical supplies and should not be subjected to extremes of temperature."

"Not a problem. We'll use our friends who run an airfreight forwarding business. The packages to be delivered within a thousand miles will be shipped by truck. All vehicles will be air-conditioned. There's no cause to worry."

Ibrahim pulled an envelope out of his inside jacket pocket, presented it to Jumblatt and said, "Our Brothers are grateful for your assistance."

80
South Waziristan

It wasn't your usual domestic scene. The Hakim, his closest aide, and an elderly visitor sat at the kitchen table in Ayman's house in Waziristan. The visitor, Hassan Abdullah Khan, a senior member of al-Qaida's Shura, looked menacing. He had a full white beard dyed red at its periphery by henna, and sun-weathered skin like wrinkled brown leather. Ayman had never seen him smile. One of Ayman's wives cleared the table from their lunch, and served tea and fresh fruits. She wore a burqa that only revealed her frightened eyes. She was alarmed by the visit of the dreaded Mullah Redbeard. The visitor was there to brief Ayman on the current status of the operation. He waited for the woman to leave before speaking.

"Ayman, my brother, things have been going well. The Waziristan factory was closed down and most of the buildings dismantled. We removed all the equipment and have it stored in a place whose location is one to which I am not privy. The remaining structures were made to appear like an abandoned ISI camp. It's still camouflaged, so it won't be detected easily from the air. There are no remaining witnesses as to what the site was used for except for the Professor and some trustworthy members of my tribe who served as security officers. The Professor is now in a remote village near the Afghan border. Although he knows too much for his own good, he is a devout believer and we may need him in the future."

Ayman closed his eyes and said, "That's good and as planned. Tell me, did the infectious agents survive the trip and will they work?"

"They did survive. Our able, physician brother in the US performed a field test of two agents and they worked."

"Can you be sure of this?" Ayman asked.

"Absolutely! The heathens even sent out doctors from their infectious diseases agency to investigate after the test. Our physician did an outstanding job and we needed to get him out of the US before the attack because he knows too much. He's another person we may need again. He's currently on his way back to Pakistan. After he visits his family in Karachi, we'll move him to a remote village up north."

Ayman scowled and asked, "What about the boys in the US? I always saw them as weak links in our chain of attack."

"They have remained well-disciplined. We used three of them to mount our test attacks. They will do as they are told. After the big day, they will leave the country and then be eliminated. We have used many layers of personnel in the American side of the operation. Even if the boys were caught, they would lead the Americans to a dead end in any investigation. Your strategy of insulated layers to the operation should work, Inshallah. Our sources tell us the Americans have no inkling as to what's in store for them."

Ayman stroked his beard and leaned forward to say softly, "Tariq and I will be leaving tomorrow for a more secure location to wait out the Great Satan's reactions. Our families will stay here. We'll use the camp in…"

The visitor abruptly held up his hand. "Don't tell me where you're going. I mustn't know. The success of the enemy's drone attacks is based as much on loose tongues as on aerial surveillance. The fewer people that know where you are, the better."

Ayman opened his vest to show two hand grenades he had attached to the lining. "If they come after me, I'll take a few of their Navy seals with me."

"I'm more worried about the cursed drones," the elder said.

Ayman continued, "When a tiger's tail is bitten, he strikes out in blind anger. It's best for all our leaders to go underground for a while."

"That is wise, but some of us will have to stay in communication with our field operatives. I will arrange for most of our Shura to disappear."

The visitor, who looked as cheerful as a relative at a funeral, got up to leave. He embraced Ayman and said, "I pray that our operation is a success and that you and I will meet again in this life."

"Inshallah. Travel carefully and safely my brother," Ayman whispered.

81
Oak Ridge

At 9:00 PM Earnest Abe was reading in his bleak apartment when his phone rang. He rarely received calls, so the ring startled him. A familiar voice said, "This is Uncle Abdullah. The materials will be delivered to you tomorrow evening at 7:30 PM. Do not talk to the deliveryman. Open the box and read the instructions carefully. Memorize them and do exactly as you are instructed. May Allah protect you." Before Abe could say anything, Abdullah had hung up. A series of identical calls were received by the other bag boys. The calls had been recorded and sent out through an overseas forwarding site.

The FBI wiretap listeners picked up the calls and called headquarters immediately.

82
Albuquerque, New Mexico

John Omar Abbott had received a phone call alerting him to the delivery of a package to his home. Abbott knew little about this package, only that he was to deliver the contents to a student in Santa Fe. Abbott was a devout Moslem whose parent's had changed the family name from Abboud to Abbott when they emigrated to the US, and he'd been recruited for this task by an elderly gentleman from Syria who attended his mosque. John had been told that his task was to help promote an important religious cause and he was to follow the directions he would receive to the letter. He suspected the Mosque elder was linked to some shadowy Islamist cause, but that didn't bother John—he believed strongly in asserting Moslem political strength in the US. He was running a successful business, and he was tired of being looked down on as a primitive religious zealot. He often thought that had he remained in the Middle East, he'd have become a jihadi; that's how much he detested the US and its corrupting culture.

Abbott had taken the morning off, and was waiting in the kitchen of his small, one-story home in the Nob Hill section of Albuquerque. At about 10:45 AM there was a knock on his front door. A dark-skinned man in a tan uniform asked if he was John Abbott and gave him a package before leaving in an unmarked white van.

John locked the door, took the package inside and placed it on the kitchen table. It was an ordinary-looking, medium-sized, brown cardboard box weighing about five pounds. With a bone-handled pocketknife, he carefully opened the top. Just as he expected, there was an envelope inside that read "Delivery Instructions." He sat down and opened the envelope, learning that he was to remove the plastic bag and place the package inside it in a paper or plastic shopping bag and keep it in a cool place until delivery. The bag was to be transported on a car seat and not in the trunk. He was to cut up the cardboard shipping box and burn it. There was a name and address of the party to whom he was to deliver the parcel and a detailed map of how to drive there. He was to memorize these details and then burn the instructions, map, and envelope as well. His arrival time at the specified address was to be 7:30 PM today and he was given no telephone number for the recipient. Impressed by the clarity and precision of the instructions, he finished dressing and set off for his work as chef and half owner of a Middle Eastern restaurant on nearby Central Avenue. He would have to pass off today's evening duties to his sous-chef.

Abbott left work early and went home where he changed into a navy plaid shirt and jeans. He read the instructions one more time and took them and the envelope to the small fireplace in the corner of his living room where he had already placed the shipping box. He had never used the kiva fireplace before and looked inside to figure out how to use the damper. He opened it and lit the paper with a match. It caught fire without flooding the room with smoke. That was a good start, he thought. He let the fire die out and closed the damper. He swept up the ashes and flushed them down the toilet.

He watched television until 6:00 PM and then prepared to leave. The drive to Santa Fe usually took about an hour and ten minutes. He thought he might need a few extra minutes in case he caught the tail end of rush hour. He loaded the shopping bag on the passenger seat, buckled up, and headed towards I-25 North. He drove west on Central Avenue and got on the highway. Traffic wasn't heavy, but he drove at the speed limit since he had some time to kill. He always enjoyed the drive to Santa Fe; the road was wide and well constructed and the desert scenery and skies were beautiful, particularly at sunset. He got off I-25 at the St. Francis Drive exit heading

to the south side of the City and following the memorized instructions, found himself in front of the student's apartment building ten
minutes early. It was in a housing development of identical looking
two-story buildings. He parked and waited, oblivious to the empty
tan van parked down the street. At 7:25 he got out of the car with the
bag in hand and walked across the street to the student's apartment
building. He found the student's bell and buzzed it. The student
buzzed back, allowing him to open the locked door. While Abbott
walked upstairs, the parked van moved slowly up the street and
stopped behind his car.

The agent behind the wheel of the van was wearing an audio
headset and spoke into the mike: "I think we have the delivery guy
visiting our boy. He's driving a maroon Chevy sedan, with New
Mexico license plates." He took a photo of the car with a small camera and read the license plate number to the agent on the other end.
He then drove the van around the block and parked it in its previous
place. An elderly man was walking his dog down the street towards
Abbott's car. He was shabbily dressed and talking to his Boston terrier as he walked. He shuffled along and stopped beside the maroon
car where he stooped to tie his shoelace. While hidden by the car,
he deftly reached under the car's rear fender, wiped an area clean
with a cloth, and secured a tracking device to the cleaned spot. He
got up and walked on. The whole operation took less than a minute.

Abbott reappeared in less than five minutes and got into his car,
pleased to have   discharged his duty as instructed. As he headed
back to I-25 for the ride home, he didn't notice a gray SUV following him or a helicopter overhead.

Abbott drove slowly on his way back to Albuquerque. He didn't
have the faintest idea of what this delivery was about, but fanta-
sized that he had made a modest contribution to the jihad against
the United States and its corrupt culture and devilish desire for
world domination. While listening to the radio, he never noticed
the changing cars tailing him. An hour later he parked his car in
the carport alongside his house and went in. That act mobilized a
large-scale surveillance operation. With knowledge of the address,

his landline phone could be tapped and his cellphone identified if he used it. He would be identified and run through the government's computers. A nondescript van with surveillance equipment would be dispatched and parked near his house. Agents with skills in tailing suspects would be brought in and situated near the house. Abbott was a link to others involved in the attack and a valuable potential informant. The FBI would smother him with coverage. He would be taken into custody eventually and heavily interrogated. He was worth his weight in gold.

83
Washington

The carefully orchestrated deliveries to the bag boys led to a massive mobilization of interdiction forces at the ten sites. It also led to the reconvening of an exhausted Task Force at FBI Headquarters. Win and the others were ordered to attend an emergency meeting at 9:30 PM.

Bill began the meeting: "Deliveries have been made earlier this evening to all ten bag boys. All deliveries were made at the same time and were preceded by a recorded phone message from their Uncle Abdullah. So it looks like an attack is imminent. We're working on tracking that call; it's a VOIP message that appears to have originated in Mumbai. The deliveries were all made by private citizens. Two of them appear to be naturalized US citizens of middle-eastern origin. I'll turn things over to Herb Armitage who'll be handling the surveillance and interdiction of the couriers and the bag boys."

Herb cleared his throat. "We now have a large surveillance program in place monitoring the ten boys and their ten delivery agents. We'll interdict the attack and try to get contact information from the boys. We're hopeful the delivery guys will lead us to their handlers so we can progress further up the command chain. At this point, we can likely thwart the attack completely. Our secondary goal is to identify the planners of this attack and nab them."

Herb looked at Bill who said, "We're now able to arrest the bag boys, assuming biologic weapons have been delivered to them. The big question is whether we move in now to make arrests or we try to catch the bag boys in the act of contaminating foods. We have two of our in-house lawyers here, Dave Harwood and Mort Sessoms. Dave, why don't you fill us in on your Department's thinking."

Dave, in a gray suit with a red tie, began. "First off, these actors are US citizens acting on US soil, so they have full Miranda rights. Second, they'll likely get charged and tried in Federal Court. Third, we'd like to have them tried as a group since this appears to be a coordinated attack with the same command. Lastly, although we likely have a strong case against them, it would be helpful to catch one or more of them in the act of spreading agents over foods. We believe we don't have to catch all of them in the act to try them successfully. Arrests will have to be closely coordinated and we have to remember the boys will be apprehended in four different time zones. We don't want the arrest of one boy to trigger an alarm for the other actors."

Roger Salay looked pained. "By arresting these bagboys and giving them public trials, we play right into the hands of the terrorists. News of the planned attack will be as terrorizing as an actual attack. Citizens are going to be haranguing their representatives in Washington to beef up food safety and security and that's going to cost our economy big time. People are going to shop and eat differently after the news of a potential biologic attack on their salads, meats and other produce. Successful attack or not, they win. The moment the infectious agents reached the bagboys on US soil, they won."

Mort, the suit with a blue tie answered, "We know this, but have no other choice. The Director has met with White House counsel and that's the strategy they've chosen. Trying to conceal these arrests will only cause more damage if the press finds out about it. The White House feels strongly that honesty and transparency will work best here. We can at least claim the success of our anti-terrorism activities in protecting the US."

Win noticed the gloom growing in the room. It was a damn clever plot and a huge mess. He wondered how well their anti-terrorism programs would have worked if he hadn't stumbled on to the cholera cases in Santa Fe and linked them with other cases at DOE sites.

Bill wrapped up the meeting by outlining the Bureau's plan for apprehending the bagboys and surveillance of the delivery agents. It looked to Win like they'd won a great battle, but lost the war.

84
Oak Ridge

It was a gray day with a heavy drizzle, so Abe, the Oak Ridge bagboy, decided to drive to work because he didn't want the paper shopping bag in which he would carry his heavy attack belt to get wet and fall apart. He had read his instructions numerous times and committed them to memory. This was to be a landmark day, the culmination of many months of planning and the launching of a new holy war against the evil US. He would achieve greatness today on his way to Paradise. He arrived at work mid-morning; his work schedule was from 10:00 AM to 6:00 PM but he would leave early because of a "medical emergency" in his family.

It was a light morning so Abe spent time chatting with the cashiers. His lunch break came at 1:00 PM and he went back to the staff lounge, feeling elated but slightly nervous. In the empty lounge, not visible from the main floor of the market, he reached into his shopping bag and removed the belt with its color-coded syringes. He fastened the belt around his waist and concealed it under his shirt worn out of his trousers as instructed. He next went over to the refrigerated storage room for produce and looked through the glass window. No one was inside, so he entered quickly and hastily emptied the contents of the differently colored syringes over different salad greens: the red over bulk salad green mixes; the green injected skillfully into plastic bags of salad greens that he resealed with a tiny dab of glue. He went over to the bins of sprouts and was emptying a blue-colored syringe when the door to the room sprang open. He was startled by the entry of two large men in orange jumpsuits that

248

said "Acme Plumbing" on their front. "What are you doing?" one man asked Abe.

"I'm freshening up our salad greens. Who are you and what are you doing here?" Abe asked, as if he owned the place.

One of the men pulled a pistol out of his pocket, pointed it at Abe and said, "Please drop what you're holding and raise your hands to the ceiling. You're under arrest by the FBI. Don't even think of doing anything else. Now raise them." Abe turned pale, dropped a syringe, and raised his hands slowly. Two other men in similar outfits came in and placed Abe's hands in cuffs behind his back. One of the agents read Abe his Miranda rights.

Comparable scenes were played out at the other supermarkets; all of the bagboys were apprehended, their apartments raided and their cars searched. None of the arrested bagboys could get to their phones. They were well trained and said absolutely nothing other than to request an attorney.

85
Washington

The atmosphere was edgy in the FBI Situation Room as they waited for the roundup of the bagboys. The stakes were too high for screw-ups. Win could feel the pressure as he watched Dan wolf down several doughnuts in a row. News started to trickle in and soon everyone in the room seemed to be on the phone.

"We have good news all around," Herb Armitage began. "We successfully apprehended all ten bagboys while they were in possession of their lethal syringe belts. All the bagboys had brand new US passports and E-tickets that would get them to Mexico City by different routes. They had printed reservations at mid-level tourist hotels, no two at the same hotel. We don't know what was next. So I propose we have agents use those tickets, go to the same hotels, check in under the boys' names and then wait. We need to see what happens next or else the trail goes cold for us. We'll have to pull some strings to allow the agents to use false names for entry to Mexico. They'll also need to be armed and our Embassy can help with that. I have a hunch the boys will be executed in Mexico. We need to do this pronto so our agents can use the boys' tickets on the same flights. Are there any disagreements?"

There were no comments, so Herb excused himself to handle the deployment of stand-in bagboys.

Bill picked up for Herb. "We now have the infectious agents in hand so we need to identify them. Mary, this is your arena. How do you plan to proceed?"

Mary read from her notes. "First, we'll try culturing all the syringe contents. That's relatively slow—a minimum of 12 to 24 hours. This won't work if any syringe contains a virus, though we don't think that's likely. If we assume the agents used include cholera and E. coli, we can perform an array of specific tests that would give us rapid answers. We also can run a battery of tests based on the most likely bioterrorism agents—the 'round up the usual suspects' approach."

"Where are you going to do this lab work, Mary?" Bill interrupted.

"I was planning to rush the samples to Atlanta to the CDC labs."

"Why don't we also send samples to our Homeland Security Lab at Fort Detrick?" Bill suggested.

"It sounds like there were multiples of the different color-coded syringes, so that shouldn't present any problem," Mary said. "Having separate labs working on identification could be valuable."

"I can help with the rapid transport of the syringes," Dan piped up. "We can get the Air Force to help since this is such an important operation. I'll get going on the logistics, if that's okay with everybody. Do we need to refrigerate or freeze the samples, Mary?"

"Probably not; they were meant to be delivered at room temperature," Mary said. "On the other hand, refrigeration shouldn't do any harm and might preserve the organisms better."

Win sat there as a passive observer; this was outside his expertise. He was impressed by the lack of turf battles between the different agencies.

Bill wrapped up the meeting and said, "We'll adjourn and let our team work on the transport and identification of the materials we captured. Why don't we reconvene at 9:00 AM tomorrow morning? We should have some more information then."

86
Washington

Next morning, Win sprang for eggs Benedict at his hotel; a celebration was in order after yesterday's successes and one day of hedonism shouldn't clog his coronary arteries. He skimmed the Washington Post and New York Times over breakfast and found no mention of the aborted attacks or the bagboys' arrests. He was still wondering how news of the failed attacks and capture of the home-grown terrorists would be handled by the FBI, and the President for that matter. If they planned to try the boys in court, news certainly would get out.

Win finished his feast and went outside to wait for his ride to Headquarters. His favorite Ethiopian doorman wasn't on duty, so he continued to read the papers. He enjoyed the coolness of the spring morning and felt relaxed for the first time since taking up residence in Washington. He'd be heading home soon and back to his neatly organized retirement in Santa Fe. He missed Julia and the dogs and his weirdo friends. He wondered if he would miss the excitement of being involved with international terrorism. His thoughts were interrupted by Roberto pulling up.

"Hey Doc, rumor at the Bureau has it that you helped pull off a great anti-terrorism coup. Is there anything to it?" Roberto asked after Win got in the car.

"Roberto, for a guy who reported me for being loose-tongued with my Ethiopian buddy, you should know better than to ask. Anyway, the answer is yes, although my role was darn small."

"I'm beginning to think you might be pretty good, Doc."

Roberto insisted on shaking Win's hand after he dropped him off at Headquarters. Win went through security and found his way to the Situation Room. He was a bit early so he went over to the sideboard and picked out a succulent-looking jelly doughnut and poured a cup of coffee. People straggled into the room, looking disheveled and dog-tired.

Bill called the meeting to order and turned the floor over to Mary who was wearing no makeup today. "We have some preliminary diagnostic results," she began. "All ten of the boys had syringes containing Cholera vibrio, but only seven had syringes containing E. coli. By virtue of the attack method used, we suspected we were dealing primarily with foodborne infections, so we did some specific tests and discovered some of the syringes contained Shigella and others Salmonella organisms. We think we also have Hepatitis A and will confirm it shortly. We don't know the contents of the other syringes yet. Curiously, the color codes used were different for each boy and different combinations of agents were used at each site."

"Damned slick," Roger Salay muttered. "They used multiple agents and simple tricks to confuse us and slow us down."

Fascinated, Win munched on his jelly doughnut. He was learning bad habits from Dan.

"Do you have any guesses as to the contents of the remaining tubes?" Herb asked.

"Our lab people think we may be dealing with uncommon or below-the radar bioterrorism agents. We could also be dealing with one or more viruses, although that would require much more laboratory sophistication on the terrorists' part."

"Don't sell these guys short," Salay added. "Our uncovered chatter from Pakistan suggests Al-Qaeda recruited some high-level university types."

"Yeah, but they would need a sophisticated lab to propagate viruses," Mary shot back.

"Never underestimate the capabilities of terrorists," Roger responded.

A phone rang in the back of the room. An agent picked it up, listened for a few minutes and passed the phone to Bill. "It's from Fort Detrick," he announced.

Bill listened and asked an occasional question. "Well, it looks like our friends at the Homeland Security Lab were also able to identify Campylobacter organisms. They suspect one of the syringes contained Brucella, but can't be sure yet. That bug requires complex testing," he announced to the group. "They haven't identified any agent for the last syringe and suspect it contains some virus."

Win frowned and said, "Can you just imagine the confusion a successful attack would have generated? Patients would present with a wide range of different signs and symptoms, the diseases all have different latency periods, different age groups have different susceptibilities, and most docs wouldn't know what on earth they were seeing. It would be extra hard to figure out what was going on, but that would just add to the terror. Pretty damn smart if you ask me."

"Nobody asked you," Dan said.

"Brucellosis is on the list of possible bioterrorism agents, but what's this Campylobacter bug all about?" Herb asked.

"It's a common cause of diarrhea worldwide," Mary answered. "It's become a big problem for hospitalized patients in the US. Immunocompromised patients, people on antibiotic therapy, children, and the elderly—these are the most susceptible groups. Some of these patients have protracted disease. It would direct attention away from foods and towards hospitals as sources. It's another clever touch. These terrorists were cunning."

"No shit!" Roger muttered.

"Okay, okay. We now need to discuss what on earth we tell the public," Bill said. "We aborted the attacks but we can still scare the average citizen to death if we don't handle this right."

They compiled a list of options for presentation to the Director and ultimately to POTUS. This would likely end up being the President's call.

Win was told to hang around for another day or two, so he decided to hike back to his hotel.

87
Oak Ridge

Clyde Roemer was eating lunch at his desk in a corner of the freight receiving room at the Oak Ridge Nuclear Facility. He'd had a busy morning and was enjoying his break playing a few games of solitaire on his desktop computer. He checked his E-mail before going back to his unloading and inventorying work. One caught his attention. It was titled: Check out my bod, Dude. I bet you have... Clyde opened it and it was a note and some attached photos. It read, "Check me out Dude. I bet you'll have a big hard-on after." The photos were titled: My tits; my ass; my cunt. He opened the first one; it was a picture of the biggest, shapeliest boobs he'd ever seen. He skipped to the third one and let out a loud whistle. It was a shot of a woman's genitalia in full color with her legs spread wide apart and her finger beckoning towards her privates. She was right; he did have an erection. He downloaded the pictures; these were worth saving, and decided to forward it to several buddies. He attached a note: "Check these pictures out; they're hot stuff! Clyde." The message was sent to half a dozen friends mostly at the nuclear facility. He was unaware it had also been sent to hundreds of other workers at his and other DOE facilities and that it had unleashed computer Armageddon. He got up and went back to his work without noticing his computer screen had gone black.

88
Los Alamos, New Mexico

William Strange, PhD, a physicist at the Los Alamos National Laboratory, was at his desk, concentrating as he edited a scientific manuscript, when his computer pinged to indicate an incoming E-mail message. Its subject line read: "Looking for my high school classmate with your name." He opened it and read that the sender was looking for someone with his name for a high school alumni publication. It was from someone named Cynthia Ross and she wanted to know if he was the person featured with her and a few other classmates in the attached photo. The name didn't ring a bell, but she did have his E-mail address. He didn't notice that she hadn't named the school or the graduation year as he absent-mindedly opened the photo. No, he wasn't in the photo.

He typed a brief reply: Sorry I'm not in the picture. WS. His train of thought had been interrupted, so he got up to get a cup of coffee. When he returned, his computer had been turned off. He tried several times to reboot it before he let out a sigh and looked in his Rolodex for the number of his Division's tech assistant; the line was busy. He waited a few minutes and dialed the number again; it was still busy so he left a voicemail. He'd work on something else in the meantime.

89
Washington

It was May 2nd; the anniversary of Osama bin Laden's death, and the Task Force was meeting to celebrate their success. Dan had brought in an iced cake that said on it, "Good Riddance Osama," and there were fresh flowers on the table.

Today, the Bureau Director, Robert Manning, joined them to attend the victory party. Bill called the meeting to order and introduced the Director, who began his remarks with a smile. "I want to thank you all for doing such a superb job in sparing us from a potentially devastating bioterrorist attack. This was a close call and we managed to nip it in the bud. We now have to round up the bad guys. I'd like to thank Bill, Dan and Herb from our Bureau and our colleagues from the CDC and the CIA for excellent work. I'd like to express particular thanks to our consultant, Dr. Winston Sage, whose prescient thinking led us to uncover this gruesome plot. We were lucky this time and I fear for the next attack from our enemies. This plot will change a lot of policies at our Bureau and other agencies I'm afraid. Al-Qaeda sent us a strong message and it's been heard." He stopped and got up to shake hands with everyone before taking leave.

Win was impressed by the Director's engaging personality, but bothered by his string of clichés and platitudes. He guessed the ability to show warmth while pleasantly saying nothing was part of the job-description for FBI Director. Manning belonged to the subspecies Homo sapiens platitudinosa. He'd make a great minister or rabbi, Win thought; with lines like, "As you stroll down life's highways together, hand in hand…" Win must have heard that line at least 10 times at weddings and it grated like chalk on a blackboard.

While they all were chatting, a phone rang. Bill took the call and the smile on his face disappeared. "I see, I see. Why don't you get your house in order and then come over here to brief us on what's happened. Thanks for the heads-up."

Bill caught the Director as he was leaving the room and whispered something in his ear. The Director pursed his lips and said, "Let me know when all the details are in. I guess I'll have to brief POTUS on this." He left the room shaking his head from side to side.

Bill reconvened the meeting looking glum. "It looks like someone's rained on our parade. I just received a call from Sam Oberdorf at DOE; he wanted to let me know there's been a massive cyberattack on DOE computer facilities. All their operating systems are down. Thus far, it looks like a sophisticated attack similar to the Stuxnet worm that took down the Iranian nuclear program's operating system. Whoever did it used highly specialized malware specifically coded to target our DOE systems. Sam will come over later to brief us on what they find. I hope this is the last of our bin Laden anniversary attacks. We took a victory lap too soon, I'm afraid. All right, let's review the loose ends that need to be tied up."

Bill reviewed the lack of progress they'd made in getting information out of the bagboys and the deliverymen. They needed information to move up the chain and get closer to the masterminds behind the operation. Bill reported that two of the agents sent to Mexico City posing as bagboys hit pay dirt. Working with the Mexican Federales they apprehended two men sent to fetch the boys. They were low-level hit men used by the drug cartels. They had received anonymous requests and thick envelopes of cash to collect the boys, take them out to the countryside and decapitate them. The heads and hands were to be disposed of at a local incinerator.

The phone rang again, and an agent in back answered. The phone was passed to Mary, who listened for a moment and exclaimed loudly, "Oh, shit! Where did this happen?" All eyes turned to Mary who was blushing. After hanging up, she slammed her fist on the table. "It looks like we screwed up and missed a bagboy. We've got a dozen cases that sound like cholera in New York; they're at a local hospital."

Bill was the first to speak. "Speed is essential now. Herb, you need to get your response team activated. Mary, I hope your mobile medical units haven't been disbanded."

Herb got up and said, "We had a dry run of our system a few days ago and it worked well. I'm going to move to a control center to handle this."

Mary too excused herself to go coordinate the medical side of the containment and treatment operations. As she was leaving, she said, "Our mobile units haven't been disbanded yet and we'll dispatch a plane to the Long Island-MacArthur airport in Islip. The attack appears to be centered around Brookhaven on Long Island. As soon as I get operations running I'm going to head out to Long Island to coordinate things."

"Mary, we'll get an Air Force chopper for you. You could land right at the local hospital. We'll assign one of our experienced agents, Orville Maybach, to accompany you. Orrie knows what to do in a situation such as you might encounter, " Bill said.

"Can I go with her?" Win asked. "I could be of some help."

"We need you here, Win," Dan snapped.

"Where the hell is Oberdorf when we need him? Do we have DOE nuclear facilities near Brookhaven?" Bill asked.

Win piped up, "We have a National Laboratory in Brookhaven that does nuclear research as I recall. I once was involved with an investigation of a cluster of childhood cancer cases near the laboratory. Local people thought it was due to radioactive isotopes from the facility getting into their water supply. So how did we miss this?"

"Remember, you cooked up the sampling method for investigating the other non-defense DOE sites, Win. Shit happens, I guess." Dan said. "Let's hope there aren't other sites attacked. Lunch is here, so why don't we eat while we get Oberdorf back here?" Food trumped emergencies for Dan.

As they went out to a lunchroom, Win commented to Bill, "What a day! We start off with a victory party and now we're in manure up to our ears.

90

Brookhaven, Long Island, New York

The Air Force chopper circled the landing site at Brookhaven Community Hospital. The pilot, a captain, pointed to a large crowd around the hospital and the many cars parked helter-skelter. "It looks like we've got a rugby scrum down there. You guys may have your hands full," he announced over the intercom.

Orrie Maybach signaled with his hand for the pilot to keep circling as he looked down to scan the scene. He used a handheld radio to call headquarters. "Maybach to base," he shouted over the motor's din. "We may have a control issue at the Brookhaven Hospital. I need you to have the police officer-in-charge at the site and the hospital administrator meet our helicopter as we land. I'll have the pilot circle for a few minutes. Good. Roger and out."

Orrie leaned over to Mary Carpenter and shouted in her ear. "Now you see why control and command is so important in dealing with a bioterrorism threat. Bioterrorism scares the bejesus out of ordinary folks and scared people panic. Panic impedes our work."

Orrie scampered up to the cockpit and crouched behind the pilot. He shouted something to the pilot who gave a "thumbs up" sign. Air Force choppers weren't designed for quiet chats.

Orrie went back to his seat and buckled up. It wasn't long before the pilot announced he was going to land. The landing site was an asphalt-paved, circular pad at the back of the hospital; it had a large red cross painted in its center and police surrounded it.

The plane set down, and as soon as the rotor stopped, a crewman opened the door for the passengers and put out a block step for them to use. Orrie got out first, and quickly spotted a portly officer who looked to be the local police chief. He extended his right hand to the chief and said, "I'm Agent Orville Maybach with the FBI. I'll be the commanding officer here until we get everything under control." He pointed to Mary and said, "This lady is Dr. Mary Carpenter from the Centers for Disease Control. She'll be in charge of all medical activities. She's an expert on the diseases at issue here. Is the hospital administrator here?"

"I'm Chief Rocco Santini with the Brookhaven Police Department and the gentleman over there with the gray suit is the hospital administrator," he said, pointing to his left. The Chief looked miffed at his summary demotion.

"Chief, you and I are going to check out the crowd situation while you brief me on what's been happening. Dr. Carpenter will go with the Administrator to check out the situation inside. We're going to unload some medical supplies from the chopper that'll need to be moved inside and guarded by an armed detail."

"Whoa, whoa, Maybach! What kind of games do you think you're playing here?"

Maybach, who was a good foot taller and a hundred pounds heavier than Santini, fixed him with a stare and said softly, "This is no game, and if you stand in my way, I'll make one call and you'll be fired by the Governor of New York. Got it?"

Santini didn't seem inclined to test Maybach's authority or heft and said, "Okay, you're going to take responsibility if things go wrong. Follow me."

Maybach clenched his teeth as he followed. It was his bad luck to have to work with a full-blown, bureaucratic martinet.

91
Brookhaven

Mary went inside the hospital with Alex, the administrator, who was pale-faced and looked scared out of his wits. She suggested they visit the Emergency Department first, and on the way inquired about the hospital's number of acute care beds, occupancy rate, staffing, and supplies of antibiotics and IV fluids. The administrator stuttered as he answered, but had an excellent grasp of the hospital's status. She sensed they were getting close to the ED by the increasing noise level.

"You can hear the noise from our Emergency Room; it's just ahead," he stuttered. "People started streaming in early this morning and the numbers got out of hand. When people started demanding care and yelling at our staff, I called in the police."

They went through a door that required a pass to open. It was noisy inside and there weren't enough seats to accommodate the waiting people, many of whom were sitting or lying on the floor. A disheveled woman holding a baby ran up to Mary and looked at the CDC picture ID she was wearing.

"You're a doctor. I want you to take care of my baby right now!" she demanded. Alex gently took the distraught woman by the arm and tried to lead her away. She pulled away from him and screeched, "My boy's dying. He needs a doctor now!" A municipal police officer came over and pulled the panicked woman back.

"Don't worry. We can deal with this mess in short order," Mary said. "Let's go inside. I need to talk to your triage nurse and the treating physicians. The door to the treatment areas also required use of an ID card to open

Alex led the way to a glass-walled room with a desk, examining table and sink. A middle-aged woman wearing green scrubs and a long white coat sat at the desk. He knocked on the door and asked, "Kathy, can I interrupt you for a minute?"

"Sure Alex." She excused herself to the patient she was seeing and came outside

"Dr. Carpenter, this is Kathy, one of our most experienced nurses. Kathy, Dr. Carpenter is from the CDC and was sent here to help with whatever it is we've been seeing here. You look tired, are you holding up okay?"

Kathy answered, "Yes, barely."

"What have you been seeing today?" Mary asked.

"Profuse, watery diarrhea with bad dehydration. Some of the patients have fever, others don't. Some have blood in their stools, others don't. My guess is we're seeing several different diseases. Our docs have been admitting those with the most severe dehydration, mostly the elderly and children, but we're going to run out of beds soon. With the last few cases, they've been treating them here in the ED."

"That's a good call, Kathy," Mary said. "I suspect the involved diseases are a mix of cholera, typhoid fever, shigellosis and pathogenic E. coli. Here's what we're going to do: take care of your current patient and then we're going to set you up with a triage station outside in the ED reception room. Alex, do you have other triage nurses you can call in?"

"Sure, I have two other experienced nurses I can call."

"Before you do that, we need some more equipment and personnel from the hospital." Mary recited a long list of needs and put Alex to work. She asked Kathy to take her inside and introduce her to the doctors on duty.

The Brookhaven ED usually had only one physician on duty, but a second on-call doc brought in to handle the influx of patients confirmed what Kathy had reported; it was diarrhea and more diarrhea. Laboratory studies on the patients only revealed that several had high white blood cell counts consistent with an acute infection and some had severe electrolyte imbalances. After the first few cases they saw, they'd been ordering stool cultures on all patients, but those results wouldn't be available for at least 24 hours.

"You've been doing an heroic job," Mary said. "I believe you've been seeing a mix of enteric infections—everything from cholera to pathogenic E. coli. More supplies are on the way. We can have a triage nurse screen the patients and dispense the drugs. We'll need you for dealing with the very sick—those with severe dehydration, or high fever, or with kids. We have stocks of oral replacement fluid that should arrive soon. In the meantime, your pharmacists can make some up here."

One of the doctors asked, "What's going on?"

"We don't know yet. We suspect some nut-case, anti-nuke group tried to poison foods near the Brookhaven National Laboratory." She changed the subject. "We're going to get a pediatrician in to help out. Our plan is to send most of the sick kids back here for evaluation. We're worried about enterohemorrhagic E. coli in kids leading to hemolytic uremic syndrome—HUS is the big killer in these infections and kids are particularly susceptible to developing it. We'll have a pediatrician evaluate all kiddie cases before prescribing antibiotic therapy, which could be harmful. Anyway, the main thing in treating kids with this disease is fluid replacement. I'll let you guys get back to work."   She didn't tell them there had been a previous attack and the infectious organisms were all found to be sensitive to the antibiotics she requested or that the patients also might have been exposed to hepatitis A virus. Hepatitis A had a much longer incubation period and they could safely intervene later with immune globulin injections or vaccination.

92
Brookhaven

Mary found Alex in the midst of a small crowd of hospital workers in the area just inside the door to the waiting room. "I was able to get just about everything you wanted," he told her. "I even found some lipstick for you."

Mary stood up on a chair and said, "Good job! Now here's how we're going to organize out there in the waiting room. I want you to set up two tables. We'll need two triage nurses, one for each table. At each table, we'll have a technician who'll take and record the patients' vital signs. We'll also need one clerk at the table to collect important information for us. We'll have a police officer lining patients up in an orderly fashion and a second officer at the door letting in new patients only as we discharge others. We'll give priority to pediatric and geriatric patients and we'll define children as those under age 15 and oldsters as age 65 plus. Pregnant women also get priority."

Mary went on, "Now here's the protocol. A patient comes up to the table and the clerk first records the patient's name, age, gender, address and phone number. We'll need to get back to them later. Don't worry about insurance information; the Government's picking up the tab. We need you to ask the patient or caretaker the names of all supermarkets and groceries at which they purchased food during the past week. Also, what towns the stores are in. The technician will take and record the patients' vital signs and pass them on to the triage nurse who'll then take a history from the patient. We'll need chairs for everyone to sit, particularly the patients. I'm afraid you nurses won't have the luxury of doing anything beyond a cursory physical exam. You'll have to sort out the very sick from the rest. The sickest will be sent back for medical attention. All others adults will be empirically treated with ciprofloxacin; we'll have a pharmacist available to give out the doses and ask patients about drug allergies. The pharmacist will give dehydrated patients oral rehydration fluids. All pediatric patients will be sent back to be seen by a pediatrician, assuming they're really sick. The only preventive measures you'll need are wearing scrub suits and rubber gloves. Our pharmacist will give you each a dose of cipro. Take it before you start seeing patients. He'll give you more when you go home."

"We're still an important Emergency Department for the area and we're going to get the occasional heart attacks, and severe accidents coming in," Alex pointed out. "What do you want us to do with them?"

"I guess they'll go to the head of the line and triage will be done outside," Mary said. Any severe bleeders or obvious MIs and strokes should be taken in immediately. Some of them may have to be stabilized and then transferred to other hospitals so we can focus on the infectious disease patients. Our main goal right now is to decrease the backlog of patients and calm them down. Okay, Alex, why don't you and I go outside and triage the waiting room."

Alex reached down and presented Mary with a megaphone.

"Where'd you get that?" Mary asked.

"This has been around my office forever. I think we used it at hospital picnics. Let me show you how it works."

The two of them went out into the even more crowded waiting room. Mary used the megaphone to announce that they'd be setting up nursing stations to help everyone get seen quickly. Walking through the crowd, she stopped and knelt down before an elderly woman who looked very sick. "How are you feeling, Ma'am?" Mary asked. A middle-aged woman sitting next to the patient answered for her. "She's been sick for the past 24 hours and she's going downhill fast. Is there anything you can do for her?"

"Yes, we'll get her seen soon," Mary said as she took out the lipstick Alex had given her and wrote a large, red P on the patients forehead. They walked around the room and Mary wrote Ps on three more foreheads. As they went back inside, Mary whispered to Alex, "The P is for priority and we need to get those patients to the head of the lines and back to the doctors ASAP."

93

Brookhaven

Mary had to restrain herself from smiling; she hated to admit it, but she'd been looking forward to this day for her whole career. This was her first chance to experience and manage a real bioterrorism attack. For years she'd had fantasies about what it would be like, but her career had been largely academic and hadn't prepared her well for a real-world attack. It was a shocker to her that law enforcement was as important as the medical management of an attack. Somehow, her training and preparation had paid little attention to the panic and chaos an attack could provoke.

Her thoughts were interrupted by Alex informing her, "Hey, doc, we just got some reinforcements of drugs, nurses and equipment. There's also a young fella looking for you." He pointed to a tall young man in a white coat who was helping at one of the triage tables.

Mary went over to the young doctor and introduced herself. He told her that his name was Irving Benjamin. "I go by Irv," he said. "I'm an EIS Officer on assignment to the Suffolk County Health Department and got an urgent message to get over here fast and help you out."

"Well Irv, I have an important task for you. We think we're dealing with a common- source exposure to several different diseases usually transmitted by the fecal-oral route. As you've seen, we've been collecting information on where the patients purchased their groceries within the past 3-4 days. I need you to go through the lists of grocery stores and look for one particular store that all or most of the patients or their families shopped at. We need to identify the source as quickly as possible. Just use the techniques you learned in your EIS training."

It wasn't more than five minutes before the young physician rushed over to Mary to say that he'd found the common source. He handed Mary a slip of paper with the store's name as if he was presenting her with a great treasure. "The store's right here in Brookhaven."

Mary took the sheet and headed out the door to find Orrie. "That is one helluva good job and damn good epidemiologic thinking," she said over her shoulder.

She found Orrie standing with a beefy firefighter alongside a fire truck parked so as to block all but one lane to the Emergency Department. There was no backed up traffic and everyone on the scene looked calm. Orrie came over to greet her.

"I think we've identified the common-source grocery and need to investigate it ASAP," Mary whispered. "Here's the name," she said as she handed him the slip of paper. "We'll need to close it down and treat it as a crime scene. Do you have an agent that can supervise the investigation?"

"Yeah; two of our agents with training in handling bioterrorism cases arrived with the last contingent of personnel and equipment; I'll put them on it. We're going to have to work on this with our martinet police chief."

"I need to get back to D.C. now to coordinate the CDC's efforts."

"We've got an Air Force chopper waiting for us. I'll be going back with you. I'll radio the pilot now and get our troops here mobilized." With that, he got on his radio and began barking out orders.

Mary walked back to the Emergency Room slowly; she was wiped out. She sought out Alex, who was running the show now. "Hey Alex, I need to brief you on the media and how to handle them when they tumble to this outbreak. They'll likely descend on you like a plague of locusts. I'm surprised they haven't been here yet. Maybe Orrie and the police have kept them away."

"I hadn't thought about that," Alex replied.

"We'll need to prevent public panic about the outbreak. One of the simplest ways to control things is to centralize the source and content of information released to the public. You're going to need to brief your staff on the importance of directing all media inquiries to you and then on to me and my higher-ups. It's not about censorship; it's about preventing panic." Mary was getting good at telling half-truths. "At this point we can't tell whether we've had a breakdown in food hygiene, like some big-time plumbing problem, or some lunatic trying to poison people. It looks like the cases all purchased food at a single store, so we need to investigate it. We'll do some public service announcements to warn people not to consume foods purchased at that store. The outbreak should be under control in short order. Just warn your nurses and doctors to keep mum about things." She handed Alex her card. "Direct all questions to me at the number on my card; someone will be available at that number 24-7."

"Gotcha, Doc. Are you headed out now?"

"Yeah; I've got to get back to Washington."

"I don't know how to thank you for coming to our rescue. You're a real pro."

"So are you, Alex. Call me if you need any help. Mind the store well."

Mary left and made her way out to the helicopter landing pad in back.

94
Washington

The mess and large crowd in the Situation Room startled Mary, although it hushed slightly when everyone noticed the two arrivals.

Bill shouted, "Everyone, quiet down; Dr. Carpenter and Agent Maybach just arrived from Long Island. We need to hear what they have to say. Which one of you wants to go first?"

"Let Orrie go first, I need a cold drink," Mary said.

Orrie stood up and went over to the white board to give his talk.

Watching Mary go to the credenza to get a drink, Win noticed she looked tired, but he thought she looked more attractive.

Orrie gave a concise and expert report of the emergency room scene and the actions of the police and other first responders; it wasn't encouraging for future attacks. He wrote his recommendations for handling any future attacks as bullet points on the board.

Mary went next; she sat as she gave her report. The group had been right that the local population would panic and overwhelm the capacity of the Emergency Room, but it sounded as if she had handled the situation coolly and expertly. It also was lucky that the local hospital administrator was competent and willing to take orders from Mary and Orrie. The good news she had to convey was that a bright EIS Officer had quickly identified the likely site of this attack and Orrie's men were there to start an investigation. Mary stopped and took a long sip of her drink.

Bill was the first to speak. "Were any reporters or cameramen at the hospital, Mary?"

"No, but I instructed the hospital administrator to refer all inquiries to me." Mary looked over towards Orrie and asked, "How about you Orrie? Did any media people approach you outside the hospital?"

"No. That surprises me. I'm more worried about the dingbat local police chief shooting off his mouth to feel important. I did tell him to keep his mouth shut and take his orders from the FBI agent-in-charge."

Bill picked up on the questioning again. "Mary, did you tell anybody what diseases were involved?"

"I thought about it and decided I had to tell the doctors and nurses what the presumptive diagnoses were. It would be unethical to withhold that information from them; they needed it to treat their patients properly. I didn't mention any diagnoses to the patients."

"You probably did the right thing," Bill said. "While you two were gone, a meeting was held at the White House regarding how to handle the media and public regarding this attack. All of the Agencies involved agreed that we shouldn't mention Al-Qaeda or the other planned attack sites. We don't want to give Al-Qaeda any more bragging rights. Most importantly, we don't want to get the public panicked about food safety and demanding enhanced security. It would have a huge economic as well as psychological impact. Similarly, everyone agreed we should hush up the cyberterrorism attack on DOE facilities as best we can. The Brookhaven attack was another matter. We were equally divided over whether to hush it up or release some information about the nature of the attack. POTUS stepped in and made the decision that we give out straight information about the outbreak, but not that it was a terrorist attack. We then came up with the strategy of painting this as a tainted food story or a rogue attack by a disgruntled Brookhaven Lab worker or some local anti-nuke group. Remember the salad bar attack of some religious cult out west? It received a modest amount of media attention and then quickly went away. We haven't had any deaths and lets hope it stays that way. That should decrease the story's shelf life. We haven't had the story picked up yet by the media, but the President wants us to get out ahead of the story by a media release from either HHS or the CDC, not from Homeland Security or Defense. It's a tough call, but I think POTUS is right."

"I think we should get the information out at the local level," Mary said. "Why not have the New York State or even Suffolk County Health Commissioner make a statement? It could be overkill and even alert the press to something larger going on if the Federal Government gets involved first. After all, don't we want to defuse the story?"

"You know, Mary may be right," Dan added. "We Washington bureaucrats only seem to think in terms of federal agency actions."

"How many of you think we should adopt Mary's approach?" Bill asked. "Let's have a show of hands." All but one hand, a DOE representative, went up. "All right, I'm going to call the White House Chief of Staff to relay this advice to POTUS. Dan, why don't you inform the Director of this recommendation?" As Dan raised his great bulk to leave the room, it occurred to Win that Dan must burn up a lot of calories just getting up out of his chair many times day. "Let's take a five minute break."

Bill reconvened the meeting. "We'll need to know urgently what infectious agents were used in the Brookhaven attack. Let's hope the EIS officer located the right attack site. Unfortunately, the terrorists used different combinations of agents at each site. All sites were to use cholera organisms and the other agents, typhoid, pathogenic E. coli, Shigella, what looks like hepatitis A, Brucella and Campylobacter, were to be used in varying combinations at the different sites. The Campylobacter was another creative wrinkle; it's not thought of as a bioterrorism agent and its presentation often mimics cholera. It's a good one to confuse our doctors. With the exception of the E. coli, none of these agents causes diseases with a high case-fatality. This attack was meant to terrorize Americans and cause economic damage, getting us to set up expensive security systems for distributing foods. That's why we need to keep a lid on things. My guess is that by creating terror with little loss of life, the terrorists thought it wouldn't trigger a massive retaliation. Sorry to digress like this. Mary, were all of the cases you saw in Brookhaven cholera patients?"

Mary was slumped in her chair and pulled herself up to answer. "It's really hard to say. Almost all of the patients presented with severe diarrhea. Perhaps fifty percent were cholera patients. Some patients had scant diarrhea without fever; these could be E. coli victims. Some patients presented with diarrhea, sometimes bloody, and fever; these could be Shigella or Campylobacter victims. It's going to take a few days to sort things out. We need to know as soon as possible whether hepatitis A, HAV in the trade, was part of the Long Island bag boy's arsenal. If it was, we're going to need to set up a vaccination program within two weeks of ingestion of the agent to be effective. Depending on the food consumption history of customers, we would use active immunization with or without immune globulin. Brucellosis presents another set of issues. It's got a variable incubation period that can sometimes be several months and like syphilis and TB is one of the great medical mimics that can present clinically in many puzzling ways. We need to determine what foods were contaminated and with which infectious agent. Fortunately, we now have real-time, reverse transcriptase-PCR method for HAV identification from foods. Identification of bacterial contamination is a lot easier, except for Brucella. The challenge is to determine which foods were selected as transmission vehicles. Our job is made easier by focusing our investigation on foods that are consumed raw or cooked lightly, like hamburger. We've also have a big job of 'shoe leather epidemiology' ahead to identify and trace all customers and find out what food items they bought."

Win sat there musing about Mary's use of the word "issues," in describing brucellosis. These weren't issues; these were huge problems.

"Can more personnel speed up the process?" Bill asked.

"Oh yes, so long as they don't trip over each other," Mary answered.

Bill said, "So let's flood the damn grocery with personnel. We need to get this embarrassing episode over with ASAP. Don't worry about the costs."

Mary got up and said, "I'll go round up more troops."

Orrie too excused himself to bring in more agents with the proper specialized skills.

An agent came over to Bill and handed him a note. Bill read it and said, "We just received a copy of the coverage of the Brookhaven attack on one of the local Long Island TV station's evening news. Apparently, the story hasn't received national or New York City coverage." He gestured to the agent who opened up a cabinet that contained a large flat-screen TV and turned it on.

A young, blond woman was interviewing the Suffolk County Health Commissioner, a jowly, middle-aged guy in a rumpled seersucker suit. They were standing outside the Brookhaven Community Hospital ED. "Dr. Snyder, could you tell us what happened here today in Brookhaven?" she asked.

"There appears to be an outbreak of severe gastrointestinal disease. A few patients came in seriously dehydrated but there are no fatalities and none are expected."

The reporter next asked, "Do you know the cause of the outbreak? Is it like the diarrhea epidemics we see on cruise ships nowadays?"

"No," the doctor answered. "This outbreak looks more like cholera. Most cases of cholera in the US nowadays are from eating contaminated shellfish or in people who've spent time overseas. In most parts of the world it's spread by contaminated water supplies. Cholera is an easily treatable and curable disease."

"How many victims are there in this outbreak?" the reporter asked.

"So far we know of 47 people who were seen at the Hospital or local doctor's offices for acute diarrheal disease," Snyder answered unhesitatingly.

"That sounds like a large epidemic. Do you know how the people caught the disease?"

"This looks like what we call a common-source exposure to some infectious agent and we're actively investigating whether the victims consumed any foods in common. If this is cholera, it would typically be contracted by ingesting contaminated water or food, particularly shellfish as I pointed out, so that's what we're investigating."

"Does the County Health Department have the resources to do this investigation?' the reporter asked.

"We're fortunate in having a close relationship with the Centers for Disease Control and Prevention, the CDC, in Atlanta, and they've sent additional personnel here to assist in the investigation. We're on top of things and hope to have answers in the next 24 to 48 hours."

"Thank you very much Doctor for that information. And now back to the newsroom."

The TV went off and Bill said, "Dr. Snyder handled her questions beautifully. He made cholera sound like an everyday event. Let's hope there are enough important news items elsewhere to divert attention away from Brookhaven. I think we have a chance of finessing this outbreak and putting the saga to rest."

Win's read on the situation was that the terrorists had succeeded with one food attack and their cyber-attack. Maybe there won't be widespread terror, but you can bet there'll be much tightened food handling regulations at great expense. This could be the death knell for selling loose salad greens in America. As for DOE, they'd need to spend big bucks on new cyber-security procedures and the replacement of damaged, expensive equipment. Al-Qaeda had mounted one helluva clever attack on the US to commemorate bin Laden's death—one that would change a lot of things. With that, they adjourned for the evening.

95
Washington

The next day, Bill thumped on the table with a coffee mug to call people to order. "We have some good news for a change," he began. "First off, there are no new attacks and no new cases. Second, we may have caught a break in Brookhaven. We don't think HAV or Brucella was used there, which should make our job easier."

Mary threw her head back and let out a loud sigh.

"The agents detected in Brookhaven are Vibrio cholerae, Salmonella, E. coli, and Shigella. We're not sure yet about Campylobacter. There was another suspicious bagboy employed in Brookhaven; he took leave for a family emergency three days before the outbreak. We presume he left for Mexico City and is now a decapitated corpse. We're doing a trace on him. As soon as we have all the agents and contaminated foods identified, we'll start a full-scale, customer tracing and recall program. We're going to have to tread lightly so we don't stir up media attention. Unless there are questions, I'll turn the meeting over to Roger. His Agency has been analyzing the attacks."

Everyone shook their heads "no," so Roger, who wore a pink bowtie today, began. "This has been a puzzling but brilliant attack from an intelligence standpoint. We had no advance Intel or warning signals. The concerted attacks had some low-tech and some highly sophisticated features and were shrewdly conceived. We've been lucky to get off so lightly, thanks to Dr. Sage alerting us in time. We have strong reason to believe Al-Qaeda was behind this, particularly since the attacks were timed to occur on the anniversary of OBL's death." He pointed to a disheveled character sitting next to him who looked like a Hollywood version of a mad scientist. "I brought along one of our senior Agency analysts, Charlie Asteway, to brief you on our analysis of these events; he has some interesting theories about the attacks."

Charlie shifted back and forth in his chair as he decided whether to sit or stand up. He finally opted for standing, cleared his throat and began. "There are so many clever features to what we've just witnessed at our nuclear sites. We've been concerned for a long time about the recruitment and radicalization of US citizens and this action proves our concerns were well founded."

Charlie sounded intelligent, but Win kept getting distracted by his appearance. Charlie had wildly untamed, graying hair that could have used a good combing. His jacket looked like he'd bought it when he was 50 pounds heavier. The thing Win focused on was Charlie's sweater-vest; it was buttoned so that the first button went into the second buttonhole and on down.

Charlie went on, "The feature our group has been most puzzled by is the choice of attack sites. Why did they target our nuclear facilities and not big cities?   We think we have the answer to that question and it's troubling. We believe the attacks involved collaboration between Iran and Al-Qaeda."   His head rotated like a submarine periscope as he scanned the room to gauge people's reactions.

He continued, "There's increasing evidence of joint ventures between Al-Qaeda and Iran. Despite the deep antipathy and religious differences between these radical Shiite and Sunni groups, they seem to have found common ground in their hatred of the US The Iranians are hell-bent on owning nuclear weapons and the US has been their main obstacle. They believe we partnered with the Israelis to create the Stuxnet worm that disabled their nuclear centrifuge operating systems. We think the Iranians got wind of the bioterrorism plot and persuaded Al-Qaeda to target US nuclear facilities while they used a new computer worm to attack our nuclear facility computers as payback for Stuxnet. The Iranian message would be:

We can play this game too—hit us and we'll hit you back harder. And they did; they did more damage to our computer systems than the Stuxnet worm did to theirs."

Sam Oberdorf said, "Yeah, tell me about it!"

Charlie went on. "We think the basic plan was hatched by Al-Qaeda. It was timed to memorialize OBL's death for starters. The style and recruitment of US bagboys fits with Al-Qaeda. A couple of minor touches also make us think it's Al-Qaeda. The final calls to the bagboys were made to appear as if they came from Mumbai, India—Pakistan's mortal enemy. The DOE malware, we discovered, was made to appear to have been launched from a government office in Israel. Al-Qaeda's current leader, al Zawahiri, is a medical man and there've been rumors of Al-Qaeda's recruitment of sophisticated university scientists. Our hunch is that this is from Al-Qaeda, originated in Pakistan and al Zawahiri was the brains behind it. Iran probably provided funds and pushed for going after US nuclear sites. The sites really didn't matter much to Al-Qaeda for creating terror, so long as there were enough of them. Fewer people might get infected in small towns, but it would still have the same impact. Luckily for us, the sites did matter and saved our skin. If they hadn't chosen Santa Fe, and New Mexico didn't have a pork-barrel bioterrorism program to identify cholera cases, and Dr. Sage hadn't figured out that we were being attacked, the picture would've been very different. Chance plays a big role in our business and as Louis Pasteur said, 'chance favors the prepared mind'." He looked at Win as he said this. Charlie sat down and missed the seat, landing on the arm of his chair.

Win snapped upright. Why did Asteway use that particular quote from Pasteur? Was the CIA spying on him?

Roger picked up, "That sums up our thinking. The captured boys aren't talking. I suspect they know little beyond how they were recruited and what they were instructed to do. We had hoped to get a description of Uncle Abdullah, their contact person. We're studying the pre-paid SIM cards in their cell phones to trace their calls. All of their calls were to a VOIP number, that's an Internet phone account, in Detroit. They all received calls from another VOIP number and we're working on tracing it. The deliverymen don't know much; their contact was an elderly Syrian gentleman who visited their mosques. This was a professionally-designed program aimed at throwing us off the scent of the perpetrators."

Roger went on, "We've come up with a decision for disposition of the bag boys; our friends over at Justice concur with it, as does the White House. We simply let the boys go free. We've been holding them incommunicado with no charges made and no legal representation. We can't hold them this way much longer. We can't risk taking them to court; the media would have a field day and scare the bejesus out of the public. They're of little further use to us other than to lead us to the people who radicalized them, if we're lucky. We suspect the guys with beards and turbans will take out the boys pretty quickly. They're more of a liability to the B and T crowd than they are to us. Remember what they had planned for the boys in Mexico. I'm sure the Brookhaven bag boy is already with the fishes. We're also covering our tracks. We have an Executive Order from the White House to expunge all reports of the involved cholera or E. coli cases from the CDC registries. We'll work out methods to do the same at State levels. We'll have to report the Brookhaven cases though; the media are already on to them."

"What about justice being served? These boys are wannabe murderers," Win said.

Dan piped in, "Remember from our past work Win, national security trumps concerns about justice. We can't alarm and panic the US population; that's what the terrorists want. Justice will be done when we hunt down and kill the perpetrators. We'll get these guys, and Al-Qaeda will take care of the boys for us."

Win was about to say something but decided to keep quiet.

Bill adjourned the meeting and announced that the Task Force was disbanded. He thanked everyone with the exaggerated insincerity of an experienced bureaucrat.

Win was approached by Bill and Dan. "Win, we both wanted to thank you for alerting us to this potential disaster," Bill said. "I thought you were nuts at the beginning, but you were unswervingly right. Our country owes you big time."

Dan leaned towards Win and whispered, "We'll pick you up at your hotel tonight at 8 PM. We have a surprise. Keep quiet about this."

Salay was next to come up to Win. "You know Sage, when Dan first brought you in, I thought he was nuts and I didn't like you and your style. I hate when amateurs get in the way of our work. But you're good, really good. You've got good instincts and would've made a good operative in our Agency. I bet you're the world's first cyber-epidemiologist. Your Harvard background shows."

"Well thanks. I enjoyed working with you. Auf wiedersehen!"

Win hated the "good ol' Harvard boys" mindset of Salay, but it had been an incredible odyssey. Just a few months ago he worried about having nothing to do and going dotty in his retirement. He was focused on lamebrain activities to recapture his youth while the US was the bull's-eye for half the world's crazies. At least, he'd demonstrated that his brain could still work and he had the perseverance to investigate suspicious observations even in the face of ridicule by the authorities. He rubbed his forehead in amazement that his amateur-night, obsessive tenacity could lead to the derailing of a major international bioterrorism attack. He got up and smiled as he realized he still had a lot of gas left in the tank and he had a talent for detective work.

96
South Waziristan

The turbulent skies overhead mirrored the rage erupting inside the house in South Waziristan. The Hakim was pacing his living room, scowling at the men sitting on the floor and ranting about the failure of their war on the Great Satan.

"I knew we shouldn't have teamed up with those heretic Iranians. Osama thought it would be expedient to accept their money and assistance. Their part of the mission, the destruction of the nuclear computer systems, was a success and ours a failure. I bet the clever jackals thought the joint timing of our attacks would lead the Americans to pin the computer attack on us."

"But Ayman, it's a victory. The Iranians were successful in ruining the enemy's computer systems at their nuclear facilities; it will cost tens of millions of dollars to replace," said a dignified, elderly man whose long, white beard matched his white turban and robe.

"That's a pittance to the Americans. I wanted terror!" Ayman interrupted.

The elderly man went on, "We were also successful at one of the attack sites. Even though only one site succeeded, the message of the vulnerability of their food distribution system will register and we didn't need mass panic to deliver it. This will cost the enemy dearly as they are certain to increase their food security systems. They always overreact to an attack after the fact."

"We mustn't be discouraged in our jihad," said a younger man. "We should strike again soon. The Americans won't be expecting an attack so close on the heels of our latest attack."

"My son, you are young. We must proceed deliberately," said a man dressed all in black.

"No. I think we should attack soon. The Sheikh and I had a back-up plan. In the meantime, we must find out who's responsible for our failure? We must set an example and execute that idiot," the Hakim raged as he walked up and back like a madman. His face was red, matching the Afghan rugs hanging on the walls.

"Ayman, calm yourself. Our operation was successful. We just didn't create mass panic," the man in black said as he raised his hands in a calming gesture.

"I wanted to avenge the murder of our Leader by causing sufficient panic and disorder to terrify the beasts and teach them to fear us and our righteous cause! How did our operation get compromised?"

"Ayman, my brother, we don't know, but we believe the American dogs somehow discovered our plan and arrested our boys as they were putting germs into foods," the younger mullah replied.

"Do you think it was the trial attack that tipped off the enemy?" Ayman asked.

"Remember, we needed to conduct a trial to be certain the infectious agents survived shipment; it was the Shura's decision," the mullah in black said.

"I had doubts about that idiot public health doctor. If it was his plan that gave us away, I want him killed!" Ayman shouted as he kicked a cushion.

"Ayman, he did an outstanding job in recruiting and placing the boys in position. He was a genius at setting up this complex operation in America. He is also a modest and devout man with a young family."

"I don't care!" Ayman bellowed. "Incompetence must be dealt with."

"You must control yourself, Ayman. The Shura has been discussing future operations. The Iranians were pleased with the successful attack on the American nuclear computer system and have offered to help fund other attacks. We may need the public health doctor as well as the medical professor if we stay with bioterrorism attacks."

One of the Hakim's wives, clad from head to toe in a black burqa with a mesh screen over her eyes, appeared ghost-like in the doorway and announced that dinner was ready.

"Come Ayman, let us take dinner. We must celebrate the successes we've had and begin planning for the future."

97
Washington

It was 7:55 PM and a black, stretch limousine was waiting outside Win's hotel. There were two men in back, the FBI Chief and another man who extended a hand as Win got in. Tilikso was up front with the driver. A black SUV waited behind the limo.

The well-dressed patrician smiled at Win and shook his hand. "I'm Jim Cooper, Director of the CIA. I'm pleased to meet you Dr. Sage. I've heard so much about you and want to thank you for all you've done."

"It's a pleasure to meet you, sir."

Cooper smiled and said, "We have a surprise in store for you. It shouldn't take long to reach our destination."

Win couldn't see through the tinted windows as the car headed down Pennsylvania Avenue. They soon stopped at a gatehouse checkpoint and pulled up alongside a large white building. The driver stepped out and opened the door. They were ushered inside via an awning-covered walkway and greeted with a crisp salute from a marine in dress blues; he was expecting them. "Welcome to the White House, gentlemen. You'll need to proceed this way through the metal detector, please." He led them through the detector manned by a second marine.

Dan and the Directors took out their IDs and hung them around their necks. The FBI Director whispered something in the ear of the higher ranking of the two marines and the marine responded, "I was instructed to do just that, Sir. There'll be no sign-in and your visit will never have occurred, Sir. I'm not to ID your guest either, Sir."

The second marine made a call and a gentleman in civilian clothes soon appeared. He led them down several corridors with carpeting that muffled sounds. Their escort opened the door to a room and led them inside.

"Jeez!" Win blurted out. "I've seen this room on TV; it's the Oval Office,"

"The President wanted to thank you personally," Cooper said.

They stood as they awaited the President. Win was swivel-headed as he took in the details of the historic room. He never dreamed he'd be standing there. "I wish I'd brought a camera. I guess I could use my cell phone for a selfie; otherwise, nobody will ever believe I was here."

Director Manning looked at Tilikso, who responded, "I'm afraid there'll be no photo ops tonight. The President insisted on meeting you although we urged him against it to maintain secrecy about the nearly successful plot. There'll be no record of this meeting and nobody saw you enter other than security personnel who were instructed to have amnesia. So soak it up and remember it well. Sorry about that."

The door opened and an aide led the President in. He smiled, came over to Win and shook his hand firmly. "I'm honored to meet you, Dr. Sage. You saved us from a catastrophe. If Al-Qaeda had been successful they'd have caused huge economic damage and the deaths of innocent civilians. Thank you very much."

Win stood mutely and finally responded, "I'm honored to be here with you."

The President smiled, and took Win by the arm and led him to a yellow, silk-covered chair. "How about some drinks to celebrate this success?" He signaled his aide who was hovering in the background, "Warren will take your orders."

The President ordered bourbon on the rocks, the two Directors scotch with a splash of water, and Tilikso bourbon, straight up. Win hesitated before asking whether they had calvados. Warren informed him that they might not, so Win blushed and ordered a Jack Daniels on the rocks as a back up.

The President, who was wearing a shawl-collared, gray cardigan sweater, red plaid shirt, tassel loafers and jeans, pointed at his outfit. "Pardon my appearance. I was having dinner with the family and some friends upstairs," he said. "I didn't want to change and make them aware I was having a meeting down here. I told them I was sneaking out to check on some reports."

"I was told you helped the FBI uncover a high-ranking spy for the Chinese at Los Alamos last year and that you were almost killed in the process. From what Jim and Dan tell me, you're a first-class intelligence agent. You deserve a medal for your work and unfortunately, I can't award you one. We don't have a system of granting secret medals like the Pope has for naming cardinals secretly—*in pectore*, I believe it's called."

They were interrupted by the arrival of drinks. Warren served the President first, the two Directors, and then Tilikso. He came over to Win and whispered, "You're in luck. Our chef uses calvados in cooking so we were able to rustle some up for you."

The President raised his glass and said, "Here's to Dr. Winston Sage, an unsung American hero." The others joined, "Here! Here!"

Win took a sip and realized this was the best darn calvados he'd ever tasted and they used it for cooking!

"I have some good news," the President said. "This morning one of our drones killed Hassan Abdullah Khan in Waziristan; he's known as Mullah Redbeard. He's a cold-blooded murderer and reputed to be a senior member of Al-Qaeda's Shura council. One by one, I can assure you, we'll get the people who did this."

The President gazed at his drink and said, "I'm not sure who really won this war. We stopped a major bio-terrorism attack, but suffered a small successful one. Maybe it was just a clever head-fake, because we also sustained a major cyber-terrorism attack. These will have a major economic impact in how we protect and market foods in the future and how we defend our country from cyber-attacks, let alone the cost of repairing our nuclear computer systems. The

CIA thinks Iran played a big role in these attacks. The bottom line is that we've entered a new era of warfare and we're going to need new tactics." He shook his head and said, "It's a big responsibility to keep our country safe." He fixed Win with a stare. "I'm informed by our two Directors that we may be in for a long siege of terrorist threats. Dr. Sage, you seem to have a good feel for espionage and terrorism; do you have any idea what the next threat might be?"

Win was sipping his drink and the question made him choke. He took out a handkerchief to wipe his chin and thought for a moment. "I get most of my information from the newspapers and the Internet, but I have some crazy thoughts about possible attacks. I'm sure none of this is new to you. As a rank amateur, I would be concerned about cyber-attacks on our electric power grid or on financial records of large institutions. Imagine the chaos if all the records of trading on the New York Stock Exchange and NASDAQ for a day or two just evaporated. We saw a sophisticated and effective cyber-attack on our nuclear facility computers this time. I would also be concerned about a bioterrorist attack on our livestock herds. I have a veterinarian buddy who thinks we're really vulnerable there. Agriculture is big business, as I'm sure you know. We're also vulnerable to attacks on our offshore oil rigs and other eco-terrorism. Remember the damage from one rig in the BP-Gulf of Mexico accident. A coordinated attack on Gulf drilling rigs by small boats wouldn't be hard to pull off. The economic and political impact of several rigs being blown up and spewing oil into the Gulf would be huge. After this plot, I've been thinking the terrorists prob-ably want to inflict economic damage on a large scale. We're such an open society and there are so many possible points of attack."

The President frowned as he looked out the window. "You're right, we're an open society, thank God, and innocent and vulner-able. I like the way you think Sage, though you scare the living daylights out of me. I'm amazed that you could just search the web and uncover a planned attack on the US while our spy agencies were sleeping. Would you be willing to serve in an advisory capacity to some of our security committees? They could use your out-of-the-box thinking."

"Mr. President I'm honored, but I'm an amateur."

"Maybe we need some of your amateur input. We'll get back to you on this," the President said while rubbing the back of his head. He sighed and went on, "Now let's get down to brass tacks. I hear you're a Steelers fan." Win remembered the President was from Cleveland and a die-hard Browns fan. They had a heated discussion of the merits of the two teams although the Steelers regularly beat up the Browns.

The President looked at his watch and got up to leave. "Thank you again Dr. Sage. I'm glad we had this opportunity to meet. Next fall, I'd like you to join me at Camp David to watch a Browns-Steelers game. I'll bring the calvados."

END

About the Author

Seymour Grufferman is a physician-epidemiologist who holds two masters degrees and a doctorate in public health from Harvard. He has held faculty positions at several universities (Haile Selassie I, Duke, Pittsburgh and New Mexico) and has published numerous articles in leading scientific journals. He taught and practiced public health in Ethiopia where he saw first-hand many of the diseases described in this novel. He has taught epidemiology and traveled widely in less developed countries ranging from Afghanistan to Zambia and draws on these experiences to create vivid images of the novel's third-world settings.

His life-long research interest has been on the question of whether human cancer is caused by infectious agents and can be transmitted from person to person. After being invited to participate in conferences on U.S. food safety, he became seriously concerned about the startling vulnerability of U.S. food supplies to bioterrorist attack.

Dr. Grufferman is "sort of retired" and lives in the desert outside Santa Fe with his wife and dog.